I0831352

Hornet's Nest

Book Five
The Blackout Series

A novel by

Bobby Akart

Copyright Information

Other Works by Amazon Top 50 Author, Bobby Akart

The Doomsday Series

Apocalypse

Haven

Anarchy

Minutemen

Civil War

The Yellowstone Series

Hellfire

Inferno

Fallout

Survival

The Lone Star Series

Axis of Evil

Beyond Borders

Lines in the Sand

Texas Strong

Fifth Column

Suicide Six

The Pandemic Series

Beginnings

The Innocents

Level 6

Quietus

The Blackout Series

36 Hours

Zero Hour

Turning Point

Shiloh Ranch

Hornet's Nest

Devil's Homecoming

The Boston Brahmin Series

The Loyal Nine

Cyber Attack

Martial Law

False Flag

The Mechanics

Choose Freedom

Patriot's Farewell

Seeds of Liberty (Companion Guide)

The Prepping for Tomorrow Series

Cyber Warfare

EMP: Electromagnetic Pulse

Economic Collapse

DEDICATIONS

To the love of my life, thank you for making the sacrifices necessary so I may pursue this dream.

To the *Princesses of the Palace*, my little marauders in training, you have no idea how much happiness you bring to your mommy and me.

To my fellow preppers—never be ashamed of adopting a preparedness lifestyle.

ACKNOWLEDGEMENTS

Writing a book that is both informative and entertaining requires a tremendous team effort. Writing is the easy part. For their efforts in making The Blackout Series a reality, I would like to thank Hristo Argirov Kovatliev for his incredible cover art, Pauline Nolet for making this important work reader-friendly, Stef Mcdaid for making this manuscript decipherable on so many formats, John David Farrell, who together with Marshall Davis has brought my words to life, and The Team—whose advice, friendship and attention to detail is priceless.

The Blackout Series could not have been written without the tireless counsel and direction from those individuals who shall remain nameless at the Space Weather Prediction Center in Boulder, Colorado and at the Atacama Large Millimeter Array (ALMA) in Chile. Thank you for providing me a portal into your observations and data.

Lastly, a huge thank you to Dr. Tamitha Skov, a friend, and social media icon, who is a research scientist at The Aerospace Corporation in Southern California. With her Ph.D. in Geophysics and Space Plasma Physics, she has become a vital resource for amateur astronomers and aurora watchers around the world. Without her insight, The Blackout Series could not have been written. Visit her website at www.SpaceWeatherWoman.com.

Thank you!

About the Author

Bobby Akart

Author Bobby Akart has been ranked by Amazon as #55 in its Top 100 list of most popular, bestselling authors. He has achieved recognition as the #1 bestselling Horror Author, #2 bestselling Science Fiction Author, #3 bestselling Religion & Spirituality Author, #6 bestselling Action & Adventure Author, and #7 bestselling Historical Author.

He has written over twenty-six international bestsellers, in nearly fifty fiction and nonfiction genres, including the chart-busting Yellowstone series, the reader-favorite Lone Star series, the critically acclaimed Boston Brahmin series, the bestselling Blackout series, the frighteningly realistic Pandemic series, his highly cited nonfiction Prepping for Tomorrow series, and his latest project—the Doomsday series, seen by many as the horrifying future of our nation if we can't find a way to come together.

His novel *Yellowstone: Fallout* reached the Top 50 on the Amazon bestsellers list and earned him two Kindle All-Star awards for most pages read in a month and most pages read as an author. The Yellowstone series vaulted him to the #1 best selling horror author on Amazon, and the #2 best selling science fiction author.

Bobby has provided his readers a diverse range of topics that are both informative and entertaining. His attention to detail and impeccable research have allowed him to capture the imaginations of his readers through his fictional works and bring them valuable knowledge through his nonfiction books.

SIGN UP for Bobby Akart's mailing list to receive special offers, bonus content, and you'll be the first to receive news about new releases in the Doomsday series:

eepurl.com/bYqq3L

VISIT Amazon.com/BobbyAkart, a dedicated feature page created by Amazon for his work, to view more information on his thriller fiction novels and post-apocalyptic book series, as well as his nonfiction Prepping for Tomorrow series.

Visit Bobby Akart's website for informative blog entries on preparedness, writing, and a behind-the-scenes look into his novels.

BobbyAkart.com

About the Blackout Series

WHAT WOULD YOU DO
if a voice was screaming in your head - *GET READY* . . .
for a catastrophic event of epic proportions . . .
with no idea where to start . . .
or how, or when?

This is a true story, it just hasn't happened yet.

The characters depicted in The Blackout Series are fictional. The events, however, are based upon fact.

This is not the story of preppers with stockpiles of food, weapons, and a hidden bunker. This is the story of Colton Ryman, his stay-at-home wife, Madison, and their teenage daughter, Alex. In 36 Hours, the Ryman family and the rest of the world will be thrust into the darkness of a post-apocalyptic world.

A catastrophic solar flare, an EMP—a threat from above to America's soft underbelly below—is hurtling toward the Earth.

The Rymans have never heard of preppers and have no concept of what prepping entails. But they're learning, while they run out of time. Their faith will be tested, their freedom will be threatened, but their family will survive.

An EMP, naturally generated from our sun in the form of a solar flare, has happened before, and it will happen again, in only 36 Hours.

This is a story about how our sun, the planet's source of life, can also devastate our modern world. It's a story about panic, chaos, and the final straws that shattered an already thin veneer of civility. It is a warning to us all ...

never underestimate the depravity of man.

What would you do when the clock strikes zero?
Midnight is forever.

Note: This book does not contain strong language. It is intended to entertain and inform audiences of all ages, including teen and young adults. Although some scenes depict the realistic threat our nation faces from a devastating solar flare, and the societal collapse which will result in the aftermath, it does not contain graphic scenes typical of other books in the post-apocalyptic genre.

PREVIOUSLY IN THE BLACKOUT SERIES

The Characters

The Rymans:

Colton – Colton Ryman is in his late thirties. Born and raised in Texas, he is a direct descendant of the Ryman family which built the infamous Ryman Auditorium music hall in downtown Nashville. His family migrated to Texas from Tennessee with Davy Crockett in the 1800s. The Rymans became prominent in the oil and cattle business and as a result, Colton inherited his skill for negotiating. After college, he landed a position with United Talent, the top agency for the country-western music industry. He eventually became managing partner of the Nashville office. He is married to Madison and they have one child, Alex.

Madison – Madison, in her mid-thirties, is a devout Christian born and raised in Nashville. She grew up a debutante but quickly set her sights on a career in filmmaking. But one fateful day, she was introduced to Colton Ryman and the two fell in love. They had their only child, Alex, which prompted Madison to give up her career in favor of a life raising their daughter and loving her husband—two full time jobs.

Alex – Fifteen-year old Alex, the only child of Colton and Madison Ryman, was a sophomore at Davidson Academy. Despite inheriting her mother's beauty, Alex was not interested in the normal pursuits of teenaged girls which included becoming the prey of teenaged boys. Her interests were golf and science. It was during her favorite class, Astronomy, in which the teacher encouraged his students to become *solar sleuths* that Alex learned of the potential damage the sun could cause.

Supporting Characters of Importance:

Dr. Andrea Stanford – Director of the Joint Alma Observatory (JAO) Science Team at the Atacama Large Millimeter Array (ALMA) in the high-mountain desert of Peru. She is a graduate of the Harvard-Smithsonian Center for Astrophysics in Cambridge, Massachusetts. Her long-time assistant is Jose Cortez.

Members of the Harding Place Association (HPA) – In 36 Hours, book one of The Blackout Series, Shane Wren and his wife Christie Wren make their first appearance. They have two daughters and live just to the north of the Rymans. Shane Wren is the President of the HPA. In Zero Hour, two other members of the HPA are important players in the saga. Gene Andrews, a former director of compliance with the Internal Revenue Service, and Adam Holder, a former banker, make their appearance. Jimmy Holder, Adam's stepson, is a key player in the story as well.

Betty Jean Durham **–** In Turning Point, we are gradually introduced to Betty Jean Durham, the only child of the infamous former sheriff of McNairy County, Tennessee, Buford Pusser. Betty Jean had a tragic childhood that shaped her into a hardened woman—Ma Durham. Following the murder of her husband which resulted in her banishment from the sparsely populated southwest Tennessee county, Betty Jean and her two young sons relocated across the Tennessee River to Savannah in adjacent Hardin County. She rose to political power the old fashioned way, via luck and trickery, and became the iron-fisted Mayor of Savannah. The solar storm wreaked havoc on the world, and ruined the ambitions of many a politician, but nobody stops Betty Jean Durham. No sirree.

Leroy Durham Jr. – But his friends call him Junior, all five of them. Junior is the youngest son of the now deceased Leroy Durham, and Betty Jean Durham. Likened to Deputy Barney Fife, Junior was elected to become sheriff of Hardin County, Tennessee at the age of twenty-seven, just like his grandfather—Buford Pusser. Junior missed out on the Pusser genes somewhere in the process. While his grandfather was nicknamed Bufurd the Bull, during his short-lived wrestling career, Junior stood five-foot-eight and weighed one-hundred-fifty pounds soakin' wet. Now, Junior didn't have a big stick like his grandfather, but he wielded power nonetheless, with the aid of his Ma, who was very encouraging. Like all great antagonists, Junior always thinks he's right.

Coach Joe Carey – Unless you've lived in Smalltown, U.S.A., it's hard to appreciate the importance and grip high school football has on a community. While some may look up to their political leaders for inspiration, most will see the coach of the local high school football team as their guide to the Promised Land. In Turning Point, we are introduced to Joe Carey, former Head Coach of the Hardin County Tigers who has taken on a far more important role—leader of an underground resistance comprised of the brave young men and women of Hardin County High who stand opposed to the tyrannical actions of Ma Durham and her son Sheriff Junior Durham. The Tiger Resistance will play a big role in the Blackout Series.

Beau Carey – son of Coach Joe Carey and QB1, captain of the Hardin County Tigers football team. He is also the undisputed leader of the *disdants*, as Junior Durham calls 'em, those members of the Savannah community that fight back against the tyrant Mayor—Ma Durham. By the way, Beau is sweet on Alex, but then, what high school boy wouldn't be.

The Bennett Brothers, Jimbo and Clay **–** twin adopted sons of Coach Carey and therefore the brothers of Beau. Jimbo and Clay's parents passed away in a tragic accident and as Beau puts it, "they were left to us in their parent's will". Now the twin starting linebackers of the Hardin County Tigers join with the Carey's as an active thorn in the side of the Durhams.

Russ Hilton and family – Retired country crooner who found his way to the tiny town of Saltillo, Tennessee located on the west side of the Tennessee River in upper Hardin County. Hilton was of Colton's first clients and the two were surprised to run into each other toward the end of the Rymans' journey to Shiloh Ranch. Saltillo immediately accepted Hilton as their adopted son so he rewarded the community with its own honky-tonk, The Hillbilly Hilton.

The Tennessee River **–** Wait, hey Bobby, shouldn't this be under the next section titled Primary Scene Locations? Not in my book. You see, throughout history, bodies of water have played major roles in the development of mankind. They are the sources of life, providing hydration and food to all species on the planet. Bodies of water are also significant geographic boundaries, or barriers, to the movement of man. Before there were boats, planes and rocket ships, the vast oceans blocked man's migration. Then the new world was discovered, but for those without the ability to sail her waters, the rivers and lakes separated whole communities of people. The Tennessee River is one such body of water, dividing Hardin County in half both geographically, and politically.

As The Blackout Series continues, and pay attention my friends because this is important, you'll find that life is like a river. It's always easier to flow with the current. To turn against the current takes effort and fortitude.

Sometimes, going against the flow was necessary.

Jake Allen and family — Jake Allen is a country music star who began his career like so many others, in a honky-tonk on Printer's

Alley in Nashville. Like Russ Hilton, Jake hired Colton to be his agent and the men remained close friends for years. The Allens live halfway between Springfield and Branson, Missouri where Jake performs in his newly created music venue. Emily Allen went to nursing school before marrying Jake and becoming a full time mom to their son, Chase. Chase is in his late teens and has a bit of a wild streak, as most boys his age have.

***Stubby Crump and his wife, Bessie* —** The Crump family has resided on the west side of the Tennessee River for many years. The small town of Crump was founded by Stubby's grandfather and the family ran a farming operation for many years. Following high school, Stubby embarked on a two year stint in the St. Louis Cardinals baseball organization during which time he married the love of his life, Bessie. He realized baseball wasn't for him and like so many other young men in the Hardin County community, he enlisted in the military. Stubby's military career as an Army Ranger found him in the jungles of Cambodia, an experience which deeply affected him. Now in his late sixties, Stubby has converted a lifetime of experiences into making Shiloh Ranch a prepper haven.

John Wyatt and his wife, Lucinda – The Wyatt's own a cattle farm just to the north of Shiloh Ranch. Their land borders the Shiloh National Park.

Primary Scene Locations

Ryman Residence – located on Harding Place in Nashville. It is located approximately two miles east of historic Belle Meade Country Club and just to the west of Lynnwood Boulevard. It is a two-story brick home similar to the one depicted on the cover of Zero Hour.

***Harding Place Neighborhood* –** The portion of the Harding Place Neighborhood depicted in The Blackout Series is bordered by Belle Meade Boulevard to the west, Abbot-Martin Road to the north,

Hillsboro Pike to the east, and Tyne Boulevard to the south. Generally, this area is southwest of downtown Nashville in an area known for its historic homes—Belle Meade.

ALMA - the largest telescope on the planet—the Atacama Large Millimeter Array, or ALMA. It's located at an altitude of over sixteen thousand feet in Atacama, Chile.

The Natchez Trace – Well, this scenic route developed in the mid twentieth century was ordinarily a leisurely trek from Nashville to the Mississippi River. In Turning Point, it became the proverbial highway to hell. In our pre-apocalyptic world, don't let the experiences of the Rymans during their bug-out influence your decision to enjoy a long drive on this four-hundred-forty mile stretch of southern hospitality. But know this, you never know what lies around the bend.

Savannah, Tennessee – the county seat of Hardin County, Tennessee, population six thousand (pre-collapse) and lies on the east banks of the Tennessee River. It is a beautiful southern town with gorgeous antebellum homes and lots of friendly faces. Historically, Savannah has played a role in the Civil War. Fictionally, Savannah represents a microcosm of the small towns across America which chooses a path after TEOTWAWKI to be feared by every prepper. Beauty is only skin deep, but evil cuts clean to the bone.

Saltillo, Tennessee – the perfect prepper hideout. Sitting on the west side of the Tennessee River in the uppermost corner of Hardin County, Saltillo still maintains its local charm from two hundred years of sleepy isolation. Larger than life country music star Russ Hilton moves there with his beautiful family and now Saltillo has a claim to fame. Russ built his own music venue, the *Hillbilly Hilton*, and the town enjoys a close knit relationship centered around country music, southern comfort food, and the Tennessee River. Prepper Utopia.

Shiloh Ranch, Tennessee – the Rymans' bug-out destination. That's all you get for now my friends. You must read on.

Previously in The Blackout Series
Book One: 36 HOURS

The Blackout Series begins thirty-six hours before a devastating coronal mass ejection strikes the Earth. Dr. Andrea Stanford and her team at ALMA identified the largest solar flare on record—an X-58—hurtling toward the Earth.

This solar flare was many times larger than the Carrington Event of 1859, widely considered the strongest solar event of modern times. Alarm bells were rung by Dr. Stanford and soon eyes at NASA and the Space Weather Prediction Center, SWPC, in Boulder, Colorado, were maintaining a close eye on Active Region 3222—AR3222.

AR3222 was a huge dark coronal hole which has formed on the solar disk. It had grown to encompass the entire northern hemisphere of the sun. As the story begins, AR3222 had only fired off a few minor solar flares, but as the hole in the sun rotated out of view, Dr. Stanford knew it would be back.

That same evening, Colton Ryman was in Dallas, Texas on business. One of his country music clients was being considered for a spot on the upcoming Super Bowl halftime show. Colton participated in a dog-and-pony show hosted by Jerry Jones, owner of the Dallas Cowboys which included tours of the Cowboys' stadium and a concert in downtown Dallas.

Via news reports and text message conversations with Madison, Colton became aware of the unusual solar activity. At first, he brushed off the threat, but as time passed he became more and more convinced.

Madison and Alex were in Nashville going about their normal routine. Alex was the first to ring the alarm that the threat they faced from a major solar storm was real. She tried to raise the level of awareness in her mother, but Madison initially brushed it off as the overactive imagination of a teenage girl.

By noon the next day, all of the Rymans were beginning to see the signs of a potential catastrophic event. While the rest of the country went about its normal routine, Colton, Madison, and Alex made their decision—*Get Ready*!

The initial reports of the solar event were widely downplayed by the media. Even the President refused to raise the alarms for fear of frightening the public unnecessarily. But the Rymans were convinced the threat of a catastrophic solar flare was real, and the three sprang into action.

Colton, unable to catch a flight back to Nashville from Dallas, rented a Corvette and began to race home. Madison, using a valuable resource in the form of a book titled *EMP: Electromagnetic Pulse*, studied the *preppers checklist* located in the back of the book which enabled her to apply a common sense approach to getting prepared in a hurry.

Madison pulled Alex out of school and they immediately hit the Kroger grocery store for food and supplies. It was during this shopping expedition that news of the solar flare broke. Society began to collapse rapidly.

After forcing her way out of the grocery store parking lot using her Suburban's bumper to shove a KIA out of the way, Madison and Alex made their way to an ATM. The lines were long, but Madison waited until she could withdraw the cash. However, she let down her guard and was assaulted by a man who tried to steal her money. While the rest of the bank customers stood by and watched, Alex sprang into action with her trusty sand wedge. She beat the man repeatedly until he crawled away—saving her Mom, and the cash.

Meanwhile, Colton's race home—doing over one hundred miles an hour in the rented Corvette—was almost red flagged when he was stopped by an Arkansas State Trooper. While he was waiting for the trooper's deliberation of what to do with Colton, a gunfight ensued between two vehicles in the southbound lane of the interstate. Having bigger fish to fry, the state trooper left Colton alone, who promptly hauled his cookies toward Memphis.

Madison, despite being battered and bruised, elected to make another *run* with Alex. They added to their newly acquired preps but encountered a group of three thugs on the way home. Frightened for their safety, Madison once again used her trusty Suburban bumper to pin one of the attackers against the car in front of her. This brought an abrupt end to the assault.

As Colton drove home, he listened to the scientific experts on the radio broadcasts talking about the potential impact an EMP would have on electronics and vehicles. He learned pre-1970 model cars were more likely to survive the massive pulse of energy associated with an EMP. This knowledge served him well when he stopped at a gas station in eastern Arkansas.

Colton was confronted by three men who took a liking to the shiny red Corvette. Not wanting any trouble, Colton made the deal of a lifetime. He traded the new 'vette for a 1969 Jeep Wagoneer. The good ole boys thought they'd gotten the better of the city slicker, but it was they who were hoodooed. Colton took off with his new, old truck and sufficient gas to make it to the house.

Madison's and Alex's exciting day was not over. After dark, a knocking on the door startled them both. It was their friendly neighbors, Shane and Christie Wren. Madison attempted to keep her conversation with them brief, and her newly acquired preps hidden, but the simple mistake of turning on a light revealed her bruised face to the Wrens. The couple immediately suspected Colton of being a wife abuser despite Madison's explanation to the contrary.

After Madison sent the nosy Wrens on their way, she and Alex settled in to watch CNN's coverage of Times Square and the Countdown to Impact Clock. Thousands of people had gathered in New York to witness the apocalypse's arrival. The drama was high as the scene in Times Square was reminiscent of a New Year's Eve countdown without the revelry and deprivation.

The girls anxiously waited as they were unsure of Colton's whereabouts. Then they heard the kitchen door unlock, and Colton entered—reuniting the family. They began to move into the living room when Alex exclaimed, "Hey, look! The clock stopped at zero and nothing happened."

The CNN cameras panned the mass of humanity as a spontaneous eruption of joy and relief filled the packed crowd. The trio of news anchors couldn't contain themselves as they exchanged hugs and handshakes. Jubilation accompanied pandemonium in Times Square, the so-called Center of the Universe, as the bright neon lights from the McDonald's logo to the Bank of America sign continued their dazzling display. Then—

CRACKLE! SIZZLE! SNAP—SNAP—SNAP!

Darkness. Blackout. It was — *Zero Hour.*

Book Two: ZERO HOUR

The central theme of The Blackout Series is to provide the reader a glimpse into a post-apocalyptic world. Book One, 36 Hours took a non-prepping family through a fast-paced learning curve. In the period of a day, they had to accept the reality that a catastrophic event was headed their way and accept the threat as real. Once the decision to *GET READY* was made, then the Rymans scrambled around to prepare the best they could with limited time and resources.

Book two, Zero Hour, focuses on the post-apocalyptic world in the immediate hours and days following the collapse event.

Zero Hour picks up the Rymans' plight immediate after the collapse of the nation's power grid and critical infrastructure. First, they accept the challenges which lie ahead and then they apply common sense to establishing a plan.

First order of business was security. Colton recalls a story from his grandfather who reminds him to never underestimate the *depravity of man.* While they accept their fate, and attempt to set up a routine, there are neighbors who have other ideas about what's best for the Rymans.

Under the pretense of banding together to help the neighbors survive, the self-appointed leaders run a survival operation of their own. Using the intel willingly provided by unsuspecting residents, the three leaders of the Harding Place Association loot empty, unguarded homes and keep the contents for themselves.

When a rift forms between the Rymans and some of their neighbors, things turn ugly. There are confrontations and arguments. One of the leaders attempts a raid on the Ryman home at night with plans to steal the generator and some supplies. A gunfight ensues which wounds several of the attacking marauders. One of the three HPA leaders later dies due to lack of sufficient medical care.

There are also undercover operations including one involving Alex and a teenage boy. Alex recognizes the family's weakness in not having sufficient weapons to defend themselves and this boy's stepfather has an arsenal ripe for the pickins. Alex befriends the boy, procures weapons and ammunition, and everything is going smoothly until she finds the stepfather abusing her teenage friend. In self-defense, Alex shoots and kills the man, who happened to be one of the HPA leaders.

The death of the other two leaders has a noticeable effect on Shane Wren, the ringleader of the HPA who is the cause of the rift between the Rymans and the other neighbors. We're left in the dark as to whether the death of his cohorts resulted in the turnaround, or simply the knowledge that the Rymans are capable of defending themselves with deadly force, if necessary.

As a new threat emerges, the HPA and the Rymans come together to repel the vicious group of looters as they make their way deeper into the neighborhood. It was, however, too little too late for the majority of the neighbors in the HPA. Many, because they were out of food, and scared, opted to leave their homes and walk to one of the many FEMA camps and shelters established in the area.

The Rymans debated and considered their options. Madison stepped up and set the tone for the next part of their journey by making a large meal and announcing that it was time to go. The family gathered their most valued belongings to help them survive. It was time to go.

Here are the final paragraphs from ZERO HOUR:

Madison shed several tears as she closed the kitchen door behind them. Colton opened the garage door, revealing the trophy received for the most cleverly negotiated deal in his career—the Jeep Wagoneer. This old truck was their lifeline now. It was their means to a new life far away from the post-apocalyptic madness of the big city.

Colton eased the truck out of the garage and worked his way down the driveway until he had to veer through the front yard to avoid the Suburban. As he wheeled his way around the landscaping, all three of them looked toward the west where fire danced above the tall oak trees. Reminiscent of a scene from *Gone with the Wind*, the magnificent antebellum homes of Belle Meade were in flames.

Madison began to sob now. "Will we ever be able to return?"

"What about our things?" asked Alex.

"Having somewhere to live is home. Having someone to love is family. All we need is right here in this front seat—our family." With that, Colton drove onto the road and led the Ryman family on a new adventure and to a new home.

They'd reached their turning point—a point of no return.

Book Three: TURNING POINT

If you've come this far, you know The Blackout Series is designed to provide an imaginative journey into life after a major collapse event. Not everyone is a prepper, and the Rymans certainly fell into the non-prepper category. However, they're learning—the hard way.

At the end of book two, Zero Hour, they'd reached a consensus as a family that Nashville and the areas surrounding their home were unfit. The unknown destination of Shiloh Ranch seemed less dangerous than the known perils threatening them on Harding Place. So they bugged-out.

The perils of bugging-out are on full display in Turning Point—especially if (a) you wait to long and (b) you don't plan for all unforeseen contingencies. My goal in writing Turning Point was to provide the reader many of the realistic scenarios one might face as they're forced to leave their home.

In our busy lives, we scurry to and fro, using the highways and the byways to move from Point A to Point B. We take this freedom of movement for granted. In a post-apocalyptic world, everything changes, especially freedom of movement.

You see, in a grid down scenario like the one experienced by our characters in The Blackout Series, your world gets much smaller. The center of your universe starts with where you live, and can only expand as far as your means of transportation will carry you—feet, horse, bicycle, old car, canoe, etc.

The Rymans, thanks to some forethought and the art of negotiation on the part of Colton, were fortunate to have a pre-1970 vehicle which was immune to the massive blast of electrical energy released by the solar storm. The old Jeep Wagoneer served them well throughout the truck, showing its ability to get shot at with both bullets and arrows.

During their bug-out expedition, the Rymans faced a number of obstacles. There were the marauders who manned overpasses, underpasses, bridges, and town boundaries. They experienced natural roadblocks including fallen trees, horrendous storms and an important factor in this saga—The Tennessee River.

Above all, they experienced the depravity of man, and child. Children will grow up fast in the post-apocalyptic world but they will still need the guidance of an adult. The boy scouts at the Devil's Backbone were led down the wrong path of survival by their scoutmaster, who paid the ultimate price at the hands of Madison, who notched a couple of kills in Turning Point. Alex has grown into a woman with nerves of steel and an eye for trouble. She has an intuition that has developed throughout her post-apocalyptic experience. She also has learned that her fellow teens are prepared to step up as well.

The quaint town of Savannah has a problem—Ma Durham and her offspring, Sheriff Junior Durham. Like every tyrant before her, she takes over everything for the *greater good* and the *protection of Savannah's citizens.* However, it's not Savannah's citizens who benefit. There are those who are prepared to resist Ma Durham's tyranny.

Enter the *disdants*, as the dissidents are referred to by Junior

Durham. Led by beloved football coach Joe Carey of the Hardin County High School Tigers, local students and athletes went into hiding for the sole purpose of fighting back against Ma Durham, and surviving. A few of these young men play an instrumental role in saving Colton from discovery and assisting the Rymans in escaping the grasp of Junior and his Ma.

But, despite their successes and evasion of imprisonment, or worse, the Rymans still have a major obstacle to overcome—the Tennessee River. The route through Savannah was out of the question. The Pickwick Dam to their south was closed and blocked by the National Guard. The bridges farther north were either blocked by locals or manned by ransom-seekers.

As luck would have it, there was another option, one that hadn't been used regularly in decades. Old Man Percy, an elderly black gentleman pushin' a hundred years old, owns the dormant Saltillo Ferry. He agrees to fire up the old vessel and tote the Rymans to Saltillo, a small town of three-hundred-three inhabitants.

And one very dear friend, one of Colton's earliest clients, Russ Hilton. Hilton and his family moved to the tiny town to make a home for themselves as his country music career faded. They constructed the Hillbilly Hilton as a hangout for their neighbors and friends. The Rymans enjoyed a night of their southern hospitality, which included a song by Colton and Russ, and a respite from the travails of the road.

Invigorated by their fun, relaxing evening in Saltillo, the Rymans head south for the final thirty miles to Shiloh Ranch. It was intended to be an easy trip until a brutal thunderstorm collided with their progress.

The Rymans had lost their windshield wipers on day one of this bug-out when a marauding woman attempted to bash in their windshield with a tire iron. Madison, who was the family expert in using a vehicle as a weapon, shook the woman who was holding onto the windshield wipers for dear life, back and forth. Finally, utilizing the age-old technique of punching the gas and abruptly stopping, Madison threw the woman, and the windshield wipers, to the asphalt pavement. The wipers were ruined, as was the skull of the marauder.

In any event, wiper less, the Rymans elected to ride out the storm after a bolt of lightning brought a tree down right in front of them. In Colton's attempt to hide the truck, he got it stuck.

So they decided to hoof it—a fifteen mile hike to the Promised Land—Shiloh Ranch.

From Turning Point …

They made their way onto Federal Road and once again took in the smells emanating from the Tennessee River. The sounds of overflowing, rain-swollen creeks became deafening as they entered the canopy of trees which enclosed the quickly narrowing road that ended at Shiloh Ranch.

Excited, yet nervous, Colton could sense Madison and Alex picking up the pace. Madison giggled a little as she broke out into a slight jog. Alex laughed as she began to run and pass her mother.

Not wanting to be left behind, Colton joined them and grabbed his girls' hands as they rounded the bend to the entrance of Shiloh Ranch, giddy with excitement—until they stared down the barrels of half a dozen rifles.

Book Four: SHILOH RANCH

The Rymans made a decision to leave their home and chose a path into the unknown. They loved one another and they loved their life together. They made a decision to survive rather than succumb to a certain fate. Madison said it best around the campfire one night—*I survived because the fire inside me burned brighter than the fire around me.*

Thus a new chapter in their lives began at Shiloh Ranch, the vacation home of their friends Jake and Emily Allen. Jake, a country singer with an entertainment venue in Branson, Missouri, had been a long-time client of Colton's as well as a family friend.

By sheer coincidence, Jake, Emily, and their teenage son Chase happened to be at their two hundred acre cattle ranch located on the west bank of the Tennessee River in Hardin County. Shiloh Ranch, which was maintained by Stubby Crump and his wife, Bessie, was ideally suited for bugging out. Over the past couple of years, Stubby and Jake had added dairy cows, extensive gardening, and alternative-energy sources with an eye towards off-grid living. Their steps toward sustainability and self-reliance paid off when the power grid collapsed at Zero Hour.

The Rymans quickly assimilated into the extended family at Shiloh Ranch and a normal routine was established. One of the aspects of life in a post-collapse world was foraging. The inner debate between looting and foraging will always be a part of the prepper conundrum. The same applied to the activities of Chase and Alex who had become a team. They would explore areas within the Shiloh / Pittsburg Landing area to find empty homes and requisite supplies.

Their rules were simple—only get what we need and be careful. Rule one was followed but rule number two, be careful, was difficult for teenage Chase to abide by. Whether it was because he was trying to impress the pretty girl, or because he was raised largely unrestrained, Chase pushed the envelope constantly. In a world where danger lurks in the form of your fellow man, unnecessary risks could get you killed.

Although Colton assumed that Junior Durham was angry over the Rymans' escape from Savannah, he didn't expect it to become an obsession. For Junior, he'd become determined to find the Rymans and punish them for embarrassing him. Determination turned to obsession, which then became *all that matters*.

When Chase and Alex let down their guard and placed themselves in a compromising position, Junior's men pounced and kidnapped Alex. She was taken to Savannah where Junior tormented her. The women of Savannah had not fared well since the blackout. Junior and his friends were sadistic. Alex faced a certain fate.

But a rescue effort contrived by ex-Army Ranger Stubby, together with the assistance of the Rymans' rescuers—the Tiger Resistance led by Coach Joe Carey and his sons Beau, Jimbo, and Clay, was mounted to save Alex. The plan was working flawlessly when the wild card inserted itself into the game.

Chase, perhaps wanting to make up for the mistake that put Alex in harm's way, or in an effort to be the *big hero*, once again threw caution to the wind. In the chaos and darkness which surrounded Cherry Mansion during the rescue effort, he undertook an ill-advised shot in Alex's direction.

He missed his target, the two men who were dragging Alex towards Junior's home, but ruptured a propane tank instead. His second shot punctured two nearby gas cans. His final shot ignited the fuel mix creating an explosion that sent fire into the darkness and which engulfed Junior's bungalow on the Cherry Mansion property.

The scene was surreal as the devastation froze all the participants in the battle, except *one*. *One* who was watched through the eyes of Ma Durham and her new companion—the spirit of a Civil War hero.

From Shiloh Ranch …

Burgundy. It was Hardin County Tigers burgundy. Number 1. Gunfire continued to fill the night air from all directions. The young man was undeterred. He'd reached his destination. Briefly, he crouched down and lifted up a lifeless body.

Number 1 began running towards the neighborhood to Ma's left. He was fired upon but escaped unscathed with the blonde hair of the young woman flowing over his shoulder.

Ma stared into the fire, mesmerized. The roof of Junior's home collapsed to the ground, causing a rush of sparks and flames to gush out in all directions. Despite the intense heat created by the burning home and the surrounding vegetation, a chill came over her body. Ma unconsciously balled up her fists, unaware that a figure had joined her in the window. It wasn't Junior.

It was an aberration — a ghost who had been in a similar position one hundred fifty years before. The hissing sounds coming from the flames provided a voice for Union Major General William Wallace, who whispered in Ma's ear.

Fight fire with fire. Fight fire with fire.

Ma gritted her teeth and set her jaw. She mumbled the words but only loud enough for General Wallace to hear.

"When you poke the hornets' nest, ya better make dang sure you kill 'em all. If you don't, you're gonna suffer their wrath."

The saga continues in — HORNET'S NEST

Epigraph

Irritabis Crabones
You will stir up hornets.
~ Plautus

*****

Some say that by fighting the terrorists abroad since September the 11th, we only stir up a hornets' nest. But the terrorists who struck that day were stirred up already. If America wasn't fighting terrorists in Iraq and Afghanistan and elsewhere, what would these thousands of killers do - suddenly begin leading productive lives of service and charity? We are dealing here with killers who have made the death of Americans the calling of their lives.
~ George W. Bush.

*****

The firing on that fort will inaugurate a civil war greater than any the world has yet seen and you will lose us every friend at the North. You will wantonly strike a hornet's nest which extends from mountains to ocean. Legions now quiet will swarm out and sting us to death. It is unnecessary. It puts us in the wrong. It is fatal.
~ Robert Toombs, arguing against the Confederate's attack on Fort Sumter

*****

The only place you'll find fairness is in the dictionary and the only place you'll find justice is in Heaven.
~ Stubby Crump

*****

Rangers lead the way!

*****

Because you never know when the day before
is the day before.
Prepare for tomorrow!

Hornet's Nest

Book Five

The Blackout Series

CHAPTER 1

Moments after Midnight
November 2
Cherry Mansion
Savannah, Tennessee

Beau Carey led Jimbo and Clay through the thicket of trees that shielded Cherry Mansion from Highway 64 to its south. It took less than a minute for Beau to find a line of sight to the rear of the property where Junior's bungalow was located.

Like tigers stalking their prey, the boys moved from tree to tree, avoiding detection. But they never took their eyes off Alex, who was being dragged along by two of Junior Durham's thugs barely one hundred feet away. The men, both armed with weapons hanging over their shoulders from a sling, manhandled Alex as she squirmed and wriggled out of their grasps.

"Whadya think, Beau?" asked Jimbo, the oldest of the Bennett twins by all of a few moments.

"I don't see anyone between them and the house," replied Beau as he craned his neck above some shrubbery while looking for signs of Junior as well. "Should we try to take them or wait for the signal?"

Before either of the Bennetts could answer, Beau's father provided the response.

Tiger Tails, Tiger Tails, KICKOFF!

The sounds of explosions and gunfire filled the air. Instinctively, the boys hit the ground and crawled on their bellies to get a better look at the hundred-yard span between Cherry Mansion and Junior's bungalow.

Alex shrieked loudly as the world erupted around her. Startled, the men pulling her along shoved her down and readied their weapons. Confusion set in as they spun in all directions, openly exposed to incoming fire.

Beau sprang out of his crouch, ready to run to the sound of Alex's cry, but he caught himself and knelt back down. He whispered to the guys, "They'd gun us down in a second if we came at them. Let's cut them off by moving closer to Junior's house."

Beau's voice was calm. He was intense, adrenaline flowing through his body, but there was no panic. Alex had been on his mind since the moment they met. He joked with his boys about how he couldn't help but fall in love with a girl who'd greeted him with a gun at the back of his head and the promise of death if he moved.

There was something about her. She was very pretty, but that wasn't what attracted Beau to Alex. He thought of it night after night as he wondered where she'd gone with her family. Then one day it came to him. It was her confidence. Alex was the type of person who made a decision and stood by it. She wasn't afraid to stand up for herself or for what she thought was right. This required courage and intestinal fortitude, a trait few people had anymore.

He pushed aside the personal feelings he'd developed for Alex and concentrated on the problem. His dad had taught the team the importance of focusing on the task at hand. High school athletics created a learning process designed to teach young people dedication, determination, and discipline. This applied to sports as well as life.

Suddenly, two of Junior's men raced across the lawn towards the river. The boats were heard through the cracks of gunfire. Alex's captors were distracted. When they hesitated briefly, seemingly choosing between the mansion and the bungalow, Beau saw his window of opportunity.

He led his fellow members of the Tiger Resistance in a low crawl through the brush, scraping their hands in the process. Beau's eyes shifted between Junior's house and Alex, constantly calculating the distance and time. He was trying to maintain awareness of the men at the entrance to Cherry Mansion and the possible return of Junior to assist with Alex. The men continued to drag an uncooperative Alex through a flower bed and yoked her up by the arms, causing her to groan.

They'd closed to within only fifty feet when the gunshots rang out. The first one sailed to their right, striking the propane tank and creating a loud hissing sound.

CRACK! TING! HISS!

CRACK!

Another shot ripped a hole through two gas cans before embedding in the wood-framed house. Beau frantically searched for the source of the gunfire. He halted his progress and held his arms to the sides to prevent Jimbo and Clay from continuing. He approached with caution. A few steps forward and they would be in the line of fire.

CRACK! TING! BOOM!

The eruption caused by the final shot forced both ends out of the propane tank. The concave-shaped disks blasted through the shrubs, and one embedded in the trunk of a tree to the boys' rear. A fireball rose into the air, igniting the trees in flames and smothering Junior's bungalow in fire.

Through the smoke and carnage, Beau regained his position, unaware that a small smoldering magnolia branch was on the back of his burgundy Hardin County Tigers sweatshirt. He searched for a sign of Alex but couldn't see her.

"If I can't see them, they can't see me," he muttered to the Bennetts, who had joined his side. "You guys ready?"

"Dang straight, QB1," said Jimbo, using Beau's title as starting quarterback for the school's football team. *One* was also his jersey number.

"I'll get Alex; you two take out Junior's boys. Can you do that?"

"We'll do what we gotta do," said Jimbo as he pulled a knife from a sheath tied to his leg.

"Let's go," said Beau as he darted into the clearing to the point where Alex was seen last. Burning tree branches were scattered in their path and the fiery leaves floated from above him, which in this surreal moment reminded Beau of those Chinese sky lanterns he'd seen in the Olympics.

He stumbled and fell over one of the men who lay unconscious from the blast. Beau landed on his belly and quickly hopped into a crouch. *Where's Alex?*

Beau dashed towards Junior's house, ducking under a burning tree branch, until he found Alex. She wasn't moving. *Is she alive?*

"Alex! Alex!" Beau implored her to respond. Nothing.

A man was sprawled out on the ground to his right. His jacket was on fire and he was groaning. In a blur, Jimbo appeared out of the darkness and pounced on the man. He put the dying attack dog out of his misery.

"Is she okay?" asked Jimbo as he wiped the blood off his knife.

"I don't know," replied Beau.

"Go! Take her to the hospital. We'll cover you."

Both of the boys jerked their head toward Junior's place as the roof of the bungalow began to collapse from a large tree limb that fell on its peak. Beau scooped Alex up in his arms. Carrying her lifeless body, he ran like the wind as sparks of fire gushed out of the house, resembling the celebratory fireworks at the end of a big win for the Tigers.

Except this wasn't a win—it was only the kickoff.

Chapter 2

1:00 a.m., November 2
Hardin Medical Center
Savannah

Beau was out of breath as he lowered the unconscious body of Alex into the backseat of the car. As he'd regained his presence of mind while running through the streets of Savannah to their hidden vehicle, he felt for Alex's pulse. It was weak, but she was alive.

He knew enough about sports injuries to realize that Alex had a concussion. Heck, his ears were still ringing from the exploding propane tank. Alex was much closer to the center of the blast and fortunately wasn't near the ends, which, by design, always bore the brunt of the outward force.

As he frantically drove toward the Hardin Medical Center, two of Junior's men raced in the opposite direction toward Cherry Mansion. With the multiple distractions employed by his father, Beau felt certain that he could make it through town undeterred. Further, he hoped that Junior's men would be pulled off guard duty to assist in the fight on the west side of the town.

He was correct, in part. Ordinarily, at least two heavily armed guards would cover the entrance of the medical center, together with one at each of the other two entrances marked *Ambulance* and *Emergency*. Tonight, luck was starting to come his way.

He chose the ER, as it was the furthest door away from where a lone armed guard stood. As Beau wound his way through the incapacitated vehicles due to the solar storm, the guard perked up and began walking towards him. When he stopped short of the ER entrance and began to slowly roll forward, the guard unshouldered his rifle and began to run toward the Careys' old Chevy. Beau made a decision.

"Hold on," he said to the unconscious Alex. Beau gunned the engine and lurched towards the guard. The man's reflexes at this late hour were slow and he fired two shots wildly into the pavement between them.

Spit! Spit!

Before he could fire another round from the suppressed AR-15, his body was tumbling over the hood of the Chevy and onto the roof before falling off to the side.

The guard's legs were broken and his knees were crushed. He lay helpless on the ground, moaning. Beau grabbed the prized rifle and the man's nine-millimeter pistol. Then he dragged his body between two parked cars.

"Sorry, bud," Beau said to the man as he pulled some duct tape out of the glove box and taped his mouth closed. Then he tied his hands behind his back but didn't bother with the legs. He wasn't going anywhere on those busted-up twigs. "Someone will find you soon enough."

Beau located a wheelchair and gently placed Alex in it. Then he quickly parked the car in the lot so it would blend in with the others. He entered the ER doors with the AR-15 raised and prepared to shoot any of Junior's men who showed themselves.

A single nurse hid behind the desk inside the facility. "Please don't shoot me!"

"What?" stammered Beau when he realized he was pointing the weapon at her. "I'm not going to shoot you. This is an emergency. My friend needs help!"

The nurse rose from behind the reception desk and relaxed. She immediately admonished Beau. "Sir, you can't come this way. Everyone must be approved by the guards and checked in through admissions."

"She's unconscious," said Beau, ignoring the instructions. "She has a concussion and needs a doctor. Now!"

"Young man," the nurse said with condescension, "that's not how things are done anymore. Everyone must be approved by the deputies. You must leave and go through the front entrance."

"There's no time! Please!"

Heavy footsteps could be heard running down the corridor from Beau's left. It was dark, as the emergency lighting only illuminated workstations. He quickly put his body between Alex and the approaching figure. He fell to one knee, pulled the charging handle on the rifle, and steadied his aim on the center of the silhouette.

"What's happening here?" said a man wearing a white coat as he emerged into the dimly lit opening. His tennis shoes immediately squeaked as he stopped and raised his arms. "Whoa, okay. No need to shoot the only doctor on duty tonight!"

Beau obliged and shouldered the rifle. "Doctor, there was an explosion. My friend was close to the propane tank and it knocked her unconscious. Please help her!"

The doctor approached and the nurse worked her way from behind the desk. "Nurse Sutton, let's get this young lady into an emergency room and check her vitals. Son, my name is Dr. Jeff Fulcher. Let's see what we can do, but I have to warn you, there's a sheriff's deputy stationed outside the entrance to the medical center. He will take issue with us bypassing their protocols."

"Not tonight, he won't," Beau said as he wheeled Alex toward an examination room.

Dr. Fulcher shrugged and helped Beau place Alex on the table. While the nurse checked vitals, the doctor examined Alex for other signs of trauma. Fortunately, there weren't any.

Then he turned his attention to Alex's head injury. "Has she regained consciousness at all? Any moans or groans? Opening of the eyes? Movement of fingers or arms?"

"No, sir."

He examined her eyes, ears, and nose. "There aren't any signs of fluids coming from her ears or nose. I don't see any abnormal eye movements and her pupils are of equal size. That's good. She clearly has a concussion. Let's see if we can wake her up."

First he examined her neck and back to look for any obvious signs of a spinal injury. Satisfied there was none, the doctor carefully rolled Alex onto her side. The doctor placed one of her arms across her chest and then he bent her top leg at a right angle to her hip. Gently, he tilted her head back to insure that Alex's airway stayed open.

"A sign of a severe concussion is repeated vomiting," said Dr. Fulcher. "We don't want her to choke."

"Aren't you going to try to wake her up?" asked Beau.

"Not right away," replied the doctor. "She's stable and breathing steadily. There aren't signs of a severe concussion, and although she is knocked out, she's not exhibiting signs of being comatose just yet. Let's watch her and set up an IV to get some fluids in her."

"I'll take care of it, Doctor," said the nurse.

Dr. Fulcher took Beau by the arm and walked him into the hallway. "Son, this is very dangerous for both of us. Sheriff Durham has been strict about the patient-admission process. In a way, he picks who gets treated based upon the patient's perceived worth to the community. Every patient gets screened by his men."

"Doc, I know. Your nurse told me. Here's the thing. I ran over his man in the parking lot. He's bound and gagged out there between two cars."

Dr. Fulcher started walking toward the exit doors. "We have to help him."

Beau ran and grabbed the doctor forcibly by the arm. "No, Doc, we don't," said Beau, holding up the AR-15. "He fired this weapon at us without a hint that that there was some sort of admission process. I defended myself by running over him. Listen, that man and the rest of the Durhams' people are like a disease infecting our town. They kill people, steal their belongings, and force our women to do unspeakable things. My friend was going to become one of their victims tonight until we saved her. That piece of crap lying in the parking lot does not deserve your attention. Alex does."

The doctor studied seventeen-year-old Beau Carey. Then he smiled and nodded. "You're right, son. It's time we get our priorities straight around here. But be mindful, it's only a matter of time before our quiet little hospital gets busy. I heard the explosions and gunfire.

All heck is breaking loose out there, and you're just the first of many visitors tonight. This will include, I suspect, casualties from Junior's men as well."

"Yes, sir," said Beau, who was about to suggest he stand guard when the nurse called for them.

"She's waking up, Doctor!"

CHAPTER 3

1:11 a.m., November 2
Savannah

"Come on, Dad," encouraged Chase. "You've got to keep up."

Jake's chest was heaving as he jogged twenty yards behind Colton, Chase, and Coach Carey. He cursed himself with every step for not staying in some semblance of shape. Jake was a tall man, so he carried his weight well, as they say. But at two hundred sixty pounds, his hefty frame was wearing on his stamina. Twice he was forced to stop and catch his breath.

As Junior's men swarmed the area like hornets, the four men found themselves without transportation. When they saw Beau racing across the grounds at Cherry Mansion, carrying Alex, they assumed he was headed toward the Chevy, which had been hidden in the adjoining neighborhood. After they arrived at the rendezvous point and found the vehicle missing, their concerns grew for the safety of both teens.

"What should we do?" asked Colton, who was short of breath as well. Only the younger Chase and the athletic Coach Carey seemed to breathe easily. Jake caught up and joined the group, who tucked themselves inside a fenced backyard.

"I never anticipated losing our transportation," started Coach Carey. "We've got to get across town somehow and through a swarm of Junior's men."

Colton's eyes darted, searching for clues in the darkness. He was starting to panic and Coach Carey tried to calm the frightened father.

"Listen, Beau must have had good reason to take it without us," said Coach Carey.

"He was carrying Alex," said Chase. "I hope she's not hurt."

Colton remained silent as all eyes fell on him. Coach Carey patted him on the back.

"This is not the time to worry or panic," said Coach Carey. "Beau knows what to do. He'll get her help, or he'll meet us back at the house."

Jake lumbered through the fence gate and collapsed onto the cold, dewy lawn. "What's plan B?"

"We need transportation," replied Colton. "We've got to find Alex and then get out of town somehow. Junior's men will be scouring the banks, looking for our boat after we sent those two roaring by Cherry Mansion."

"Junior has a motor pool about three blocks from here," said Coach Carey. "It's surrounded by a fence with razor wire. It usually has a couple of guards stationed there but maybe not tonight. It's worth a try."

A car roared down the street across the way, causing everyone to join Jake on the ground.

"Maybe they're preoccupied," said Colton. "Let's go for it."

"It's all we got," said Jake as he hoisted himself off the ground. "Saddle up, boys. Let's see about a new horse."

Coach Carey led them through the backyards of Savannah's deserted neighborhoods as they approached the car depot from a secure angle. There was a stretch of a hundred yards where they'd be exposed before they could hit the woods again. Coach Carey gathered them at the edge of the clearing.

"The compound is on the other side of those trees," he explained, pointing across the road and toward a large vacant lot. "Once we cross the road and the clearing, we'll have lots of cover to assess our options."

Chase rose out of his crouch. "Let's go, then." He began to bolt into the clearing when Jake grabbed him by the arm.

"Hold up, Chase," said Jake. An old pickup with two armed men in the back sped down the street in front of them towards the river. "You've got to slow down, son. Coach Carey knows this area. Let him call the shots."

Chase dropped to a knee and his chin hit his chest. Coach Carey gave the young man a pat on the back in encouragement.

He'd mentored and coached teenage boys most of his adult life. These young men came from all walks of life. They were rich and poor. They came from broken families as well as two-parent homes. Unlike the adult world, where political animosity seemed to rule the day, high school football was about teamwork. He taught his players, both black and white, to be color blind. He told them that the concept of teamwork was *not about me, but we.*

Coach Carey believed that a lot of the problems of the world could be solved if people talked to each other instead of about each other.

He'd coached young men like Chase Allen before. They seemed on a mission to impress, which resulted in taking unnecessary risks. On the playing field, it might result in a fumble or a missed tackle. In life, miscalculated risks in an attempt to prove something could result in death or injury.

Coach Carey provided Chase some positive reinforcement. "All right, here's the play. Chase, you're the quickest among us and you're very good with that rifle. We need you on the other side, providing cover. Also, you'll have a clear line of sight up and down the road. I need you to get in position across the way near that stack of firewood. Once there, check for traffic, vehicles and anyone on foot. If you're sure it's clear, I'll send Colton next."

"Okay," replied Chase eagerly.

"You guys provide cover as I send Jake after Colton. I'll bring up the rear. By going one by one, we'll draw less attention, and this way we'll have rifle cover on both sides of the road. Sound good?"

"Yes, sir," said Chase, which drew a quick glance from his father. Coach Carey concluded that the words *yes* and *sir* weren't used very often between Jake and his son.

"Go!" said Coach Carey, and Chase took off in a flash. He swiftly crossed the road and took up his position as instructed.

Colton was next and promptly took up his position near Chase.

Jake, who'd recovered from the jaunt through the neighborhood, immediately joined his son and Colton.

Before Coach Carey crossed the open space to join the others, he thought to himself, *There's a big difference between calling a play in football and the task of crossing the road in a dangerous, post-apocalyptic world. In the end, teamwork results in achievement that an individual may not be able to reach.*

He took a deep breath and ran across the road, knowing that he was covered.

CHAPTER 4

2:00 a.m., November 2
Sheriff's Office Motor Pool
Savannah

The Hardin County Sheriff's Impound Facility had been converted to Junior's motor pool. Within the eight-foot-tall chain-link fence topped with razor wire were a variety of vehicles, both new and old. A large forklift commandeered from a scrap metal company outside town sat in the middle of the enclosed yard. New vehicles were unceremoniously tossed into piles along the fenced perimeter. They created another layer of protection for the prized antiquities centered in the facility—older model vehicles taken from people as they entered Savannah after the power grid collapsed.

"Yup, this is where our Jeep Wagoneer would have ended up," said Colton as the men stealthily walked around the fence to get a better view of the gatehouse and its guards. All four men heard a heated conversation taking place between the two deputies assigned to protect one of the most valuable post-collapse commodities—operating vehicles.

The two were arguing about abandoning their post and heading toward the river, where the action was taking place. However, it had been fifteen minutes since any gunshots could be heard. One man wanted to go out of curiosity, but the other refused, not wanting to abandon his post and incur Junior's wrath.

"Should we take them out?" asked Chase.

"That's one option," said Colton. "We can't use the guns. They'll draw too much attention."

"We could get the jump on 'em," said Jake. "I'm itchin' to throw a few punches!"

"Patience, fellas," interjected Coach Carey. "Let's try a diversion first."

Coach pulled his two-way radio out and called the play. "Tiger Tails, Tiger Tails, blue left. Blue left. KC Masterpiece. Pull trap. Repeat. KC Masterpiece. Pull trap. Go!"

"What the heck?" Jake laughed.

"There's an Indian historic site just to the north of Cherry Mansion," replied Coach Carey. "They installed a monument to pay tribute as part of the Trail of Tears National Historic Trail. It's a beautiful sculpture depicting the Indians as they were driven to the west."

"*Blue left* represents the northwest quadrant of town," added Colton. "*Pull trap* signals to the Tiger Resistance to create a diversion."

"Very good, Colton," said Coach Carey.

"What about the *KC Masterpiece* part?" asked Jake. "That's a dang good barbecue sauce."

"We tried to come up with a variety of metonyms for locations around town," continued Coach Carey.

"Look here, Coach," said Jake. "I'm still figurin' out the play callin' and you gotta go using words like metropolitan."

The men dropped to one knee as a car raced past the entrance of the motor pool. "No, Jake, not metropolitan. Metonym. It means a word or a name as a substitute for something else. Here's an example. When you need a copy from a copy machine, you say you need a Xerox. In the south, everything is a Coke. In a restaurant, the server doesn't ask if you'd like a soda. She wants to know if you want a Coke or sweet tea."

"I get it," said Colton. "Like when we complain about those fools in Washington, we're not talking about the city. We're talking about the government."

"Exactly," said Coach Carey. "In this case, KC Masterpiece refers to the beautiful Indian work of art. KC stands for Chiefs, like the football team, or Indians in our case. Masterpiece applies to the sculpture."

"Coach, this is brilliant," said Jake. "Even though some might say it's politically incorrect."

"Well, it's easy for us to understand but over the head for Junior's Neanderthals." Coach Carey laughed. "Plus, political correctness isn't really very important anymore."

Chase stood up and peered over a partially crushed Subaru. "Everybody, the guards are gone."

"Great!" exclaimed Jake as he allowed his six-foot-six frame to rise above their cover position.

"No, it's not," said Coach Carey as he grabbed Jake by the waistband and pulled him back down. "Nothing's happened yet. They're roaming around somewhere."

Everyone hit the dirt next to the fence and began to scan their surroundings. The men had either returned inside the guard shack or abandoned their post after their earlier discussion. Or they overheard the group talking and they were coming after them.

"Should we abort?" asked Jake.

"Let's fan out," replied Colton. "I don't like us bunched up. If something happens, run back to the edge of the trees near the woodpile and we'll regroup.

Just as the men began to allow some separation between them, staccato gunfire erupted to their north. Coach Carey caught everyone's eye and provided a thumbs-up.

Colton mouthed the word *gunfire?*

"Firecrackers," replied Coach Carey.

The favorite diversionary tactic of the Tiger Resistance, the boys had quickly emptied the local fireworks stands that were full of inventory for the Labor Day weekend festivities. Initially, the Tigers only had a few weapons. They had increased their arsenal substantially through their insurgent attacks since the grid collapsed. However, they were very low on ammunition, so it was saved for important missions and defense. Fireworks were still the method of choice when attempting to get the attention of Junior's men. By using empty barrels or other sound-modifying tools, a simple pack of firecrackers could sound like an automatic weapon from a distance.

The crack of a tree branch behind them caused the group to snap to attention. Heavy footsteps could be heard ambling along the trail parallel to the chain-link fence. More steps were approaching.

Nobody breathed as they listened to every step hit the ground. *Were they discovered?*

Everyone raised their weapons and prepared to fight. The two guards from the motor pool were searching for them.

The first man quickly moved past their position. But the trailing guard stopped only twenty feet away. He crouched and looked under the tree canopy created by the leafless oaks. He swung around and trained his rifle on the path he'd just used. He whipped his head back and forth. He sensed something.

Colton raised his gun and placed the man squarely in his sights. His finger eased onto the trigger. He waited. He had the shot, but he waited.

CHAPTER 5

2:00 a.m., November 2
Hardin Medical Center
Savannah

"Young man," said Dr. Fulcher as he exited Alex's room. "You can come in now. Again, she's stable, but these next few hours are critical to her recovery. She's also responsive to my voice, but she won't answer any questions that I pose to her beyond medical matters. I need you to help us check for memory loss. Please come in."

Beau slowly walked into the room. Alex was connected to an IV line on a portable line-stat stand. The IV bag provided a steady drip of fluids to help her body recover from the trauma. Alex slowly turned her head toward him and beamed. She raised her left arm to reach for him and he quickly joined her side.

"Beau," she whispered as he held her hand, "is this your idea of a date?"

Beau started laughing and turned to Dr. Fulcher and the nurse. "She's gonna be fine. She remembers me and the last time we saw each other. Thank you both."

"Good," said Dr. Fulcher. "Alex, I don't want you to overexert. Rest is critical right now and we still need to monitor you for internal injuries. Do you understand, young lady?"

Alex smiled and nodded. She squeezed Beau's hand, who responded on her behalf.

"She'll be a good patient, Doc. I'll make sure of it."

"We'll check on you both in a little while," said Dr. Fulcher as he turned and left the room. "Nurse, let's see about the man in the parking lot with two broken legs."

"Broken legs?" asked Alex.

"Yeah," replied Beau proudly. "I ran over one of Junior's men in the parking lot. He's tied up between two cars at the moment."

Alex managed a giggle and then winced in pain. "Thank you, Beau."

"No problem. Do you remember what happened?"

She tried to lift herself up in bed but immediately fell back onto her pillow. Beau helped her adjust to get comfortable.

"Junior had me at the jail and then took me to meet his mother. She was creepy."

Beau laughed. "That's bein' too kind. She's creepy and crazy. Did she hurt you?"

Alex shook her head and pointed toward her water cup. Beau held it for her while she sipped water through a straw. Alex smiled and nodded when she was done.

"Ma asked a lot of questions about my parents and where we've been. I refused to answer and then she called me names. Beau, she described the nasty things that Junior was going to do to me. You know, like she'd watched him before or something. Anyway, the last thing I remember was being pulled towards Junior's house."

Alex hesitated and tears welled up in her eyes.

Beau gently wiped them away with his hands and leaned into her and whispered, "It's okay, Alex. You're safe now. I'm with you, and the others will find us soon. Don't worry."

Alex took a deep breath to calm her emotions. "Beau, he was gonna rape me. Like the other girls. He was going to make me *his* sex slave." Alex lost it and began to cry. Beau tried to console her as Alex wrestled with the happiness of being alive versus the potential horrors that Junior had in store for her.

"You're safe now," he said. "We'll get you healthy and then all of us will come up with a plan to deal with Ma and Junior once and for all."

SMACK! SMACK!

"Where is everybody?" screamed a man from the main entrance to the hospital. "We've got wounded out here! Hey! Who's on duty anyway! Where's the deputy?"

SMACK! SMACK!

The man yelling in the hallway was slapping each of the hospital room doors, looking for anyone—patient or staff. He was getting closer to Alex's room.

"Hallooo!"

He was yelling now and clearly agitated.

Beau pressed his back against the wall and pointed the handgun toward the center of the door. The shadow of the man's feet blocked the light under the door. He was prepared to shoot him if he burst in.

SMACK!

He was at the room next door.

THUMP! THUMP!

He was hitting the walls with the back of his fist.

"Sir, sir!" yelled Dr. Fulcher. "May I help you, sir? I'm, um, the ER doctor on duty tonight."

"Where's my guy on the front door?" the man shouted in response. "Where's your staff? What's goin' on around here? Junior will be real pissed when he hears how you run things."

Beau saw the shadow of Dr. Fulcher's feet join Junior's man. "Deputy, I can assure you that your injured friends will be taken care of first. Let me help you get them in."

The footsteps trailed off as Dr. Fulcher led the way back to the front entrance. Without warning, the door burst open. Beau raised his weapon and found the trigger.

"No!" whispered Nurse Sutton. "Don't shoot me."

Beau lowered the pistol and tucked it into his jeans. His hands were shaking. He subconsciously wiped them on his sweatshirt to remove the sweat from his palms.

"What can we do?" he asked.

"We have to move her," replied the nurse. "There's a closed-off corridor at the back of the east wing. No patients are taken there and it's only used for storage. If they have wounded, this room will be needed."

Nurse Sutton raised the side protection bar on the bed to hold

Alex in place. She unlocked the wheels at each of the four feet so the bed became mobile. Finally, she attached the upper half of the IV pole to a bracket welded to the bed. Alex was ready to move.

She nodded toward the door. "Is it clear?"

Beau eased his head out into the dark corridor. There was motion in the hallway near the main entrance. The doctor was using the available wheelchairs to bring the injured men inside before going out to retrieve more. His movements were slow and deliberate. Beau recognized that Dr. Fulcher was stalling for them.

"Let's go," said Beau as he readied the AR-15 and moved into the hallway. Nurse Sutton easily moved Alex's bed on her own. She turned left and quickly pushed Alex through the well-lit ER reception area. As they rushed past the double doors into another dark hallway, Beau saw the man he ran over in the parking lot slumped over in a wheelchair. Dr. Fulcher had pulled him inside the door and left him there to intercept Junior's man coming down the hall.

Voices were raised near the main entrance.

What kind of hospital is this?

There's only one doctor?

You ain't got no nurses?

Nurse Sutton hurriedly pushed Alex through a set of double doors, entering a pitch-black hallway. Beau, walking backwards to detect any onlookers, helped the swinging doors come to a stop before shouldering his weapon. He let the air rush out of his lungs, unaware that he'd been holding his breath since they'd left Alex's room.

She pulled a penlight out of her nurse's uniform, used for conducting swinging flashlight eye exams. In the pitch blackness of this unused wing of the hospital, the small LED light illuminated the space for thirty feet.

"Use this to find a suitable room," said the nurse. "The rear exit is at the hallway to your right. We'll try our best to check on you, but it appears we have our hands full and we'll be scrutinized as well."

Beau moved ahead of her in the hallway, lighting up the entrances to each room as they went. "We understand. They're gonna be looking for us."

"Stay out of sight. When we can come check on you, we'll use a light like this. Anything else, and it might mean trouble. Okay?"

Alex answered this time. "Yes, ma'am, and thank you!"

Nurse Sutton patted her on the leg and then hustled back toward the ruckus that had entered the ER. When she moved through the double doors, Beau could hear a healthy combination of groans and curse words emanating from Junior's men. *Good.*

CHAPTER 6

2:30 a.m., November 2
Sheriff's Office Motor Pool
Savannah

Jake clasped his fingers together to provide a foothold for Chase to push through the broken window. The trailing guard had been summoned to join his partner and they'd both jogged off towards the river. The group had waited ten minutes to watch for the guards' return before making their move. Chase hoisted himself into the window and slithered through like a snake. A loud thud followed by a grunt indicated Chase had a rough landing.

"Hang on," said Chase as he fumbled through the building toward the only door.

Snap. Click. Creak.

"Now we're open for business," announced Chase to the group as he opened the squeaky door.

"Jake and I will stand watch," said Colton. "We need keys for everything—vehicles, the double gates, anything you can find."

Coach Carey and Chase could be heard rustling through desk drawers and cabinets. Jake and Colton continuously scanned the perimeter, watching for Junior's men. Savannah had grown quiet again and it was a matter of time before the guards returned to their post.

"I found a safe," said Chase. "The keys are probably in there."

"Here's a padlock key hanging on a nail," said Coach Carey. "Colton, try this on the gate locks."

Colton retrieved the key while Jake moved to the center of the driveway. Although they were in an open area, it was dark that evening, so they could move freely without immediate detection.

First, Colton tried the big gates where vehicles passed through. It wouldn't work. Then he tried the smaller swing gate and it worked.

"We're in," Colton said as he rejoined the group. "Now, how are we gonna start the cars?"

"And get out?" added Chase.

Jake walked around the building toward Chase, who was standing in the doorway.

"Son, did you see any tools in there? A screwdriver, wrench, or pliers?"

"There's a fishing tackle box," replied Chase. "Let's see what's in it."

Chase rummaged through the dark building and found the tackle box. He handed it to his father, who spilled the contents onto the front steps. Jake studied his options and then picked up a set of needle-nose pliers, a crescent wrench and an adjustable wrench.

"Chase, take these wrenches and remove the hinges from the tall gates. There's a tall stepladder leaning against the fence over there. Remove the bolts from the top first and work your way down. The weakest point of any gate is not where it's locked, but where it's attached. If we can't unlock the gate, we'll just tear it off at the hinges."

"Okay, Dad."

"I'll watch the front, but how are you gonna start the car?" asked Colton.

"Listen, back in the day, before there were computer hackers," started Jake, "there were guys who aspired to be automotive engineers. Automotive Engineering 101 required you to hot-wire a car. Let's see if I've still got it."

Jake spun around and marched through the entry gate with a purpose. Coach Carey laughed and trotted to catch up.

"There aren't many to choose from," said Coach Carey. "Obviously, the older cars will run. Is there a particular brand that's better than others?"

"I learned on Oldsmobiles," said Jake. "I wish there was an old

442 on the lot. I'd be one happy camper."

"Hey, here's an Olds," said Coach Carey. He approached a tan two-door Oldsmobile Delta 88. "It's a Holiday 88, whatever that means."

Jake tried the passenger door, which was locked. He worked his way around to the driver's side door and smiled as he opened it. The vehicle was in excellent condition other than the dust it had accumulated while sitting in the motor pool.

"Let's get to work," said Jake as he dropped to his knees and slid his large frame under the steering column. The model had a center shift console, which prohibited him from sliding along the floor from the passenger side.

"First, I'm gonna remove the plastic cover under the steering column. This will give me access to the main wire electrical bundles."

"Why don't you jam a screwdriver into the keyhole and twist like in the movies?" asked Coach Carey.

"That's one method," replied Jake. "The idea is to break the locking pins in the ignition, but it's very difficult to do. We don't have time to experiment."

Jake tossed the cover on the ground and then he fumbled with the wires. "On the Olds, there are three sets of wires. Two lead to the column- and dash-mounted controls like wipers and cruise control, but the third set leads to the battery, ignition and starter."

With a firm tug, he pulled out the starter bundle containing red, yellow, and brown wires. Jake fumbled with his large hands to detach the wires from the plug. He used the needle-nose pliers to strip the red battery wire and then he moved it to the side. Next, he took the brown ignition wire and stripped it to a similar length.

He put the two together and twisted them. The lights on the dashboard lit up as electricity was delivered to the vehicle's components.

"Okay, this is the part where you gotta pay attention," said Jake. "I'm gonna strip the yellow starter wire. All I need to do is touch it to the battery wire to create a spark. This should start the car."

Sparks flew out from under the dash as Jake touched the wires together. The car tried to turn over.

"Crap!" he exclaimed as he twisted his body to position his elbow against the gas pedal. He sparked the wires again, this time revving the engine to encourage the Olds to turn over. The big Rocket V8 motor roared to life. Jake pumped the gas pedal again and then released the starter wire. They were good to go.

Just as Jake worked his way out of the car to one knee, Chase came running from the front gate.

"They're coming back," he said under his breath. "We have to go."

Colton joined them. "Too late, they're almost here."

"What about the gate?" asked Coach Carey.

"The large gate's bolts are removed," replied Colton. "It's hangin' on but barely. I put the ladder back by the fence and closed the entry gate."

"Maybe they won't notice," said Jake.

"They'll notice," interjected Colton. "We left the gatehouse door open with the tackle box stuff everywhere. First, they'll see that and the motor will be running on this monster. We've got to get ready for them."

"Fellas, we need a plan," said Coach Carey.

Everyone stood silently for a moment. Then Jake moved into the driver's seat. "Hop in, boys, we're gonna play *Smokey and the Bandit.*"

CHAPTER 7

3:00 a.m., November 2
Hardin Medical Center
Savannah

Beau and Alex had been catching up on the events of the last five weeks since they'd parted ways up on Clifton Road by the creek. They both laughed about the cheerleader comments and then Beau revealed how much he'd enjoyed their kiss. Alex became silent and then admitted she'd liked it too.

"I think I need to rest, Beau. Will you stay with me?"

"There's something I should've done already," he replied. "It'll just take a few minutes, but I'll be right back. Okay?"

"Please hurry," said Alex.

"I will," said Beau as he carefully worked his way in the dark corridor. He took a moment to let his eyes adjust. The batteries on the LED penlight were wearing down and he wanted to use it sparingly.

Beau quickly moved to the set of double doors, which led to the next corridor of the hospital. He paused there for a moment to listen to the activity in the emergency room. Dr. Fulcher was trying to explain that the injured man was found in the parking lot. He was being brought in for treatment when the rest of the injured arrived.

Junior's man was belligerent and it was causing the doctor to get agitated. Beau didn't care as long as everyone stayed occupied and away from Alex.

He pulled a gurney and blocked the doors. Beau maneuvered several other gurneys into the middle of the hall and locked the wheels in place. He was trying to create an advance warning system in case one of Junior's men decided to take a stroll. Dr. Fulcher and his nurse would use their lights to find their way through the maze of hospital gear. Junior's half-awake men would bull through the obstacles, creating an alarm system for Beau to get into position.

Beau checked on Alex to make sure she was resting comfortably. She was in a deep sleep, which ordinarily wouldn't concern him, but considering she'd received a minor concussion, it gave him pause.

While he had a moment, he positioned other pieces of furniture like metal cabinets and lounge chairs in the hallway in front of their location. If he had to get into a gunfight, at least he'd have some cover.

Finally, he confirmed their exit option. He left this unobstructed for a quick retreat. *But to where? Nobody knows where we are and I don't have my radio. It must've fallen on the ground during the chaos at Cherry Mansion.*

He couldn't worry about that right now. Retrieving his own car was out of the question because it was parked near the ER entrance, which was now filled with Junior's wounded deputies.

So he waited.

Beau fought sleep as he sat on the floor in the dark hallway. Faint sounds of voices and furniture sliding caught his attention from time to time. He thought about Alex and the certain fate in store for her. What the Durhams had done to their community was immoral and unforgivable.

When he reunited with his father, he was going to insist that it was time to take a stand. Beau realized the Tiger Resistance was outnumbered and outgunned. But tonight they'd shown they were capable of beating back Junior and his thugs. Enough was enough. The Tiger Resistance needed to become more than an opposition to the Durhams. It was time to rid Savannah of these tyrants.

The clanking sound of metal on metal woke Beau out of his half-conscious state. He immediately scrambled into Alex's room and found her sleeping soundly.

"Stupid thang!" shouted a man's voice from the end of the eighty-foot hallway.

Not the doctor or nurse.

Beau needed to intercept the man without raising attention. He left the AR-15 by Alex's side. He remembered that was her favorite weapon. If she woke up, at least she'd know how to use it. Besides, he wanted to stop this guy without firing a gun. Gunshots would create an uproar throughout the hospital.

He listened as the man moved methodically down the hallway. He was stopping at each door and moving inside the rooms. He didn't have a flashlight, but was using the ambient light coming from the outside to guide him. Beau planned on doing the same and using his familiarity with the surroundings to surprise the interloper.

He pulled his fixed blade from a sheath looped through his belt. Beau had never attacked anyone with a knife, but his mind was focused on protecting Alex. He transformed himself from a high school kid to a man who would do anything to protect the one he loved.

Beau moved through the scattered gurneys at a low crouch, constantly watching the movements of Junior's man. After entering and exiting the sixth room down the hallway, the man shouldered his rifle.

Good. Let your guard down.

Using the minimal light available, Beau stalked the man, studying his method and routine. As the man, who was short and stocky, moved into a room, Beau would move forward to a concealed position. Within moments, he was only ten feet away from the last room the man entered.

Catlike, Beau moved against the wall and waited for the man. It was taking longer than normal. He kept waiting.

Beau grew impatient. He slipped into the room and scanned every corner. The man was gone. Disintegrated. *Where did he go?*

Then Beau smelled it. Rancid. Junior's man was taking a dump.

Beau's mind raced. Should he jump the guy while he was sitting on the toilet? Or surprise him when he came out?

He waited. His answer came with the roar of the flushing toilet. Apparently the hospital auxiliary power to their internal water system still functioned. The noise masked Beau's next move.

Beau pushed in the door and it slammed into the back of the heavier man as he struggled to buckle his belt. He lost his balance and crashed into the shower stall, breaking open his forehead on the tile. The man quickly regained his footing, but Beau took the butt end of his knife and crashed it into the wound on the man's forehead.

ARRRRGGGGHHHH!

Junior's man fell back into the shower in a heap. Beau grabbed a bedpan off the bathroom sink and slammed it into the man's temple, knocking him out.

Breathing heavily, Beau raced into the hallway, where he immediately caught himself and slid against the wall. He listened.

No one heard them. There was no activity outside the double doors. His heart was beating out of his chest and he took several deep breaths to calm himself. He had to finish the guy off.

Beau had never killed anyone. In this post-apocalyptic world, he knew it was inevitable. He hesitated. This was the most difficult decision of his life.

When someone killed another by choking, stabbing, or other physical contact, the action was typically accompanied by a high level of rage and even a personal connection with the victim. Stabbing someone was visceral, graphic, and provocative. The act was very emotional—*close and in your face.*

Beau had been prepared to stab the man and kill him. He was acting defensively, reacting to the threat the man posed to Alex. Now, despite the man's potential threat being the same, he lay semiconscious and harmless—at least for the moment. For Beau, killing him under these circumstances felt more like murder.

He reentered the room and found the man lying on a shower floor full of blood. Once again, Beau had to make a choice with regard to the life or death of Junior's men. Allowing him to live flew in the fact of his plans to rid Savannah of these scum. Killing him in cold blood made him sick to his stomach.

Beau backed out of the room and slumped against the wall. He asked God for a sign.

Nothing this time.

He was on his own. Beau paced the floor, subconsciously patting his knife in its sheath. His eye caught an EKG machine shoved into the corner of the room. Several multicolored wires were plugged into it. He took the wires and hog-tied the man by tying his arms behind his back and then binding them to his feet. He ripped a pillowcase into strips and gagged the man.

"You'll live, this time," said Beau under his breath.

Beau gathered up the man's weapons and then found a prize tucked in his belt—a two-way radio. He immediately found channel 1, his jersey number, today's channel, at least until the sunrise reset.

"Tiger Tails, Tiger Tails, injury time-out."

Beau looked through the windows to get his bearings. He repeated the play.

"Tiger Tails, Tiger Tails, injury time-out. Strong side formation. On one. Go!"

CHAPTER 8

4:00 a.m., November 2
Savannah

Jake put the Holiday 88 into drive and opened up the four-barrel carburetor. The powerful V8 turned the rear tires, pelting all the vehicles behind it with gravel. After a slight fishtail, Jake brought the rear end back into line and burst through the chain-link gates, which partially flipped over the roof of the car, and the rest dangled from one bolt on their left.

"Whoa, look out!" exclaimed Colton as he gripped the headrest of Coach Carey's passenger seat. Jake slammed on the brakes to avoid shooting across the street into a drainage ditch.

CRACK! CRACK! CRACK!

Gunshots rang out as Junior's men ran down the road toward them. Undeterred, Jake swung the car around and headed directly for the assailants.

"Shoot 'em!" he shouted to no one in particular.

Colton reached his right arm through the open car window and began firing at the men with his pistol. The scene resembled a cops and robbers scene from a sixties B movie.

Jake gripped the steering wheel and swerved the mighty Olds back and forth to avoid getting hit by the deputies' errant shots. When Colton returned fire, they jumped for cover behind a parked car.

"Keep going this way!" shouted Coach Carey as he pointed straight ahead. "They'll identify the car and report we're going north. It'll throw them off."

"Got it!" exclaimed Jake as he roared up the road and put sufficient distance between them and the men who were firing frantically in their direction.

"Woo-hoo!" shouted Chase, jubilantly exchanging high fives with Colton. The four men were celebrating when a faint sound came over Coach Carey's radio. The static could barely be heard.

"Shhhhh, everybody. Quiet!" Coach Carey adjusted the squelch and turned up the volume. They waited in silence as Jake slowed the Olds to a crawl while keeping his eyes on the rearview mirror.

"Listen."

The two-way squawked to life.

"*Tiger Tails, Tiger Tails, injury time-out. Strong side formation. On one. Go!*"

"That's Beau!" shouted Coach Carey. "Turn right up here. Right. Right!"

Jake gave it the gas, turned on the next street and headed east. He glanced toward the head coach of the Hardin County Tigers. "What's it mean?"

Coach Carey shifted in his seat to face Colton. "I don't want you to be alarmed. This doesn't necessarily mean something's wrong."

"What? What does it mean?" asked Colton, a look of fear having overcome his face.

"That was Beau, and we know he has Alex. He's at the hospital somewhere on the right side, probably the east wing. He wants us to come quickly and find him. He's by himself with Alex."

"Jake," said Colton.

"I'm on it, brother," said Jake, acknowledging Colton's concern. "Just guide me in there, Coach."

"Keep going just a few more blocks. We'll hide the car behind the cancer center to the east of the hospital. He'll be watching, or we'll find a rear entrance. Junior's men will have the front covered."

"Guys—" started Colton before Coach Carey interrupted him.

"Stay calm, my friend," he said. "We'll get our kids outta there."

Jake made the final turn toward the rear of the hospital as instructed. He cut the lights and then coasted into the back parking lot of the adjacent buildings undetected. Jake and Chase agreed to set up a perimeter watch while Colton and Coach Carey went in the rear entrance. If there was a problem, they'd be coming out in a hurry. Jake was instructed to get the car and Chase would provide cover fire while the teens were extracted.

As Colton and Coach Carey approached the rear exit, a small light flashed on and off several times from the third window to the left of the door. Suddenly, the door slowly opened and Beau stuck his head out into the night air.

Colton ran toward Beau.

"Alex?" he asked.

"She's gonna be okay, Mr. Ryman. Come on in. We have to hurry."

Colton pushed past Beau and stumbled into the dark corridor.

"Hey, Dad." Beau gave his father a hug.

"You okay?"

"Yes, sir. Follow me."

Colton followed Beau, but when he turned toward the third door, Colton raced past.

"Alex, oh, honey. Alex, are you okay? How're you feelin'?"

"I'm fine, Daddy. My head hurts and my ears are still ringing a little. The doctor said I'll be fine with rest."

"Thank God, Allie-Cat. Thanks to God that you're okay."

"Shhhh. Someone's coming," said Beau as he slipped into the room. Beau's father immediately readied his gun and the two Careys prepared for the worst.

A flashlight illuminated the hall. Beau took a chance and stuck his head out of the doorway. The light was swinging from side to side, but in so doing, the white lab coat of Dr. Fulcher came into view.

Beau took a risk and entered the hallway, allowing himself to be seen. He flashed his penlight in Dr. Fulcher's direction, who immediately returned the contact with two flashes. Dr. Fulcher moved past the scattered gurneys and greeted Beau.

"How's my patient?" he asked nonchalantly.

"She's fine," replied Beau. "Her dad's here now."

Colton and the doctor exchanged pleasantries before Colton received a full analysis. After the two spent time alone, Dr. Fulcher provided some instructions to Alex.

"Young lady, you're very lucky in more ways than one. There's a lot of love in this room prepared to protect and support you. Do not let them, or me, down by trying to do too much. You need bed rest and plenty of fluids. Do not overexert. Are we clear?"

"Yes, Doctor. Thank you for saving my life."

"Well, I don't know about that." He chuckled before continuing. "I believe that young man in the number one sweatshirt should be thanked for his efforts. Just don't undo what we've accomplished, deal?"

"Yes, sir."

Dr. Fulcher turned toward Beau and his father. He handed them a set of keys. "I'm going to give you my car. It's an old Chevy Suburban that has been retrofitted into an ambulance. You are no longer safe in Savannah. Junior's men are already dubious about the man with two broken legs."

"What?" asked Coach Carey.

"I'll explain later, Dad," replied Beau. "Doc, there's another man in a room up the hallway. He, um, slipped and fell in the shower. I tied him up so he couldn't hurt himself."

"Yeah, sure, I'll deal with him when you folks have hit the road," said Dr. Fulcher. "The ambulance is parked at the north loading dock. Everyone is preoccupied up front for now. I suggest you avoid the main entrance."

Beau shook his hand. "We will. Thank you, Doc. We'll probably see ya around."

CHAPTER 9

4:40 a.m., November 2
Savannah

Alex was carefully transferred from her bed to the stretcher located in the back of the old Suburban-turned-ambulance. Beau and Coach Carey occupied the front seat while Colton sat in the single rear seat, watching over his daughter for changes in her medical condition.

Chase waved from the side street in the direction of his father. "They're all inside. We're good to go."

The two vehicles needed to cross the open space created by Highway 64 and then work their way through the neighborhoods over to Florence Road. The most direct route to their destination was along Highway 128, where Coach Carey's house was located, but that part of town was buzzing with Junior's men. The fifteen-mile trip would take longer through the east part of the county, but they were far less likely to encounter trouble.

Beau led the way as the two cars crossed the main drag without incident. They had kicked Junior in the teeth and he was surely hoppin' mad. The town was starting to settle into the early morning hours, but deputies were sure to be buzzin' about. Undoubtedly, daylight would bring quite the gathering at the Hardin County Detention Center.

Just past the entrance to the Kroger store, Coach Carey instructed his son to pull over into the parking lot of the U-Haul Center.

"Here's where I get out," he said, turning to Colton. "We have several apartments down at the Savannah Village, which are used for lying low. I suspect the town will be busy in the morning. It's best I stay away."

"Coach, thank you for helping us," said Colton. "I don't know what we would've done if it wasn't for you, Beau, and the rest of the team. God bless all of you."

"Don't you say another word, Colton. We're in this together, and I, for one, despite the circumstances, am glad that you folks are still around."

"I agree with Dad," said Beau. "I'm sorry Alex had to go through this, but it was very nice to see her again. And, um, you too, of course." Beau slumped down in his seat and pulled his sweatshirt hoodie over his head.

"Oh, I see how it is," said Colton, laughing. "The hometown hero only wants to save the pretty girl. Sure, okay."

"I'm just kiddin', Mr. Ryman," protested Beau.

Coach Carey laughed and patted Beau on the shoulder. "I'm proud of you, son. Now listen, you know where to go, right?"

"Yes, sir. I'll be out of radio range. Can I stay with Alex for a couple of days?"

"Sure, but how about this. Make your way up to the Pentecostal Church at Scooter Road around noon each day and check in. An *all clear* on both ends will let us know you're okay. Plus, I wanna hear how Alex is doin'."

"Deal," said Beau, who gave his father a fist bump.

"Colton, you wanna sit up here?"

"No, thanks, Coach. I need to keep an eye on Alex."

Coach Carey closed the door and gave his son a thumbs-up. He waved to the Allens as they passed and then he jogged into the dark streets of Savannah.

Beau drove along in silence until they reached two stalled cars blocking the road at Walkertown. They approached slowly and Colton readied his weapon. He looked to the Oldsmobile driven by Jake and saw that Chase had the barrel of his rifle pointed out the window.

"We're about to intersect with Highway 128, but we could push just a little farther east and take the airport road down," said Beau as he stopped short of the stalled cars. The road forked and an unobstructed option appeared to his left.

"Do that," said Colton. "None of us are in the mood for any more trouble tonight."

Beau turned down a country road and led them on a more circuitous route along the edge of the Hardin County Airport.

Colton constantly checked on Alex. She was so peaceful. Madison had raised her to become a beautiful, intelligent young woman. He wasn't sure what the key to success was in raising any child. Perhaps it was the fact that Alex was an only child and they could devote all of their attention to her. Maybe it was the way they'd treated her growing up, like a small adult. The Rymans always included her in conversations. They spent time discussing current events and were active in her school lessons. Even as Colton's career demanded more of his time, he'd find a way to engage his daughter in conversation in the evening or on weekends. Raising a kid took some effort, but moreover, it took dedication.

Beau continued past the airport, where a large banner read *American Barnstormers Tour: Fun Fly Savannah.* Several vintage aircraft were parked on the tarmac near the small terminal. They looked like extravagantly painted crop dusters although one plane resembled the plane flown by the Red Baron in his infamous battle with Snoopy.

Just shy of the intersection of Highway 128, Beau slowed to a stop and jumped out of the car. He ran back to Jake and spoke for a moment before returning.

"Is everything okay?" asked Colton.

"Yes, sir. I wanted to remind them that this road may have Junior's men traveling up and down it, although I doubt it. I also told them that if we get separated for some reason, Nixon's Loop is the first right after the fourth church."

"Over the river and through the woods, right?" said Colton, laughing.

"I guess so," replied Beau, who seemed confused by the reference to the old song. "Anyway, first we have the Methodists, then the Baptists, followed by the Episcopalians, and last on the right are the Pentecostals."

"That sounds like the correct order," said Colton under his breath.

"Sir?" asked Beau, looking into the rearview mirror at Colton as he eased southbound on the highway.

"Nothing. How much farther?"

"Maybe ten minutes or so," replied Beau, who picked up speed on the deserted highway with the Olds right on his bumper.

Colton began to nod off when Beau turned off the highway. He made a series of turns and loops that would require dropping bread crumbs to find their way out. This was what Colton meant by *over the river and thru the woods.* It reminded him of the road out to Old Man Percy's place. He hoped the old guy was okay.

The faint glow of the sun rising allowed a little better view of his surroundings. They were in the middle of rich bottomland along the east bank of the Tennessee River. Small farmhouses dotted the landscape, including an occasional abandoned tractor. Occasionally, a cow stood solemnly in a field, chewing its cud.

A long thicket of trees created a natural fence along a creek that ran parallel to the river. Beau crossed a wooden bridge made of railroad ties, and the thumping against the Suburban's old frame woke up Alex.

"Daddy?"

"Hey, Allie-Cat. You've been a good sleeper." Colton used the words from when she was a child. Alex would always be his little girl in many respects.

She tried to turn her head toward the front of the car but winced in pain.

"Beau?"

"Hey, Alex," he replied. "We're almost there."

The road opened up into an enormous farm completely surrounded by a white fence. They were greeted by the black-and-white faces of more than two dozen dairy cows.

"Well, hello," said Colton as Beau drove past several onlookers.

"They're Holsteins," said Beau. "This is Croft Dairies."

Colton saw the sun peak over the horizon to their rear. Like the ranches on the west side of the river, this represented a world that those in the city could never understand. Peace, serenity, and privacy were the norm. People should strive for this, not the prime corner unit in the newest high-rise.

"Give me a minute," said Beau as he parked the truck and turned off the engine. The door slammed closed, leaving them in silence.

CHAPTER 10

6:00 a.m., November 2
Croft Dairies
Nixon, Tennessee

Rhoda Croft was the widow of Master Sergeant Willie Croft, former U.S. Army Ranger. The Croft family had lived in and around Hardin County since the Civil War. Willie's ancestors were slaves used by the Confederate Army to run supplies up and down the river to Pickwick Landing. While the Battle of Shiloh had been fought on the west of the river, the Confederates had planned an ingenious attack upon Savannah by circling around the rear flank of Grant's Union Army. The opportunity never arose, as the Confederates became bogged down and were unable to supply sufficient manpower for the incursion from the southeast.

Following the war, the Croft family settled in the rural community of Nixon, Tennessee, and were given a forty-acre parcel of river bottom to farm. The family later expanded and by the mid-1900s, they owned over a hundred acres. As the TVA waterway system came to fruition, the entrepreneurial Croft family saw an opportunity to create a thriving dairy business on their land and Croft Dairies was born.

Rhoda Croft had volunteered her facilities to the Hardin County School system to enhance their FFA program. FFA, originally known as the Future Farmers of America, was an organization dedicated to the agricultural education of young people. It was through this program that Rhoda met Coach Carey.

Coach Carey wanted his players to consider getting involved in skill-learning activities during their off-season and many came to

Croft Dairies to learn from Rhoda. Miss Rhoda, as the local families came to know her, targeted the teenage girls of Hardin County for the FFA program.

She felt in today's society, every young woman should learn to be self-reliant and grow up with an entrepreneurial spirit. During her introductory remarks to her new charges, Rhoda would remind them that achievement would lift young women to levels of confidence and respect, not whether they could burn their bras or abort their babies. She felt strongly that young women were being misguided by political slogans to their detriment. Her beliefs resonated, and as a result, most high-school-age girls volunteered at least one summer at Croft Dairies as part of the FFA program.

Following the collapse, when it became apparent that the Durhams intended to enslave the young women of Savannah to do their bidding, Coach Carey immediately approached Rhoda about taking the girls in and hiding them. She agreed without hesitation and encouraged many of her neighbors to do so as well.

As a result, the bend of the Tennessee River stretching from Pickwick Dam to the south and along Nixon Loop to the north became the homes for wayward girls, so to speak. Thus far, Junior's activities had avoided this sparsely populated part of Hardin County.

Rhoda warmly greeted Colton and the Allens into her home. With their help, she escorted Alex inside on the stretcher, where several high school classmates of Beau's awaited. Naturally, they fawned over the handsome star football player, so when he asked them to welcome Alex and take care of her, they were eager to please.

"For now, we'll set her up in the guest bedroom on the first floor," said Rhoda. "When she's capable of getting on her feet, we'll move her upstairs near me. We'll be glad to take care of her for as long as it takes."

"Rhoda, you have no idea how much this means to her mother and me," said Colton. "Madison doesn't know what's happened and she'll insist on coming to see her." Colton suddenly stopped speaking and began peering through the windows.

"What's wrong, Colton?" asked Rhoda.

"How are we gonna get across the river?" he asked.

"Don't you worry your head about that, mister," replied Rhoda. "They're not much, but we've got a couple of flat-bottom aluminum boats with trolling motors. We'll get you back and forth as long as the current's not too swift."

"Thank you," said Colton, who then turned his attention to Jake. "Jake, would you and Chase mind returning to Shiloh Ranch and fill in Maddie? She needs to know what happened and I'm sure she'll insist on seeing Alex."

"No problem," said Jake. "We'll leave now if that's okay with Miss Rhoda."

"Absolutely. Ladies, would a couple of you escort these gentlemen to the dock and point them in the right direction?"

"Yes, ma'am!" replied at least five of the girls gathered in the spacious foyer.

Rhoda laughed. She leaned in to whisper to Chase, "You have several admirers."

"Appears so, ma'am," he replied.

The front door swung open and allowed the full sun to light up the interior of the beautiful home built prior to 1900. Painted portraits of the Croft family adorned the walls as well as a painting of President Lincoln. Miss Rhoda was proud of what they'd accomplished.

Jake and Chase said their good-byes and followed a few of the girls toward the boats. Colton turned his attention back to Rhoda.

"May Madison and I stay a few days, you know, until Alex has recovered?"

"Of course. I wouldn't have it any other way. Colton, you're among good people here. We live in troubling times and it's good to be among friends. In fact, when you're under my roof, you're family."

Colton spontaneously hugged Miss Rhoda and thanked God for the blessings of friends and family.

CHAPTER 11

8:00 a.m., November 2
Tennessee River
Shiloh Ranch

Jake steered the flat-bottom boat along the west bank of the river. They passed Rock Pile, where Jake and Colton had visited the other day. Jake needed to have a talk with Chase and he regretted not doing it in the car when they were alone earlier. It had been a frantic, tiring night and he didn't feel like addressing what had happened at Cherry Mansion, but shortly they would have to explain everything to Madison. She didn't need to hear the details just yet, but Chase needed to understand that the upcoming conversation wasn't about him. It was about Alex.

He took a deep breath and tried to let go of the tension. In the past, when dealing with Chase, Jake would take his son's bad behavior personally, as if it was intended to cause his father aggravation. The end result of these father-son talks was a blowup and everyone running to their own corner of the house. This time, he had a captive audience and he wanted this conversation to be different.

Jake started the discussion over the sound of the trolling motor. "Son, we need to talk."

"About what?"

"About last night. About what happened at the RV park. A lot of things."

Chase turned his back to his father and stared downriver. His body language spoke volumes, but Jake persisted.

"Son, you've been put in a horrible position. All of us have, but you more than others. You are our designated risk-taker. You have to seek out a stranger's home, make sure that there isn't a gun barrel greeting you at the door, and then return with valuable supplies that keep us alive. This is a lot of weight to place on a teenager's shoulders."

"Sure is, but I like it."

"I'm glad, son. You've grown up fast the last month and now you carry a lot of responsibility on your shoulders. I hope you understand that your mother and I worry about you."

"Thanks," replied Chase curtly.

Jake didn't know what to make of the conversation. *Was Chase trying to avoid talking to him? Was the cold shoulder gonna be the new norm? Or was he simply tired?* He pressed on.

"We had the conversation about being safe out there and how to avoid getting into bad situations. What happened last night was reckless." Perhaps a poor choice of words, thought Jake, but he couldn't retrieve them.

Chase snapped his head around. "I was trying to save Alex. Do you think I intended for that to happen?"

Jake got defensive too. "No, son, of course not. You need to learn to look before you leap. Calculate the consequences of your actions before you act on them."

"I had the shot!"

"No, you didn't. It was too dark, there was too much movement, and you didn't consider what was behind your target if you missed."

"You know I usually don't miss. It was just bad luck. Besides, I told Alex that I was sorry."

They were approaching Lick Creek and Jake saw horses approaching from the direction of the main house. The perimeter patrols must've picked up the sound of the boat. He had to bring the conversation to a conclusion.

"Chase," said Jake sternly, "forgiveness doesn't exonerate you of the consequences of reckless actions. You talk about luck. We're lucky that you're not apologizing to her parents as they buried their daughter! And that's if we could find her body to bury!"

"Screw you, Dad! You know what, maybe we'd all be better off if I left. How's that? Maybe I can save everyone a lot of trouble and find someplace else to live."

Jake hoped the sound of the motor masked Chase's words as he approached the entrance to Lick Creek, where Javy stood and waved. As usual, their conversation resulted in a blowup and silence. Mission failed.

Javy helped them tie off the boat and instructed two of the hands to relinquish their horses. Chase rode ahead and Jake encouraged his horse to catch up. Their arrival at the main house brought Madison, Emily, and the Crumps out of the house in a hurry.

Chase dismounted and tried to rush past them into the house, barely acknowledging his mother as he walked by. Tears immediately flowed from Madison's eyes. She covered her mouth with her hand and couldn't speak.

Jake dismounted and ran over to the group. "Madison, they're fine. Don't worry, they're gonna be fine."

"Gonna be?" said Madison, still crying.

"Yes. Alex was injured as we rescued her, but she received medical treatment at the hospital and now she's safe with Colton. She needs to rest a few days before she can be moved."

"Oh my! I have to see my baby. Where are they?"

Jake spent the next several minutes providing a summary of the events of the last twelve hours. Madison gradually calmed down as the reality of Alex's safety set in.

"Can I go see her?" asked Madison.

"Of course, Colton and Miss Rhoda expect you to," replied Jake.

Madison started walking toward the horses when Emily shouted after her, "Madison, wait. Why don't you come inside with me? We'll pack some fresh clothes for Alex and Colton. You'll want to take a few things also. It'll just take a moment."

"Do that, Madison," added Stubby. "I'll send a hand down with some fuel for the boat. We'll get everything ready for the trip."

Madison reluctantly agreed and took Emily's arm as they entered the house. She turned and smiled at Jake as she walked past the entry, mouthing the words *thank you.*

"There's more, isn't there?" Stubby immediately queried.

"Yeah," said Jake as he nervously kicked at some rocks. "I didn't want to go into it yet with his mother and Madison."

"What happened?"

"The explosion occurred because Chase tried to take a few risky shots at the men holding Alex. It was dark, Stubby. She was wiggling to get away. There were bullets flying in all directions. I don't know what he was thinking." Jake shook his head and then ran his fingers through his hair.

"What caused the explosion?" asked Stubby, seeking answers from his tormented friend.

"Chase fired and missed, hitting a propane tank instead. He fired twice more, also missing, but hit something to trigger the explosion. A massive fireball flew in all directions and knocked Alex unconscious. She got her concussion from the blast."

"Reckless."

"Yeah. I tried to talk about it with him on the way across the river, but it didn't go well. Now he's sulking. It's par for the course."

Stubby nodded and put his hands in his pockets. He shouted to one of Javy's men and instructed them to bring his horse and Madison's too. He also told him to take gasoline down to the boat at Lick Creek.

Madison and Emily emerged from the house with a couple of duffle bags. She sheepishly asked Stubby if this was too much and he smiled and took her bags without answering. Emily helped Madison get settled on her horse.

Stubby whispered to Jake, "Listen, I'm no parent, but it seems to me that in this world, most of the rules of the road don't apply. I love Chase's spirit, but we've got to figure out a way to harness it."

CHAPTER 12

3:00 p.m., November 2
Croft Dairies
Nixon

Three of the girls staying at Croft Dairies met Stubby and Madison at the dock. They immediately helped Madison out of the boat and took her bags. Stubby was left to fend for himself as Madison bolted up the hill toward Miss Rhoda's home.

Stubby chuckled. "Go ahead, don't mind me!"

Madison, who was already halfway there, turned and waved for him to join her. Stubby just laughed and waved back as he tied a perfect pile hitch around a post on each end of the dock to hold the aluminum boat in place. Stubby wanted to give Madison plenty of time with Alex before he visited with her.

He took a moment to take in the surroundings. This side of the river looked very much like Shiloh Ranch's shore, grassy fields gently sloping into the river. Occasionally, a stream would find its way into the river which it fed, cutting through the turf and getting larger over time. Croft Dairies was a couple of miles closer to Pickwick Dam and the signs of erosion were more prevalent. Stubby noticed the Croft property was at least two feet lower in elevation than Shiloh Ranch. That could be a real problem if flooding occurred like in October. December was coming, the region's rainiest month.

"Hey, Stubby," yelled a jovial Colton, "you're invited too."

Stubby waved and walked up the bank towards the house. "I'm comin'. Just lookin' at the river from a different perspective."

The two men shook hands and then embraced. As they walked up the hill, Stubby filled Colton in on his conversation with Jake. He got an update on Alex's condition and naturally asked when she could be moved. There was no definitive date. They'd have to evaluate day by day.

Beau was talking with a couple of the girls and Colton introduced him to Stubby. Stubby thanked Beau and complimented him on his heroics. Stubby engaged Beau in a conversation about the Tiger Resistance, the other reason he wanted to escort Madison across the river.

Beau provided Colton and Stubby with more details on their numbers and weapons capability. The planning and communications between Coach Carey and the boys was remarkable. Stubby was in awe at the play-calling scheme, which to a non-football player sounded complicated. Beau assured them that the play-calling was the easiest part of being a member of the Tiger Resistance.

"I thought a lot about this while I was watching over Alex last night," said Beau. "It's time we did something. Ma and Junior have to go or our town will never get back to normal. We proved last night that we are capable of winning. Now we need a plan."

Stubby got serious. "There's a lot to discuss, but I can assure you, if we don't take the fight to them, they'll surely bring it to us. Especially now."

Rhoda strolled around the corner of the house and interrupted the conversation. "Gentlemen, we have sweet tea on the front porch and I don't believe I've met our other guest."

"I'm sorry, Miss Rhoda," said Colton. "This is Stubby Crump. He and his wife, Bessie, are longtime residents of Crump. They run Shiloh Ranch."

Stubby shook hands with Rhoda and smiled. "You have a beautiful place here. We're practically neighbors, only separated by the river. Your place looks very much like Shiloh Ranch."

"Well, it's a pleasure to meet you, Stubby. Come join us for sweet tea and then I'll show you around. Maybe we can share some ideas."

She took Stubby by the arm and they walked toward the front of the house. Colton and Beau joined them where a dozen teenage girls gathered around. They were discussing things like milk production from the Holsteins, repairing a broken fence, and transferring hay from a remote barn to the primary grazing area for the cows. The conversations weren't that different from those at Shiloh Ranch, except it was an all-girl crew.

Madison emerged through the double front doors and approached Rhoda. She immediately gave her a hug. "Thank you for taking care of my baby, Miss Rhoda. She's so comfortable in there. She couldn't get better treatment in any hospital."

"You're welcome, Madison. You stay with us for as long as you'd like. It's no bother. Alex will tell us when she's ready."

Madison turned to Stubby. "She's asking for you."

Stubby couldn't suppress his smile. "Is it okay?"

Madison patted him on the chest and nodded.

"Excuse me," Stubby said politely to Rhoda. "Let me go check on my protégé."

"Protégé?" she asked as Stubby hurried inside.

Stubby spent several minutes with Alex as they discussed how she was doing. There was the obligatory conversation about her getting plenty of rest in order to recover. Then Alex's brow furrowed and she looked past Stubby to make sure they were alone.

"Stubby, something has to be done. Those people are evil. I've never seen anything like them, in real life or on TV. I'm afraid of what they're capable of doing to all of us."

Stubby also looked over his shoulder and leaned down to Alex's ear. "We've really pissed them off now, I'm afraid. There's no turning back. We're gonna have to fight."

Alex nodded. "I learned a lot yesterday. They're weak-minded. We can do it." Alex let out a sigh and closed her eyes. Stubby gave her a kiss on the forehead and brushed the hair out of her eyes. This remarkable young woman was destined for great things if she could recover from her concussion.

Stubby returned to the porch and refilled his sweet tea. Rhoda instructed two of the girls to get the Rymans settled. They hadn't slept in a couple of days and were on the verge of collapsing.

"How about that walk?" asked Stubby, anxious to learn more

about the Croft Dairy operations.

The two walked to the milk house and through the barns closest to the residence. They found that their two farms had a lot in common. It turned out that Stubby had some spare parts that Rhoda needed for a broken-down tractor.

Likewise, Rhoda revealed that she was a ham radio enthusiast and had had six Baofeng UV 5R radios stored in her gun safe when the solar storm hit. They work perfectly, although she hadn't attempted to communicate with anyone. She was afraid Junior's men might try to trick her.

She still had a decent supply of farm diesel to run her whole house generator. At some point, Rhoda acknowledged she'd have to search the surrounding area for more. Her solar panels on the milk house were in good shape, but the charge controller was fried. Stubby thought he had a replacement for her.

Throughout the conversation, they learned that they shared common goals and sought mutual benefits. Although Stubby hesitated at first, he brought up the issue of weapons and learned that Rhoda was in dire need of something more powerful than a .22-caliber rifle. Also, she really didn't have anyone trained in shooting. This would be a real problem if Junior and his men began to search this part of the county, searching for Alex and her family.

"Didn't your husband have any guns? You mentioned a gun safe." Stubby stopped and put his foot on the lowest rail of the fencing as he admired the cows.

"He had a few that he accumulated after his service in the Army, but after he died seventeen years ago, they either broke or disappeared somehow or another. I just never replaced them."

"Your husband was so young. How did he pass?"

"It was heart disease, which ran in his family, but he wasn't so young at sixty-eight."

Stubby thought for a moment and Mr. Croft's age didn't add up. If he died seventeen years ago at sixty-eight, he would be about eighty-five now.

"If you don't mind me saying, Miss Rhoda, but that would put your husband at twenty years older than me. You look so young. It just caught me off guard."

Rhoda laughed. "Well now, thank you for the compliment, Stubby. But I'm much older than you think. I'm guessin' at least ten years older than you."

Stubby studied her face. "But your skin, it's so healthy."

"Whadya sayin', Stubby. Black don't crack?" Rhoda laughed.

"No, I didn't mean anything by it. It's just …" stammered Stubby, concerned that she was offended.

"Black don't crack," she continued, with a giggle. "It's an old saying. A black woman's skin ages better than a white woman's does. We look at least ten years younger."

"I never thought of that."

"It's okay to agree with me," Rhoda said, laughing at the awkwardness. "People need to realize that black folks are different from white folks. Too many of us are running around looking for perceived slights and scream racism when they find one. What we all need to do is knock that chip off our shoulder and move on. We're all unique in our own way. Big deal."

Stubby nodded, not sure what to say.

Rhoda continued. "If folks would focus their energies on making a better life for themselves and their families, then the rest of that nonsense wouldn't matter."

"Miss Rhoda, I agree," said Stubby; then he changed the subject. "Did you say your husband was in the Army? So was I."

"My husband was part of the 1st Army Ranger Company that fought in Korea. He ventured north of the 38th parallel many times."

Stubby shook his head and smiled. "Small world. Of course, being younger, I missed Korea. I was part of the 3rd Ranger Battalion. I saw action in Cambodia."

"A ridiculous war," said Rhoda. "They wouldn't let our boys fight."

"Don't I know it. You'll get along great with my Bessie."

"I look forward to it," Rhoda replied as she took Stubby's arm and began walking back to the house.

"Rhoda, we think alike and we'll make a great team. We're gonna need to."

"Why's that?"

"A war is coming and we're gonna fight it together," replied Stubby.

"Rangers lead the way."

"Yes, Rangers lead the way."

CHAPTER 13

4:00 p.m., November 3
Cherry Mansion
Savannah

Ma Durham resumed her normal pace as she and the Brumby Rocker reunited. The vintage rocking chair had taken a direct hit courtesy of a fifty-caliber bullet from nearly a mile away, breaking through the ornate woodworking that made up its back. This was just one of many chores Junior would have to complete before he could go chasing ghosts around Hardin County.

"Ma, the windows are either replaced or boarded up temporarily until we can find more like them," said Junior as he exited the front door onto the porch overlooking the river. One of the flat-bottom boats used in the attack remained flipped over at the shoreline, bullet-ridden more out of frustration than purpose. "Tomorrow, I'll have the men fix the roof."

Ma, deep in thought, continued to rock without responding. This was a tactic of hers she'd used for many years since her troubled childhood. Human beings were naturally chatty, especially when nervous. Ma had been questioned by police at an early age. After she murdered the Tindle family on Election Night in 1976, fingers immediately pointed at the Pusser family. Her grandmother was the first suspect, but the teenagers of Adamsville immediately raised the possibility of another—the reclusive Betty Jean.

Betty Jean was brought into the police station and immediately isolated from other people. When she was hauled out of school, nobody bothered to mention this to her grandmother. She was alone in the interrogation room, surrounded by men, effectively employing the Reid technique, which had been so effective in eliciting confessions in the past.

Good cop—bad cop. In this case, frail Betty Jean saw mainly bad cop. They started out declaring her guilt. She would receive the maximum penalty by law, the death penalty, which had been recently reinstated. Both officers berated Betty Jean with their version of the facts—*the working theory*—which was remarkably spot-on except they missed the stolen car as a getaway vehicle.

My daddy would've put two and two together immediately.

Betty Jean remained stoic, lips pursed. At a young age, she remembered her daddy saying many times that *all he had to do was get them talkin' and they'd hang themselves.* In that interrogation room, Betty Jean didn't hang herself. The good cop and the bad cop thought they were studying Betty Jean to determine her culpability when, in fact, Betty Jean was learning how to keep calm under pressure. It had served her well over the last forty-some years.

"Ma, Ma, did you hear what I said?" asked Junior.

"Yeah, I heard you," Ma bristled. "You brought this down on us. I can go back and rehash the screwups you've made since they came into town, but what's the point? This ain't some kind of teachable moment. I want my home cleaned up and then we'll talk about what's next for you."

"But, Ma," Junior plead, "every hour that goes by gives them a chance of getting away. I need my guys out there—"

Ma cut him off. She stopped rocking, but didn't make eye contact. "Now, you listen here. I've given you full rein on runnin' things around here and you've messed it up. You'll follow my instructions now. Fix this place, secure the routes into town, and make sure these people toe the line. I don't give a *tinker's damn* whether they're talking behind your back. You get your house in order before you make another move."

Junior slumped against the porch post and then slid to a seat on the front step. He sat quietly and stared at the river. Ma sensed the rage in her son and knew it had to be carefully controlled. She'd been in this state of mind herself in the past, and the result didn't bode well for others.

She continued, but softened her tone. "Son, I know this is important to you, but it has taken us off our program, which is to maintain control and profit from this collapse. We were doing very well on both counts until these folks showed up."

"I know, Ma. Now it's escalated and we've got to tamp it down. When they, or the locals, see that we can be shown up like that, well, it's just a matter of time before they try it again."

Ma continued rocking. He was right. This couldn't stand.

"Let's talk about where we stand on security," said Ma as she decided to approach this logically, creating an actual teachable moment. "Give me an assessment of the damage we incurred at the west bridge entrance."

"We lost a few men, but there are plenty to fill the slots in security," replied Junior. "The Jeep Wagoneer was flipped upside down and exploded, ruining our two vehicles on the bridge. Today we relocated the barriers with the fork truck and tomorrow we'll drag the burnt vehicles out of the way."

"Good," added Ma. "We don't want to leave them to scare off any future guest workers. This can be completed by tomorrow?"

"Yes, ma'am."

"What about the hospital?" she asked.

"I've talked to Dr. Fulcher and Nurse Sutton," replied Junior. "Either they're very good liars or they're telling the truth, but I don't think they treated the girl knowing she was a fugitive. The fella that brought the girl in talked like he was acting on my orders. In fact, as the story was relayed to me by the doc, it sounded like the guy was here when it happened."

Ma slowed the rocker and closed her eyes. She replayed the events of that evening following the propane tank explosion.

"Did he describe what the man was wearing?"

"Yeah, a burgundy Hardin County sweatshirt."

Ma stopped and looked Junior in the eyes for the first time in the entire conversation. It was beginning to make sense to her now, but she didn't want to reveal her thoughts to Junior. He had enough on his platter without going on a witch hunt here in town.

"What?" questioned Junior.

"Nothing, just had a thought," replied Ma. "Where are you gonna live?"

"I'd like to move into one of the guest rooms, if that's okay?" he replied.

"Junior, I'm not gonna have any of that carousing in the house. No smokin', no drinkin', and most certainly no hussies. Bill knows these ground rules and, technically speaking, this is his home. He follows the rules."

"I agree, Ma. I need to focus on the task at hand. I'm gonna clean up our town, shore up our security, and with your permission, devise a plan to ferret out these weasels. I need revenge, Ma, and I won't be able to live with myself until I get it."

Ma heard the words and relived the moments in her life when she'd uttered the same. She understood, and after seeing a marked changed in Junior's attitude, she acquiesced.

"Okay, let's talk about that now," said Ma, picking up the pace in the Brumby. "You found their boat, right?"

"We think so. Our patrols check most areas every day or two, and the boat they found south of the bridge wasn't there the other morning."

"How many people could it hold?" asked Ma.

"Two or three."

Ma's working theory began to come into focus. There was a presence within *her Savannah.* The existence of *disdants*, as Junior said, was bigger than they imagined. She would help Junior exact his revenge, but she'd better make sure an uprising didn't boil up right under their noses.

"You move in here with me, son," said Ma. "We can strategize together. First order of business is to clean up and secure the town. Second, we need to send a message to the townspeople that those who oppose us will be dealt with immediately."

"What do you have in mind?" asked Junior.

"Find a scapegoat and execute him," she replied brusquely. "No, make it a woman. It will have a greater impact. Show the good people of Savannah that dissention will not be tolerated. Do it in the Court Square, as a hanging."

"Right next to the gazebo," interjected Junior. "That's where all the political speeches are made. We'll be making a statement of our own, right?"

"Yes, son. A clear message will be sent. Then you may send out patrols looking for your fugitives."

CHAPTER 14

8:00 a.m., November 5
Croft Dairies
Nixon

Colton and Beau assisted Miss Rhoda in setting up a perimeter watch. Over the last three days since their arrival, Colton learned that nearly five dozen young adult women lived in the five-mile radius surrounding Croft Dairies. Few were armed and even fewer were organized to put up any kind of defense against Junior's men. They intended to rely upon hiding or running to avoid capture.

Colton immediately realized how tenuous this was and worked with Beau and a few of Miss Rhoda's charges to gather together representatives of the neighboring farms. Fifteen to twenty people had arrived at Croft Dairies to listen to Colton's proposal. After a breakfast of corn pones, a southern delicacy combining corn meal, creamed corn, butter, eggs and sugar, Colton laid out his proposal.

He unfurled a bedsheet, mapping the area south of Savannah with a Sharpie. Each of the farms represented were noted by a smaller star with Croft Dairies represented by a large red star. Most of the farms shared a property boundary with Miss Rhoda's place and all of the farmers knew where it was located. Over the years, trails had been carved through the woods in this direction, as folks mainly traveled by horse to visit rather than car. This backwoods highway system would serve them well under Colton's proposal.

"The idea is to discourage Junior's men from traveling this far away from Savannah," Colton began. "If we provide them an easier route to search, such as Highway 69 towards Walnut Grove, they'll hopefully choose it."

Miss Rhoda added to Colton's thought. "Junior knows the Pickwick Dam is closed to traffic. If he's chasing after Colton and Alex, he'll most likely send his men toward the only highway open to Mississippi—Highway 69."

"Exactly," said Colton. "If they do come this way, I propose that we block the roads with barricades and trees. This will inhibit our own vehicular traffic, but we have ways to circumvent the blockades. How many of you own chainsaws and, just as important, have gas-oil mix to run them?"

A few hands rose into the air. Colton invited them forward to point out on the map where they were located and logical tree-cutting points were established. The main highway was too wide to block with trees without tractors to pull them across, but the side roads and long driveways could easily be done. This worked out for the best anyway because the open road would encourage Junior's scouts to follow the path of least resistance toward Pickwick Dam, which was a dead end.

Each of the chainsaw owners committed to a schedule to accomplish their tree barricades by the end of the next day. In the meantime, scouts were assigned to each of the four churches along Highway 128. If Junior's men were spotted, the scouts on horseback would use the trails cut through the woods to alert the farms. Colton envisioned a Paul Revere-inspired warning system, which gave the residents enough time to either establish a defense or hide.

"What about weapons?"

"How do we know when to fight or run?"

Colton nodded, understanding the context in which these questions were made. He'd been through this same thought process many times.

"We're behind in our planning, but better late than never," he replied to both questions at once. "We will bring you some additional weapons, but in the meantime, here's a rule of thumb that I've adopted since the collapse. Never enter a battle you can't win. If you have the option, find a place to hide. Don't worry about your homes, your belongings, or anything except your lives and the ones you love.

Everything else can be replaced and you can live to fight another day."

The group began to grumble at the thought of this. Colton could overhear a couple of conversations concerning how they would survive and not wanting to give in to Junior. He needed to make them understand.

"Everyone, please, listen up," said Colton. "I feel ya. My family went through this in Nashville. We loved our home. Alex was raised there from an early age. But it would've meant nothing if we're dead."

The group continued to whisper among themselves and some were becoming animated. Colton wasn't getting through, so he took a dramatic approach to open their eyes. He continued. "Excuse me, everyone. Do not doubt me here. How many of you have ever been shot at?"

Nobody raised their hand in response to Colton's question.

"Really. Nobody?" Colton asked. Time for the drama. "Okay, no time like the present. I want everyone to step back ten yards and spread out. Now, I'm going to pull my weapon and shoot at you. Okay?"

"You're crazy!"

"This is nuts!"

"I'll have no part of this!"

Colton started to pull his sidearm and one girl shrieked. The others began to turn and run until Colton yelled, "Stop!"

Beau looked at him wide-eyed as well and Colton gave him a slight smile. He worked to diffuse the situation.

"You're wrong, I'm not crazy, but Junior and his men are. They're nuts too. But the person who insisted they'll have no part of this gave the correct answer. You have no idea what a gunfight looks like. It's not like television where the good guys hit their mark ninety percent of the time and the bad guys always miss. I've been in gunfights. People die. Their bodies come flying apart. This could just as easily be your family or friends. Then what? You could die along with them."

Most in the group lowered their heads for doubting Colton and moved forward toward the porch. Beau, who was looked upon as one of them, spoke up to the group for the first time.

"I've seen what Ma and Junior are capable of doing," said Beau. "It has to stop and we all agree on that. Our opportunity to fight back and take our town back is coming, but Colton is right, we're not ready. In the meantime, we need to protect what we've got."

"When do we fight back?"

"Very soon, I suspect," replied Colton.

CHAPTER 15

10:30 a.m., November 6
Croft Dairies
Nixon

"Well, that didn't take long," said Madison as she walked out of Alex's room. "Alex is feeling much better and is ready to go home. She asked for her AR-15. It's like a security blankie."

"I've never seen her attached to something like this before, much less a gun," added Colton. He gave Madison a kiss and invited her to join them in the parlor. Rhoda had brewed up a pot of tea and whipped up a batch of campfire doughnuts with powdered sugar. "Miss Rhoda has a treat for us."

Madison immediately stopped and stared at the oak coffee table. It was adorned with beautifully designed teacups with a matching kettle and a plateful of doughnuts.

"Are those …" Madison began.

"Doughnuts." Rhoda laughed. "Yes, we make campfire doughnuts using the basic ingredients we have stored like flour, sugar, and cinnamon. The butter and milk required for the recipe come from our babies out there. A little vanilla extract would've been nice, but it doesn't affect the taste, really."

Rhoda offered the plate to Madison, who scurried to grab one. Madison allowed the flavors to circulate through her mouth and she closed her eyes, yearning for a Krispy Kreme store again. Then she came back to reality as a horse could be heard approaching down the long drive. Colton looked outside and hustled toward the front door and grabbed his rifle.

"Stay here," he said. "I'll see what's up."

Madison nervously drank some tea and dunked her doughnut in it. She made conversation while they awaited a report from Colton.

"I realize that there are families who've suffered as a result of the grid collapsing," said Madison. "But I also believe that if everyone could've come together, more would've survived. There is no excuse for people like Ma and Junior taking advantage of folks in a weakened state. That's not only a crime against man, but also a crime against the laws of God."

"Give, and it will be given to you," said Rhoda. "It doesn't matter if you give a lot or a little, it's what's in your heart that matters. The Durhams are takers and have used their position and power to further their goals."

Colton returned to the parlor with a rolled-up piece of copy paper in his hand. His face was red with anger.

"Colt, honey, what's wrong?" asked Madison.

He hesitated and then handed her the paper. He reported the news about Junior's men. "As predicted, a two-vehicle scout team was sent in their direction, asking questions. They handed this out to everyone they saw."

Madison gasped. "She's wearing a nurse's uniform. Is it …? Please, NO!"

"Beau confirmed it," he replied. "That's Nurse Sutton from the hospital who treated Alex. They executed her in town last night."

Madison began crying and Colton held his wife to give her comfort. Rhoda took the paper and studied the image.

"Animals," she mumbled. "What's the point of killing this woman? She was just doing her job."

Beau entered the room and stood in the large entry. "Junior's men have been handing this out and telling everyone that Nurse Sutton was guilty of harboring a fugitive. They're trying to frighten people into giving up the Rymans. Heck, all of us—me, the girls, and the Tiger Resistance."

"Beau's right," said Colton. "By violently murdering an innocent woman for the whole town to see, Junior intends to flush us all out by turning the public against us."

"It won't work," said Beau defiantly. "The town will stand with us."

Colton shook his head and addressed Beau. "I'm sorry, Beau. It will work. Maybe not with everyone, but a few frightened souls will begin to talk to save their own lives or gain favor. This type of display will turn public opinion against us."

Everyone in the room stared silently into space, ignoring the tea and doughnuts. The silence was broken by a voice in the foyer. It was Alex.

"This has to end."

Beau swirled around and took to Alex's side, helping her by supporting her weight as she walked into the parlor.

"Honey," said Madison, who leapt to her feet, "you need your rest. You shouldn't be on your feet."

"I'm fine, Mom," said Alex. "Besides, I could make out a few words of your conversation anyway. You know how when you're trying to sleep, you can hear a TV in the other room but only bits and pieces of what's said. You strain to hear the words, which keeps you from sleeping. It was the same thing here. Plus, I heard the word *doughnuts*." Alex managed a laugh.

Colton stood and prepared the sofa for Alex. "Come sit here, Allie-Cat. How about a little hot tea and a doughnut? That would be okay, right, Maddie?"

Before her mother could respond, Alex replied, "It doesn't matter if she says no, Daddy. I'm havin' a doughnut and y'all are gonna tell me what's goin' on. Don't sugarcoat it—the information anyway. Extra sugar on the doughnut, if you don't mind."

Alex's joke, especially in her weakened state, relieved the tension in the room and gave everyone a reason to feel good. She had recovered, mostly, and she came out of her concussed condition fighting mad.

She chomped on a doughnut as she was brought up to speed. When Beau and Colton had finished the update, Alex finished off her second doughnut. Her appetite was back, which Colton knew was a good sign.

"What day is it?" asked Alex.

"Wednesday," replied Madison. "Five days after the attack."

"Today's the first day you've heard from Junior?" asked Alex.

"Yes," replied Colton. "What are you thinkin'?"

Alex stood with the help of Beau. "Mom, Dad, we've got to get home. We've got to get ready."

"Alex, you need more rest," said Madison. "You can't travel across the river like this."

Colton nodded and tried to encourage Alex to sit back down. She pulled away and stood taller.

"Please, trust me on this," insisted Alex. "I've seen these people up close and personal. They will not stand for the disrespect we've shown them. I'm surprised they haven't done something already. Seriously, we've got to get back to Shiloh Ranch."

"Colton?" questioned Madison.

"If she feels up to traveling, it would be better for us to bring Jake and Stubby up to speed and work out a plan. If trouble is brewing, we don't want to return right in the middle of it."

Madison studied Alex and then returned her attention to Colton. "Let's get our things together, but what about Miss Rhoda. I feel terrible about leaving her here without protection. Maybe Beau can stay for a while?"

"I suppose I could …" started Beau before being interrupted by Alex.

"Mom, we'll work that out here in a few minutes," said Alex. "You and Daddy get us started and I'll meet you at the boat. Beau will bring me down, won't you, Beau?"

"Of course," he replied.

Colton and Madison left the room to pack their things, but Colton stayed within earshot. He sensed that Alex was trying to get rid of them for some reason.

Rhoda cleared out the china and leftover doughnuts and Alex began to speak.

"Beau, can you round up the girls and bring them here?" asked Alex. "We need to have a real frank discussion."

"Sure." Beau immediately hit the front door in search of as many of his classmates and friends that he could find. Within a few minutes, Alex was surrounded in the parlor by well-wishers.

Colton watched from across the foyer. Alex had full command of the room as the group looked to her for inspiration and guidance. During the conversation, Alex passed along her strength and experience. She secured the trust of the displaced women of Savannah. Her final words before the girls exited to leave Alex and Beau alone to say their good-byes brought tears to Colton's eyes.

"This difficult situation can't stop you. Obstacles can't stop you. Even other people can't stop you. The only one who stops you from taking back your home is yourself. I've learned that the only difference between winning and losing is not quitting. I'm not a quitter and neither are you guys. We'll fight this battle together, and we'll win!"

CHAPTER 16

4:30 a.m., November 6
Cherry Mansion
Savannah

The afternoon meetings between Ma and Junior had grown to include Bill Cherry and Junior's senior deputies. Junior was proud to display his leadership abilities in front of Ma, not realizing that she was using this as a tool to keep him on a tighter leash. Junior would never admit that he'd potentially screwed things up over this obsession with this family from Nashville, but the reality was the Durhams' firm grip on the town was close to imploding.

Junior was afraid of losing control of the town, but also the respect of his men. They needed another boost of confidence like their attack on Adamsville. He was anxious to lay out his plan for the ranchers of West Hardin County. And, although he never admitted it out loud, Junior was obsessed with the girl. There was something about her. Once he touched her and *smelled her*, he coveted her that much more. In fact, he hadn't felt the need to visit any of the town's brothels since that night.

"We've been looking for a reason to advance into West Hardin County," said Cherry. "Those ranchers have cattle to feed us and provide us dairy products. They have rich farmland, which we can cultivate. I'll betcha those rich suckers have gold and silver buried all over the place. We've got one of those metal detectors, don't we, Junior?"

"We sure do," replied Junior. "We busted into the Tennessee Bureau of Investigation Field Office and picked up a number of goodies, including the metal detector and some mighty fine weapons."

"That gun safe was a bugger, wasn't it, Junior?" chimed in one of the deputies.

"That it was," said Junior. "At least all of the electronics inside still worked even though their stash of cash is now worthless."

"Whadya reckon the TBI needed with all those greenbacks?" asked Cherry.

"Bribes, I guess?" surmised Junior. "Probably both incoming and outgoing." Everyone laughed.

Ma got down to business. "Are you confident in your search to the south?"

"We are, Ma," replied Junior. "Nothing has changed down that way except for a few fallen trees across the roads. The farmers all said they'd been harassed by folks coming up from Mississippi, so they blocked the roads to prevent vehicle access."

"Do you believe them?" asked Ma.

"I do," replied Junior. "Most of our confiscated vehicles from the south had Mississippi tags. It would make sense that the refugees would peel off a few side roads to see what they could find. I can't blame the farmers for what they did."

"What about to the north of town, toward Clifton and Decatur County?" asked Ma.

"That's on tomorrow's agenda," replied Junior. "Bill has good coverage on the roads leading in from the other parts of town. I'll need to take more men as we search the north. But we can cover it in a day."

"You're going?" asked Cherry. "I'm not sure it's a good thing for you to leave town."

"Why not, Bill?" Junior exploded. "Can't you handle it?" Cherry was not pleased that Junior had moved into the mansion. Over the last several days, Junior had gained the ear of his mother to Cherry's exclusion. Junior had seen Cherry attempt to flex his muscles a couple of times in the last two days.

"Of course I can handle it," replied Cherry. "It's just we don't know for certain how the town will react to the execution of that nurse. There could be an uprising."

Ma raised her hand and stopped rocking. She spoke in an eerily calm voice. "Now, Bill, don't be dramatic. There ain't gonna be an uprising while Junior is gone. Besides, you've got all the men at your disposal, with weapons, to shut 'er down. Junior will make sure we're covered on all sides before we head across the river."

Junior smirked at Cherry. *You're done, buster. Don't be surprised if you disappear soon.*

"Out of setbacks come opportunities," said Junior. "Winter will be setting in very soon and we need additional food sources. Why should these ranchers hog all the hogs and cattle for themselves, right? I think it's time to spread the wealth around, don't you think?"

"Heck yeah!" shouted one deputy.

"A nice rare steak sounds good to me too!" said another.

Ma began rocking slowly and raised her hand to quieten the jubilation over a victory not yet won.

"Gentlemen, don't forget that the ranchers have a different kinda mind-set," Ma began. "They're independent, self-reliant, and used to taking care of themselves."

Cherry spoke up and added, "Ma's right. If it were up to them, there wouldn't be a dang government."

"What's that got to do with us taking them out?" asked Junior, incredulous that Cherry had the nerve to speak again.

"Just keep in mind that their resistance will be born out of love of farm and family, not fear," replied Cherry.

"Bill's right," said Ma. "We need to focus here on a strategy that accomplishes two goals. First, we want to flush out this family that's tormented all of y'all since they rolled into town. Second, we need to tamp down any attempts by the ranchers to resist our authority. You never know, they might give these people up to maintain the peaceful coexistence we've enjoyed since the solar storm."

"Are you saying we should make a deal with them?" asked Junior.

"Maybe," replied Ma. "You'll know their attitude when the party starts, so to speak."

"Would you like me to approach them, Ma?" asked Cherry. "Like an emissary?"

Junior roared with laughter. "Ambassador Cherry, just what we need!"

"It's not a terrible idea, Junior," said Cherry. "Let me approach them as if I'm not totally on board with all of this." Cherry gestured, sweeping his arms from the bridge across town and back to the river.

"A double agent." Junior laughed. "Great idea. And what happens when they offer you a bottle of wine and a juicy steak? Are you gonna be a turncoat on us? Your family has a history of that, you know."

Cherry's face grew red with anger and he balled up his fists. Junior knew Cherry wouldn't dare swing on him, but his hostility was showing. Junior would definitely have Wild Bill Cherry disappear, sooner rather than later, perhaps.

"Enough!" shouted Ma. "Bill's got a point. Tomorrow. One-day offer only. Spread the word among the ranchers to give up the fugitives by the end of the day tomorrow or all bets are off."

"But, Ma," whined Junior, "it ain't gonna work."

"It may not, but nothing is gonna happen until you check North Hardin County. Now, all of you make your arrangements and leave me be. I got a few more minutes of sunset to enjoy and y'all have all given me a headache."

"Okay, Ma," said Junior as he provided her a rare showing of affection and patted her on the shoulder. As he was the last to leave, she stopped him.

"Junior, there's one more thing. Send some of the boys down to the high school and make sure no one is hanging out down there. If you find any, bring them to me. Also, fetch me the most recent copy of the Hardin County High School yearbook. What did they call it?"

"*Tiger Tales*," replied Junior. "Why?"

"I think it's time to do a class roll call of those absentee students."

CHAPTER 17

Early Morning, November 7
Northwest Hardin County

"It was nice of John Wyatt to loan us his old Chevy pick-em-up truck," said Jake as he slid his large frame behind the oversized steering wheel. He fired up the bondo-splotched stepside and popped the clutch. The truck lurched forward and Jake quickly reached for the shifter to move it into second gear. "Three on the tree, baby. It's been a long time since I've driven one of these."

Two of Javy's men perched in the back of the truck struggled to hold on as Jake got comfortable with the clutch and the lack of power steering. Colton gave them a wave in solidarity as they laughed uncontrollably at Jake's driving. Colton was glad they were having fun.

Colton unfolded a map of the county and looked at the farms marked by Stubby. There were a total of sixteen, although six key locations on the north side of the county would accomplish their purpose. Those six landowners could notify their neighbors of the meeting scheduled for the ninth at the Shiloh Battlefield Visitor Center at Pittsburg Landing.

"We're gonna loop out to the west to avoid being seen by Junior's men around the bridge," said Colton. "Besides, there were a lot of fallen trees blocking our route near where we stashed the Wagoneer, God rest her soul."

"She did her duty," added Jake.

"Sure did," said Colton. "If the Wagoneer was a horse, she would've received a Purple Heart or Medal of Honor, like Teddy

Roosevelt's horse—Little Texas."

"How do you know about these things?" asked Jake.

Colton folded the county map into one big square that isolated the roads north of Highway 64. He pointed toward a side street for Jake to turn on.

"Make the next right and then head straight up for probably six miles," said Colton. "We'll see Russ first."

"He'll be surprised!" exclaimed Jake.

"He sure will," said Colton. Then he continued with the story. "Anyway, Little Texas was his horse when he fought the Battle of San Juan Hill in the Spanish-American War. Against all odds, Roosevelt led the charge of the Rough Riders and turned back the Spaniards. It was a turning point in the war and Roosevelt received the Medal of Honor and ultimately became President. His horse became famous."

The men sat quietly as they observed the countryside. There were few noticeable signs of life. Occasionally, a dog would be seen walking along the side of the road. Most of the cattle owners had moved their herds well off the main streets, protected from the prying eyes of passersby. Life existed, but in rural communities like this one, it had hunkered down.

Jake cleared his throat then broached a subject that he and Colton hadn't discussed alone. "Chase means well. He's very sorry for the pain he's caused Alex and you guys."

Colton's chin was resting on his fist as he stared out the passenger's side window. Any animosity that he'd harbored toward Chase had quickly subsided as Alex recovered and they returned to Shiloh Ranch. He and Madison had discussed where the relationship between the two teens would be allowed to go next.

"Jake, your family, which includes Chase, took us in without hesitation and we'll always be grateful for that. None of us hold Chase responsible for anything. Do we wish things had gone smoother, without incident? Absolutely. But what the heck can we expect in a screwed-up world like this?"

"I know, Colton, but still," replied Jake. "Things are messed up enough without bringing more aggravation on top of our heads. I've asked Chase to slow down and consider the consequences of his actions before he does things."

"In the heat of battle, which we all agree is coming, that's not always possible," said Colton. "The kids have established a rapport and have worked well together in the past. They know each other and neither of us has an issue with that relationship continuing. Seriously, let's put it behind us."

Jake looked his friend in the eye, smiled and nodded. "Fair enough." He extended his hand to shake Colton's when he pulled back and swerved to miss a man lying in the road underneath a mangled bicycle. Jake whipped the truck left, and he squealed the tires as he pulled it back to the right to avoid a ditch. Just as he regained control, Javy's men both tumbled across the bed of the truck.

"Weapons," yelled Colton as he grabbed his AR-15 and jumped into the street. Both of Javy's men took positions behind the protection of the truck fenders and searched the woods for signs of movement.

Jake moved along the side of the truck and kept his weapon trained on the man, whose blood was forming a pool on the pavement. "Cover me," he whispered to Javy's men as he walked by.

Colton walked sideways, focused on the stand of pine trees that lined his side of the road. The large field on Jake's side was devoid of activity.

Jake approached the older man cautiously and pulled his arms away from his broken body. "There's no sign of a weapon, not that it matters," said Jake. "His skull is fractured and he bled out on the pavement.

"Hit-and-run maybe?" surmised Colton.

"I think so. Look at how the body was dragged along for twenty feet. Colton, this must've happened this morning. The blood's still fresh and the old guy is still fairly warm."

Colton shouldered his weapon and looked around the scene. "You know what else, there are no skid or swerve marks. Whoever ran him over didn't care to avoid the contact. It was deliberate."

"And they were headed toward Saltillo!" yelled Jake as he ran towards the truck. "Let's go!"

They raced towards Saltillo, fearing the worst. Junior's men might be on the warpath and the poor old guy in the road was the first casualty of the day. Colton became very afraid for the safety of Russ Hilton and his family.

Jake and Colton were on edge as they made the final turn into Saltillo. A roadblock was in place and two men immediately moved to a defensive position behind a makeshift barrier of railroad ties. A tractor with a trailer full of manure blocked a dirt road that led around the barrier.

"Stop about a hundred feet short," said Colton. "I'll go talk to them." As Jake pulled to a stop, Colton exited the truck with his hands raised in the air. He slowly walked closer to the men until they ordered him to halt.

"That's close enough, mister!" said one of the guards.

"State your business," hollered the other.

"My name is Colton Ryman and I'm a friend of Russ Hilton's. I was here a little over a month ago. You might remember. We stayed with the Hiltons and I played a few tunes with Russ that night."

The two men crouched lower and talked for a moment. Then one man rose and summoned Colton to come closer.

"You can put your arms down, Mr. Ryman. Would you mind telling us why you're here?"

"I need to speak with Russ, but I also need to warn you. Someone may be coming this way that ran over and killed an old man about five miles back toward Crump. Have you seen anybody?"

"No, not yet," the other man replied as he shouldered his weapon. "Any idea of when it happened?"

"Recent," replied Colton. "Do you have a roadblock like this one on the south side of town? They may be approaching from there first."

"We do," responded one of the men. "Crap! We've got to warn them. Let me move the tractor so you guys can come in."

While the vehicles were rearranged, Colton instructed Javy's men to remain at this entrance to assist one of Saltillo's guards. Jake and Colton would drive the other into town so they could warn Russ. If Junior or his men were coming, Colton might have arrived just in time.

As they eased into town, Russ was having an animated conversation with Cherry. Colton immediately ducked beneath the dash so Cherry didn't recognize him.

"Stop. Stop. Stop," instructed Colton.

Jake pulled into a side street and immediately turned off the motor. They sat quietly and listened in.

"This is disgusting and atrocious," bellowed Russ. "What's wrong with you people? You can't hang people anymore and especially because she wouldn't kowtow to your demands for information. We can't help you, Mr. Cherry. You should leave now before other folks in town see this and get really pissed off!"

"You've been warned, Hilton!" yelled Cherry as he motioned for his men to get into the car.

Three men on horses rode alongside Cherry's vehicle as he spun gravel and headed back to the south end of town. Colton contemplated chasing after them, perhaps making some kind of citizen's arrest for the death of the old man on the bike.

"I know what you're thinking, buddy," said Jake. "We could grab him. He might make a good prisoner for a hostage swap someday. We could use him as leverage for another purpose. Or we could hang them all for killing the old man and send a picture of that back to Ma."

"Yeah, all of the above," Colton growled. "But the timing is awful. I also suspect Cherry is expendable; otherwise Ma wouldn't send him on this errand with only two guards. If it was important enough, Junior would be here."

"Whadya think Junior's up to?" asked Jake.

"Probably the same thing we're doin, all the more reason we need to get our ducks in a row before we antagonize Ma and Junior further."

Jake patted Colton on the shoulder. "Good thinking, my man. Let's go see a fellow country crooner."

CHAPTER 18

Late Morning, November 7
The Stables
Shiloh Ranch

Snowflake was the happiest pony on the planet. She and Alex had developed a bond that few horse trainers would understand, and it was certainly beyond Stubby's comprehension, who'd been around horses all his life. He marveled at the two as Alex allowed Snowflake the opportunity to sniff her and nuzzle her neck. Once that first step was accomplished, Alex eagerly scratched, stroked, and hugged the much larger animal. They were one together.

"Look at her spirit, Stubby," Alex gleefully exclaimed. Snowflake was hopping around the horse pen like a young child running around a room in utter excitement, not sure which way to go first. "She's ready to ride."

"Alex, I see that," said Stubby. "I'm not sure you are. This ain't the Kentucky Derby and you're still recovering."

"I'll take her slow," Alex insisted. "Come on, you can ride with me and we'll talk. I have things to tell you."

Stubby weighed the risks. He and Colton had discussed her recovery earlier this morning and Alex was approved to ride at a slow pace. They needed to ease her back into the saddle, so to speak. Alex was an integral part of their operation and she'd be needed in the days to come.

"Okay," Stubby said somewhat reluctantly. "I'll have the boys saddle them up."

"Come here, Snowflake," said Alex. Snowflake trotted towards her. "You and I get to ride. We gotta take it slow, deal?"

Snowflake responded with a whinny as she raised her nostrils into the air to smell the opportunity to be freed from the confines of the barn and pen.

Within a few minutes, the two riders rode into the fields towards the river. Snowflake was content to have Alex in the saddle, and likewise, it seemed Alex didn't want to lose the opportunity she'd been given to ride. They were both on their best behavior.

"She's a warhorse, Stubby," started Alex. "She's not some namby-pamby pony named Snowflake. She's ready for battle."

"I don't disagree, Alex," said Stubby.

"Well, I want you to know that neither am I. I'm not weak, nor am I afraid. I'm ready to take care of the Durhams and I intend to help." Alex pulled the reins back and Snowflake responded by stopping. Alex, and her horse, stared at Stubby defiantly.

"Why are you two giving me *the look*?" asked Stubby. "I've never thought otherwise."

Alex continued to stare at him for a moment and then continued. "I know you well enough now. You're planning something. Something big—against the Durhams. I'm better now and I want in. I want to help."

Stubby dismounted and gestured for Alex to do the same. They walked their horses to a relatively flat muddy beach at the river's edge and allowed them to drink. Snowflake also chomped on some tall grass protruding out of the water.

"You know that your role in my plans is totally dependent on your parents," started Stubby. "They love you and it's up to them to determine your well-being. Naturally, I can think of half a dozen ways for you to help with what I have in mind."

"I'll talk to them tonight," she said. "If you're putting together ideas, I should be included in the planning and the attack itself."

"Alex, what makes you think that we're going to attack?" asked Stubby.

"Because it's the only way to push them out."

"Not necessarily," said Stubby. "But let's save that conversation for later when I work out the details. If you can satisfy your parents that the effects of the concussion are gone, then you're in. Fair enough?"

"Yes," she replied. "I have another thing to talk to you about."

"Go ahead."

"I need to address the issue of Chase," she began. "This will also relate to what you may or may not have in mind in your plans."

Stubby and Alex pulled their horses away from the water and began riding again towards the north end of Shiloh Ranch. Stubby wanted to check on a fence that had become damaged by the recently rising Tennessee River. Javy had repaired it and Stubby wanted to see how it was holding up.

"Chase is impulsive, which makes him dangerous," said Stubby. "I've watched him grow up, largely without the direction of his father. The end result is a high-spirited young man who is constantly seeking attention, sometimes without regard to the consequences of his actions."

"Stubby, I feel bad," said Alex, turning in the saddle to look directly into his face. The tough exterior she'd portrayed a moment ago softened and her eyes welled up in tears. "This is his home, not mine. He's not even speaking to his dad, and his mom cries about it. I feel responsible because everything he's gotten in trouble for has involved me."

Stubby pulled to a stop and explained the difficult relationship between Jake and Chase. "Since I've known the Allen family, Jake and Chase have been at odds. This happens sometimes. You do realize that the world doesn't hold hands and sing kumbaya every night, right?"

"I know, but they're family—" started Alex before Stubby cut her off.

"Yeah, but not like yours," said Stubby. "What you have with your mom and dad is unusual nowadays. The Allens love one another. They have issues that you don't have. At the end of the day, however, they are family and will stick together. As for Chase, with age and perhaps a change of scenery, he'll become a mature young man. All teenage-boy screwups don't end up in the hoosegow and all golden-boy prom kings don't end up being president. A lot can happen in early adulthood."

Alex contemplated this for a moment and made a mental note to never marry before she was at least twenty-five, and hopefully the man of her dreams ended up being much older than her. She wasn't ready to tame a teen.

"Okay, anyway, I have a suggestion," said Alex. "Before I left Miss Rhoda's, I talked with Beau and the girls about something. They all want to help."

"That's good," said a noncommittal Stubby. "But they would be best served defending their own farms. We don't need them to get involved in our troubles."

"Stubby, they don't see it that way. The people of Savannah want their homes back. They're tired of hiding. Honestly, they see the Durhams as *their problem, not ours.*"

"What are you sayin'?" asked Stubby.

"They want to organize and band together. They want weapons and they want training. They need leadership. When it's time to make a move on Junior over here, they want to approach Savannah from the south and within the town using the Tiger Resistance."

Stubby laughed. "This ain't a made-for-TV movie."

"They know its real life," argued Alex. "They want their homes back."

Stubby slowly continued the ride as the north fence line came into view. "Who's gonna lead this *band of brothers*? You?"

"No, not completely," replied Alex. "I propose we send Chase over there. For one, it gets him out from under the shadow of his dad. Second, it separates us as we move forward, which will probably please my parents. Third, he's a good trainer and really helped show me the ropes. If we send him with guns and ammo, as well as a sense of purpose, I think he'll do a great job and it will surprise the heck out of the Durhams too."

Stubby chuckled as he rode alongside Snowflake and Alex. "How old are you?"

"Fifteen."

"I don't believe it."

"Yes, sir, it's a true story. I'll be sixteen in a couple of months. Does that mean you agree with me?" asked Alex, beaming with pride.

"Maybe, we'll see."

CHAPTER 19

Afternoon, November 7
Northwest Hardin County

Jake let out a huge belch as his protruding stomach filled with catfish expanded beyond his jeans. "Excuse me, but I'm stuffed outta my mind. I've never had catfish this good, Lisa."

"Well, thank you, Jake," replied Mrs. Hilton. "Boys, there's plenty more where that came from. Anybody ready for a final helping?" She received a variety of groans in various octaves in response.

"We look like a bunch of bears getting ready to hibernate," said Russ. "At least they have to get off their butts and catch fish. We get to lay around and belch."

Colton managed to hoist himself out of the Hiltons' dining room chair and became the proverbial party pooper. "I'm afraid we've got to get goin'. While I really appreciate that you can take some of these names off my contact list, there are a few closer to the bridge that we need to see ourselves."

"Okay, I get it," said Russ. "Listen, there's not a chance Junior moves on us before we get together in a couple of days, is there?"

"Always a chance, Russ," replied Colton. "Be ready. I believe Junior's making plans like we are. Cherry may have been here as a last-ditch effort to flush us out, but he also might be gathering intel. Whatever you do, beef up security and focus on the task at hand."

Lisa approached the table with a large paper bag full of catfish wrapped in aluminum foil and some hush puppies. "Take this back to your families. At least they can get a nibble too."

Colton hugged Lisa and assured her that Madison would get some of her catfish. He then picked up baby Wyatt T. Hilton out of his crib and gave him a tickle under his chin. The newborn wiggled in appreciation.

One of Javy's men agreed to stay behind to escort Russ and the other farm owners of Northwest Hardin County to the meeting site. Although most knew where the Shiloh Battlefield Visitor Center was located, they were not aware of the roundabout route that was the safest to travel.

With only a few stops left, Jake and Colton made good time. They added the other ranch hand to the front cab of the Chevy pickup and Colton took over the wheel. Jake had difficulty maneuvering the old truck anyway, especially with a third person on the bench seat.

The trip was uneventful and the evening began to set in as they made their final stop at the home of the man who had provided critical cover fire during their rescue of Alex. This was the most dangerous of the stops on their list.

The man was an ally in terms of his relationship with Coach Carey and his willingness to help, but he'd never met Jake or Colton. Colton would have to approach unarmed and be prepared to talk his way out of a bullet very quickly. If this reclusive man wasn't so important to Stubby's plans, Colton would have avoided the risk altogether.

"Ain't no way we're drivin' through those iron gates," said Jake. "Look at what's on top of the block pillars."

"Are those anvils?" asked Colton. "Like they used in the old days?"

"I reckon so," replied Jake. "How do you wanna do this?"

Colton pulled the truck up to the gates and shut it off. The driveway sloped down the east side of a ridge and the sun was setting on the other side toward Memphis. He needed to get going because he really didn't want to knock on the man's door in the dark.

"Stubby says this guy is real important," replied Colton. "He also was a big help to us when we rescued Alex. I need to thank him and ask him to help us once again."

"Here's the portable ham radio and charger, *new in box*, as they say on eBay," said Jake.

"You know what else," started Colton. "Since I come bearing gifts, why don't I give him the catfish and hush puppies too. It might help ease any tension caused by my trespassing up his driveway."

Colton exited the truck with only his sidearm and his arms full of catfish and the Baofeng radio. He slowly walked up the winding, tree-canopied driveway towards a small ranch house at the top of the hill. Colton was completely unaware that a rifle scope had drawn a bead on his chest from the moment he came into sight. On the other end of the scope, an iconic marksman who'd served more tours in the Middle East than any other sniper from the Gulf War until the present—Charlie Koch.

As Colton reached the top of the drive, the gravel narrowed as a result of large rock formations rising twenty feet on either side of him. A normal road width would be larger than fourteen feet. Colton doubted the driveway chiseled through the stone could meet that standard.

He walked into the man-made tunnel and clutched the packages. He raised his hands as the house came into full view. It was a simple log home, with a large front porch and a green metal roof. Colton thought it could've been made out of Lincoln Logs, the toys he'd played with as a child.

"Stop!" a voice boomed down the hill toward him.

"Okay," said Colton, raising his hands just a little bit higher and farther apart. "Please don't shoot me."

"If I was gonna do that, you'd be dead at the gate. What do you want?"

Suddenly a red dot illuminated on his chest. He'd seen enough military programs to know what that meant.

"My name is Colton Ryman, a friend of Coach Joe Carey. You helped me rescue my daughter, Alex, a week ago. I'm here to thank you and talk to you about something else."

Colton could hear the faint sound of two-way radio chatter. He couldn't make out the words, which were very few anyway. Probably code, he surmised.

"Come forward, hands held high. No sudden moves."

Colton reached the front steps, sweating profusely and breathing heavily. He was relieved when a woman approached from behind him and began to pat him down. She took his weapon and relieved him of the packages.

"Thank you, Vanessa," said Charlie Koch. "Mr. Ryman, come on up so we can talk. My wife just fixed some coffee. I'd like to hear what you have to say."

Colton walked up the stairs and shook hands with his host. The three of them took seats on rocking chairs and looked out over the tree line toward the few flickering lights of Savannah. It was beautiful.

After some breaking pleasantries and allowing a moment for them to indulge in the catfish and hush puppies, Colton thanked Charlie for his assistance. He gave the Kochs an update on the events that followed the explosion and the state of Alex's health. Then he broached the subject of the upcoming fight with the Durhams.

"Not my fight," said Charlie abruptly. "I'm here to take care of my wife and our home until the lights come back on or the rest of the savages out there kill one another, whichever comes first."

"I understand that, Charlie," said Colton. "Rescuing Alex wasn't your fight either, yet you helped us."

"I owed Coach Carey a favor," grumbled Charlie. "We're even."

"That's true," countered Colton. "But wouldn't it be in your best interest to take out vicious people like the Durhams, which makes it safer for Savannah and all of the neighboring residents, like you."

Charlie stood up and looked across the treetops. "Listen, Colton. We're not the CIA. Our job is not regime change. Besides, you run off the Durhams and somebody else just like 'em moves in to fill the void. Sure, there may be peace and tranquility throughout the land, but it won't last. In case you hadn't noticed, you're only runnin' things until a bigger and badder set of hombres shows up and takes you out."

"You're pretty pessimistic," stated Colton dryly.

"Realistic," he shot back. "I've seen it before throughout the world. The United States goes and meddles in other countries' affairs, like Libya, Egypt, Afghanistan, or Iraq, to name a few, and then Washington loses interest. Sometimes, they're pressured politically, and other times, they really didn't have an overall plan to begin with. Either way, this is not my fight, so count me out."

"What if we pay you?" asked Colton.

"I'm not a mercenary, so don't insult me," said Charlie.

Colton was losing. "Charlie, we have garnered the support of all of the farmers and ranchers in West Hardin County. There are young women who've fled their homes in Savannah to avoid being forced into sexual slavery. Junior is a tyrant as bad as any of the scum you took out overseas."

"I get that," said Charlie.

Colton pulled out the photograph of Nurse Sutton hanging in the Savannah town square. "Look at this. Her name is Nurse Sutton. Junior hanged her for all to see. Her crime? Saving my daughter's life and refusing to admit it to him. This is why our fight is your fight. It should be every decent human being's fight."

Charlie took the paper from Colton and held it under the lantern light. He studied it for a moment and then handed it to his wife, Vanessa.

He returned to his rocking chair and fell in a heap. Just like his counterpart who rocked in silence nearly a mile away, Charlie reached a decision.

"What do you need me to do?"

CHAPTER 20

Morning, November 8
Colton's Birthday
Shiloh Ranch

"Alex and I have avoided Colton this morning, so either he thinks we forgot it was his birthday, or under the circumstances, he lost track of the date and doesn't know," said Madison to Bessie and Emily as they expertly spread icing on Colton's triple-layer chocolate cake.

"He'll be in for a big surprise," said Bessie. "I've always kept a variety of cake mixes and icing on hand for impromptu special occasions. As I started to stock the pantry for an unforeseen event like this one, I vowed to have the ability to create a birthday cake for every member of the family and the ranch hands for a year."

Madison hugged Bessie and smiled. "Thank you for making this day special for my husband. He'll be thrilled and I believe we all could use a dose of the old normal for at least an hour or two."

"Alex has recovered remarkably fast," said Emily, changing the subject. "She isn't showing any symptoms of a minor concussion, and although recovery periods vary based upon the extent of a patient's injuries, from my observations, she appears fit as a fiddle."

"I agree with Emily," remarked Bessie. "Over the years I've had to deal with some of the guys takin' a serious knock on the noggin'. Alex's injuries came from the shock wave following the blast, which I guess is a little different. Either way, you must be relieved."

Madison wiped her hands off on her apron and took it off. She approached the wall where Emily had attached several hooks for aprons, jackets, or hats.

"I know the guys need her, but I'm still not sure she's ready," said Madison. "Believe me, she wants to grab her gun and go after them. In fact, I'd probably join her. But another day or two will help a lot. Hopefully, we can have a few days of peace."

The side entry to the kitchen opened and startled the women. It was Stubby, who was about to enter before he remembered to kick the mud off his boots. He came in and removed his coat.

"It's gettin' cold out there," he said. The woman stared at him and didn't respond. "Did I interrupt something?"

"No, not really," replied Madison. "We were discussing Alex's recovery while we put the final touches on this cake."

"A birthday cake?"

"Today's Colton's birthday," said Madison. "We thought we'd call in everyone a little early this afternoon to wish him happy birthday and to enjoy a little time away from the madness. You know what I mean?"

"Oh yeah, the *madness*," said Stubby, laughing. "I'm afraid we will have to talk about that later, but a birthday celebration can certainly come first. Madison, can you and I talk about Alex?"

"Sure. Ladies, may I be excused?" asked Madison with a chuckle.

"Of course, dearie," replied Bessie. "We'll hide this away until later."

Madison and Stubby entered the living room and sat by the fire. The first real cold snap of the fall had arrived this morning and it was getting colder as the day went on. A weather app would reveal a cold front approaching from the northwest, but in a post-apocalyptic world, survivors were introduced to the weather in real time.

Stubby began. "Madison, I won't downplay this with you. We are gonna have a frank conversation with the group this afternoon about what our options are, but before I can make a plan of attack, I need to know whether one of my key assets will be available."

"Alex?" asked Madison.

"Yes, the fifteen-year-old teenage girl who is braver and stronger than most of us. I've never seen anything like it, but your daughter has ice water running through her veins. Cool as a cucumber. It's truly amazing."

Madison rubbed her hands together, more out of nervousness rather than chill. The room was very warm from the roaring fire. Now she knew what a mother felt like when a young male suitor came around asking to marry her daughter. Stubby was building up Alex's capabilities before he asked permission to send her off to war.

"I agree, Stubby. We love her very much."

"Madison, um, I need you and Colton to talk about whether Alex is ready. Ready to fight."

"You want to take my child off to war with you," stated Madison calmly. "You do realize how absurd that sounds, right?"

"Under normal circumstances, yes."

"Under any circumstances, Stubby."

Madison leaned back in her chair and Stubby used the poker to adjust the logs, which generated a lot of sparks. Madison was upset with herself because she didn't have the skills and the ice-water veins to perform the tasks that Stubby needed. Instead, she had to consider sending her teenage daughter out there to fight the Durhams and their thug deputies.

Madison continued. "Stubby, you can't place her on the front lines, you know, toe to toe in some gun battle. That's not fair."

"Okay," said Stubby. "The first phase will keep her completely out of harm's way."

"Is there a second phase?" asked Madison.

"Yes, it involves a surprise for Savannah. She'll be leading the deciding blow that will bring the Durhams down."

Madison thought about the prospect of living on Shiloh Ranch without fear of being harassed by the people who proclaimed to be the local governmental authority. It would be a new beginning for them and the entire community.

"I'll agree so long as Colton remains by her side during both phases. He knows her best and she'll respect his instructions. Their relationship, especially since the grid collapsed, has grown, and they seem to understand how things work now. I'm still trying to get a handle on it."

Stubby stood and Madison rose to accept his hug. A couple of tears dripped from her eyes as she whispered to Stubby, "She's still a child. Please don't let her get hurt."

Stubby gave her a reassuring smile but made no promises.

CHAPTER 21

Afternoon, November 8
Colton's Birthday
Shiloh Ranch

The last of the laughter died down after an impromptu birthday celebration for Colton took place. There were plenty of embarrassing stories told by Alex and Madison, and a few barbs were thrown his way by Jake, who'd been a friend and client for many years. This resembled any other family gathering for a loved one's birthday, until the elephant in the room reared its head once again.

"Everybody, I hate to put a damper on things," said Stubby. "We have a very big decision to make as a group and then we need to discuss what's next."

Maria and Bessie stood and began gathering everyone's plates. There was no evidence of the chocolate cake anywhere. Bessie commented how she could just place these plates on the shelf for tomorrow's use.

"I don't need to rehash the predicament that we're in," continued Stubby. "There's a storm brewin' across the way and I feel certain Junior is planning something. It's been a week since we rescued Alex. In my gut, I feel the clock windin' down."

"Stubby, should we take the fight to them, or wait until they come to us?" asked Jake.

Stubby stood so that he could face the group. He unfurled a set of construction drawings for one of the outbuildings. On the back were pencil markings depicting a map of the area and arrows drawn in several directions.

"That's the first order of business," replied Stubby. "If we take the fight to them, then we willingly start a fight that may have to be fought on their turf. If we let Junior make the first move, then we defend our positions that are familiar to us. You can win a battle by having a superior defense."

"Also, by waiting for him, it might not happen at all, right?" asked Madison.

"That's true, but not likely," said Stubby. "I know these folks. Don't underestimate their penchant for revenge. Ma has quite a history on that front, all impossible to prove, of course."

Emily raised her hand and spoke. "We can prove their atrocities now."

"Maybe, but to whom?" asked Stubby. "They're the authority around here. No, I feel like we need to prepare for the inevitable conflict. That's why we've called all of the major landowners on this side of the river to get together tomorrow at Shiloh's visitor center. We need to be a hundred percent on board."

"My vote is to get ready with a strong defensive plan," said Alex. "Let's catch them off guard when they cross that bridge. Maybe we can just turn them back around."

"Or inflict early losses on them, which might break their spirit," added Colton.

Stubby nodded and smiled at Alex. "I believe your approach is best, Alex. Does anybody disagree?"

"No."

"I totally agree."

"I agree, so what's the plan?"

Stubby sat on the hearth and spread the drawings out on the floor. Everyone leaned forward to focus on his proposal.

"There are two aspects to this plan, one which I will share with the ranchers tomorrow and the other is for our eyes only."

"Let's hear it," said Jake.

Stubby pulled a pencil from behind his ear and circled spots on both the north and south side of Highway 64. "This is one of the Indian Mounds. It provides a nice two-hundred-foot drop towards the bridge into Savannah. On the north side is our new friend

Charlie, who is an expert sniper. I propose to embed Colton and Alex on the Indian Mound as part of a two-man sniper team."

"Excellent!" shouted Alex, drawing a stare from her mother. She quickly tamped down her enthusiasm.

"When Junior's men enter this kill zone, here," said Stubby, pointing to a circled area on the map, amidst a gasp from Emily. "Alex and Charlie will open fire. One of two things will happen. Junior's men will retreat, or they'll turn off the road toward the north. It will provide them the path of least resistance as an escape route."

"What if they keep coming towards us?" asked Colton.

"Then you guys bail out of there and make your way back to Shiloh Church, where I'll set up a headquarters, and give us a report," replied Stubby. "Your role in this will not last long because I expect Junior to throw everything he's got at us. With luck, he'll turn north and give us some time to dig in. If he comes south, well, the Second Battle of Shiloh will be upon us."

"Stubby," started Jake, "you mentioned a second part of the overall plan. Tell us about that."

Stubby walked behind Chase and patted him on the shoulders. "We'll have a very important role for Chase in this aspect of the plan. Tomorrow afternoon, after we meet with the ranchers at the visitors' center, Chase, Alex, and I will travel to Nixon with weapons and ammo. We'll get Chase started in training the young ladies of Savannah who've been displaced by the Durhams. They want their town back and we're gonna help 'em."

"A surprise attack," interjected Colton.

"Yes, and you will be a part of it as well," said Stubby. "After you report in to Shiloh Church, I want you and Alex to cross the river to Miss Rhoda's. From there, you will lead a contingent into the south side of town to circle up with Coach Carey and his Tiger Resistance."

"Won't Junior or his men be waiting?" asked Madison apprehensively.

"I don't think so and here's why," replied Stubby. "Junior is very arrogant and egotistical. He sent search squads out a few days ago and they returned to Savannah with nothing. In his mind, that was good enough to go after the real prize—revenge on the Rymans. He's gonna assume that one of the ranchers has been harboring these rotten fugitives. He'll send everybody in a show of force, like he did in Adamsville."

"His backside will be exposed," added Jake, who used a stick from the kindling pile to point to the south side of Savannah. "While we whoop him over here, the rest of the good guys will sneak in and cut them off from returning to Savannah."

"They'll be trapped on our side of the river, or on the bridge, where, hopefully, we can put the squeeze on 'em," said Stubby.

"We'll get to capture their queen," said Alex quietly.

"Yup, that's the plan, Alex," said Stubby, smiling. "This part of the plan has to be kept secret from the others. Its success will depend on its trickery. Loose lips sink ships."

Everyone leaned back and relaxed in their chairs, taking in the complexity of Stubby's plan. It had a number of moving parts and there was the potential for miscalculation.

"It's a solid plan," said Colton, who was joined by other members of the group nodding their heads in agreement. "As a negotiator, I always had to know what our bottom-line, worst-case scenario was. What's the fallback position if Junior's men are too powerful for us?"

Stubby looked to Javy, who gave him a thumbs-up. "Earlier, I sent Javy with a couple of horses full of supplies and backup weapons down to Char Wolven's place. If we have to bug out, we'll hightail it down Federal Road and then through the woods to Childer's Hill. Her place is heavily wooded, obscured from the road, and she has agreed to put us up until we can regroup."

"You mean we might have to leave Shiloh Ranch?" asked a worried Emily.

"If necessary," replied Stubby. "I've discussed this with Bessie already. Tomorrow, I'll need you and Madison to work with Bessie in hiding certain supplies around the property. We don't want to make it easy for Junior's men to loot our place if they overrun us. At Childer's Hill, we'll lick our wounds and get ready for whatever is next."

"What about us?" asked Colton.

"If you have to run, stay safe and hidden first," replied Stubby. "Then make your way across the river to Rock Pile. It's a straight shot to Childer's Hill from there. Just remember, all three of you, we may not be able to come and get you this time. Keep your radios on and don't push your luck. We can always find another place to live."

CHAPTER 22

Morning, November 9
Pittsburg Landing Road
Shiloh Battlefield Visitor Center

Amongst the well-preserved battlefields of the four-thousand-acre Shiloh National Park was the two-story colonial-designed visitor center. Thousands of Civil War buffs passed through the halls of this beautiful building containing artifacts and historical accounts of this deadly Civil War battle. Prior to the collapse, a driving tour was suggested for the visitors that took them to the major battle scenes in The Woods, Grant's Last Line, and the Hornet's Nest.

After breaking in the back door, Jake, Colton, and Stubby walked reverently through the building. The sun was shining brightly that morning, allowing plenty of light to enter the grand exhibit hall.

"Kinda gives you the chills, doesn't it?" asked Jake.

"It sure does," replied Colton. "History had lost its importance in America, or it was diminished somewhere along the line."

"I agree," said Stubby as he unlocked the front doors to allow a rush of cold, fresh air to enter the building. With the two doors open on both ends, a nice breeze swept across them. "History's important because it tells us how we got here. It also can guide us in our decision making. What we face is a fittin' example. We're going to fight an enemy on the very soil where two major armies fought one another over one hundred fifty years ago."

"Yeah," started Jake, running his fingers along a map posted on the wall. "Do you think it's symbolic that we're fighting on the Confederate side of the skirmish line?"

"In terms of what?" asked Colton. "Political ideology?"

"No." Jake chuckled. "I was thinking more in terms of winning and losing. Grant had reinforcements that outgunned the Rebs. The Union, whose army was on Junior's side of the line, won the battle."

Stubby joined the men at the map. "They did, but only because the rebel advancement got bogged down here, at the Hornet's Nest."

The sound of a car approaching caused the guys to abandon the conversation and ready their rifles. Peering through the windows, they watched as two vehicles slowly made their way down the gravel entry to a parking space in front of the building. Two groups of men exited the vehicle, led by Russ Hilton, providing everyone a sense of relief.

Colton was the first to greet his old friend. "Welcome to Shiloh!"

"Hey, Colton!" Russ bellowed back. "I've got some other folks with me that you haven't met."

A man in his early fifties extended his hand to Colton. "My name is Ben Arnold, and this is my son, Bennie. We have a place up on Hooker's Bend, about halfway between here and Saltillo."

"Colton Ryman, and my friends Jake and Stubby. It's nice to meet you both and thanks for coming." Colton noticed that neither Mr. Arnold nor his son was armed. Considering the world they lived in, that seemed odd to Colton.

More introductions were made as the landowners from north of Highway 64 arrived first and wound their way through the visitors' center. More neighbors began to find their way to the meeting until everyone who was expected to be there took up seats in the theater, which showed the award-winning film *SHILOH: Fiery Trail* to the park's visitors. Today, Stubby would describe the reenactment of this famous battle, except the participants were sitting in this room.

Over the next hour, he described the various scenarios and received input from the attendees who lived toward the north. Stubby knew the geography well, having lived in the area all of his life. He was, however, unfamiliar with many of the residents.

"I regret that I haven't spent any time up in your neck of the woods to meet you folks before," said Stubby at one point. "I know your land and, finally, under these unusual circumstances, I've come to know you folks."

Stubby began to roll up his maps when an arm was raised in the back of the darkened screen room. It was Mr. Arnold's son, Bennie. "Have you considered talking with the sheriff? Maybe some type of compromise can be worked out?"

"We've thought about that," said Stubby. Prior to the meeting, Jake and Colton agreed that Stubby would take the lead on all of this. He'd be respected as being ex-military and a longtime resident of the region. "The Durhams have shown no desire to be reasonable on any matter. Their approach, as you all know from the Adamsville massacre, is shock and awe, my way or the highway. No, sadly, they only respect force."

The young man persisted. "That's what's wrong with this world. Everybody just wants to fight. There's never an interest in reasonable minds having a discussion."

Russ chimed in. "Listen, I tried to talk to Junior and then his cohort Bill Cherry on two different occasions. Junior burned down Old Man Percy's house, maybe with him in it. We can't find the old codger. As for Cherry, he demanded that we give up some people on the run that weren't in Saltillo. To scare us, he showed us a picture of an innocent woman hanging from a tree branch. Trust me, they're not interested in compromise."

The attendees began to mumble among themselves and Stubby saw that the meeting had reached an end. It was time to send everyone on their way to get prepared. He still had a long day ahead with Chase and Alex at Croft Dairies.

"Okay, you know your assignments regarding scouts and communications," said Stubby. "When Junior's men make their move, don't hesitate to notify your neighbors to get ready. To our north, set up your defensive positions along Coffee Landing and Saltillo Road. Those of us in the south will hold the line at Highway 22 and then farther south at Pittsburg Landing. Remember, if we can't split Junior's men in two, then we'll try to box them in to prevent their retreat across the bridge. Otherwise, we'll try to push them as far west as we can, where we can circle in behind them to cut off their access to the bridge. Everybody clear?"

"How will we know when it's time?" asked one of the property owners from the north side.

"First, you'll hear the sniper fire. The sound of your neighbor's fifty-caliber weapon is unmistakable. Second, we'll be raising you on the handheld ham radios we gave some of you earlier. Radio operators will spread the word face-to-face. Got it?"

"Got it!"

"We'll be ready!" yelled John Wyatt.

"Keep us posted by radio!" said Russ Hilton.

Everyone shook hands as they exited the building. Jake and Colton each took up a seat on the park benches on the front porch of the building. For several minutes, Stubby stood with his hands on his hips, watching as the last car pulled out of the park entrance.

"Stubby, whatcha thinkin'?" asked Jake.

"I'm thinkin' it's all we've got."

CHAPTER 23

Afternoon, November 9
Croft Dairies
Nixon

The skies were becoming overcast and the wind was picking up as the trio comprised of Chase, Alex, and Stubby made their way toward the dock of Croft Dairies. Whitecaps could be seen up and down the river as a beautiful sunny morning turned into a more typically damp, cold late fall afternoon. Even before Rhoda and two of her girls tied the flat-bottom boat off on the posts, Stubby decided that an evening return to Shiloh Ranch was out of the question. He regretted the need to make these frantic, last-minute preparations, but the coming storm could be seen as a sign of things to come.

"Here ya go," said Chase as he handed over the ammo cans and gun bags. "They're really heavy, but if we don't get them out of here first, the boat might flip with all of us going overboard."

Stubby was the last to disembark and pushed himself up from the deck. This cold weather didn't suit his old bones. He removed his 75th Ranger Regiment cap and wiped the raindrops off his face. *I'm gettin' too old for this.* Then he laughed at himself for the fact that *this* was about to become much worse.

"Welcome back, Stubby," greeted Rhoda. "I look forward to the day when we can all get together and talk about dairy cows or old war stories rather than the ones yet to be created."

"Don't I know it," said Stubby, who bent down to pick up the military-style duffle bag, but Chase quickly took it and slung it over his shoulder. "Thanks, Chase."

Chase walked well ahead of the two stragglers and Alex was

already out of sight with two of the girls from Savannah. Stubby and Rhoda ambled up the hill toward the house as the rain stopped.

"Why don't you stay the night, Stubby?" asked Rhoda. "It's gonna get powerful nasty out here on the river as the evening sets in. I promise I'll let you and Alex spend as much time with the girls as you need. I've already arranged for the other farms to be here for a meet-and-greet with Chase."

"I'm glad you asked. We have a lot of ground to cover in addition to some basic weapons training. These are things that can be handled in the evening hours. The more time I can spend with the girls and Chase, the better."

Rhoda cleared her throat and then asked Stubby, "Several of the girls were asking questions about Chase. Beau filled them in on what happened the night Alex got injured. They're concerned about Chase's ability as a leader and as an older guy surrounded by teenage girls. Are you completely comfortable with his ability to stay focused and avoid trouble?"

Stubby nodded and slowed them down as they reached the corner of the house. "These are all legitimate concerns that I've covered with Alex at length and then with his parents before they made the decision to let him do this."

"Alex approves?" asked Rhoda.

"Absolutely. In fact, it was her idea. She will, at some point, discuss this issue with the girls directly. Chase has admitted to being awkward around girls because he thought their sole interest in him was Jake's notoriety as a famous country musician. Alex claims he has never done anything out of line while they were working together and, with the proper encouragement, will be an excellent choice to get this important aspect of the operation prepared."

"What's our role in all of this?" asked Rhoda.

"I'll explain this evening, but I believe it's a winning strategy."

For the remaining daylight hours, Chase and Alex, under the watchful eye of Stubby, trained those with little gun experience on the proper use of firearms. Using .22-caliber weapons, Alex led the handgun training while Chase focused on rifles.

Although Alex was the better shot between the two, Chase had never fired a handgun on a regular basis. Alex recalled all of the details of the practice sessions her family had engaged in while at Harding Place.

Overall, Stubby was pleased with the progress and especially the fact that the girls were not squeamish around the weapons. He commended Rhoda on handpicking young women who would be ready to fight rather than run and put the rest of the group at risk.

Their actual role would be better defined when the group from Nixon met up with Coach Carey and the Tiger Resistance. In the meantime, Stubby would have them trained, to an extent, but also prepare them mentally for the battle ahead—the latter being critical to their success.

As darkness set in, Stubby informed Bessie that they would be staying the night and she promised to inform him of any signs of Junior. Despite a house full of teenage girls and one handsome guy, Rhoda's home was remarkably serious and solemn that evening.

Alex was making the rounds after dinner, taking plenty of time to get to know each girl. Chase, appearing to relish his role as commander of this unit, did the same. Stubby didn't see any hint of bravado on the part of Chase, and Alex seemed to have the full attention of everyone she interacted with. Stubby couldn't have hoped for better.

"Everyone, may I have your attention, please," started Stubby as he climbed a couple of stairs in the foyer in order to better address the group. "I wanna say thank you to Miss Rhoda for feeding us this fantastic bean soup with biscuits. On a dank, clammy night like this, hot soup and fresh buttermilk biscuits really hit the spot."

The rest of the girls filed into the spacious foyer and now Stubby had everyone's attention. "You guys did great today. I was very impressed with your seriousness. Learning to handle a weapon isn't fun or glamorous. A mistake can get you killed. We'll have some more training in the morning before Alex and I return to Shiloh. Chase will then take all of you through some live-fire drills he and I designed. Shooting on the move is much different than having your feet planted and pointing at a target. Chase and Alex have practiced these types of drills. The practice time tomorrow will be invaluable."

"Are you able to tell us the plan now?" asked one of the girls in the front.

"I will, but I need to tell you a little about what to expect," replied Stubby. "Your involvement in our mission will not be like a gun battle you might see in a movie. You will be pairing up with your friends, like Beau, to undertake guerilla warfare."

"Like in the jungle?" asked a girl from the rear, drawing a few snickers.

"In the past, guerilla warfare may have been fought in the jungle, but not in our case," replied Stubby. "We plan to draw the bulk of Junior's men across the bridge into West Hardin County. Once that happens, several scenarios could be played out and we've tried to account for each of them. You guys, on the other hand, will use paramilitary tactics like ambushes, creating distractions, and hit-and-run sabotage to aggravate the men Junior left behind to protect Savannah. Working with Coach Carey and the Tiger Resistance, you'll be able to move faster, in the shadows, and aggravate the piss out of 'em."

Everyone began laughing at the reference by the crusty old warrior. It wasn't Stubby's intention to make them laugh, that was just the way he spoke. But he was pleased to see that their attitudes were loose and confident.

"Why do we need the guns?"

"Just in case," Stubby replied. "We're going to catch Junior and his people off guard. In fact, he might not even be there as y'all start your mission. Unlike a battlefield, which is what we'll face across the river, victories for you guys include taking out individual guards or securing strategic buildings. In essence, while the cat's away, the mice will play."

"Yeah!" was shouted by several of the young girls as they exchanged high fives.

"I love your enthusiasm," said Stubby. "Let me mention one more thing before we sit down and discuss your local knowledge of

Savannah. Guerilla warfare is not about being an expert marksman or the ability to overpower your opponent. You fight smart, like in a chess match, where you use distraction and other methods to gain an advantage over your opponent."

"Hey, I play chess," said one particularly studious young woman in the group. "In chess, we use gambits to gain an advantage."

"Exactly, very good," said Stubby. "Like any good chess player, Coach Carey will evaluate the board, or in this case, the conditions on the ground before he makes any moves. Across the river, we are employing a gambit-like strategy. Our plan is to lure Junior and the bulk of his men away from Savannah by giving ground. Hopefully, this will make them think they have an easy route to infiltrating the west side of the river. Our goal is to divide them. If we can't divide them, then we'll steer them to one side of the highway or the other and then close off the bridge behind them. This will cut off their reinforcements and retreat."

"What will we be doing while that's going on?"

"We'll be taking out his men, one by one if necessary. We'll try to commandeer specific buildings of importance like the Detention Center, the hospital, and if possible, Cherry Mansion."

"You mean we get to capture the queen?" asked the chess player in the group.

"Yeah, but she's mine," said Alex without emotion, or argument from anyone in the room.

CHAPTER 24

Just after dawn
Veterans Day, November 11
The Bridge
Savannah

Every battle had its stories, both told and untold. Throughout history, as one man tried to exert his dominance over another for a myriad of reasons, heroes were lauded with accolades, and others were rewarded with martyrdom. But the untold stories of battles won and lost tilted the scales of victory to one side or another.

Colton and Alex lay prone under a makeshift tent created by a camouflage-pattern tarp and some paracord. Their sleeping bags provided the padding necessary to avoid becoming completely soaked by the rain-soaked ground beneath them. The fitful night's sleep was conducive to the task at hand, but after they'd received word that there was a significant amount of activity on the town square of Savannah, Colton and Alex knew what they had to do.

With Snowflake loaded down with her rifles, ammo, and camping gear, Alex rode slowly through the woods of Shiloh's historic battlefields, taking in the aura it produced. She inhaled the hidden scents of battle—the cries of the wounded, the moans of the dying, and the cheers of the victors. Her vision of the events of the Battle of Shiloh rolled through her dreams as she tossed and turned to get comfortable on an Indian Mound holding the dead of battles past. If Alex didn't believe in ghosts before, she certainly did now.

"They're removing the barricades on the outbound lane of the bridge," said Alex as her steady hands held the rifle's scope tight to her eye. "The right lane barricades are too permanent."

"I'm glad they're on that side of the bridge," said Colton. "We can steer them toward the north and away from us."

"I'd rather take the fight to them, on our terms," mumbled Alex.

Her father didn't respond.

"Okay, Daddy. They're loading up in the cars. It's time."

"Charlie One, this is Juliette One. Over," said Colton into the handheld ham radio. Charlie One, or Charlie Koch, had a number of deer hides with a clear line of sight to the highway. He'd been alerted to the activity the day before and was ready.

"Roger, Juliette One, I see."

"He's a man of few words," said Colton.

"Bessie said the world would be a better place if more men were like that," quipped Alex.

"What?"

"Nothing, Daddy," replied Alex. "I've got a dozen men on foot and at least eight vehicles approaching the bridge from town. They're coming."

Colton cued the mic again. "Alpha One, do you copy?"

Static came across the radio and then Stubby's familiar voice filled the air. "Five by five, Juliette One. Sitrep."

"Eight vehicles, fully loaded. Another dozen men on foot. They're beginning to slowly cross the bridge."

"Roger that. Hit 'em straight, Juliette. Out."

Alex laughed. "Yeah, I'll hit them straight down the middle all right—center mass."

Alex turned her cap around and wiggled her body into a comfortable spot. She was waiting for the signal from Charlie to open fire. The agreed-upon signal was the first shot and, most likely, the first kill.

"Daddy, spot me but no extra talk, okay? I've got to focus."

Stubby had entrusted Alex with his Remington 700. It was the weapon she'd practiced using in the ravine at Lick Creek several weeks ago. Although her AR-15 never left her side, she agreed the .308 was better suited for *bad-guy target practice.*

"Good," Alex mumbled. "They're bunched together."

Junior's men walked slowly behind the vehicles, which were cautiously rolling forward ahead of them. This didn't make sense to Alex. *Does Junior know there's an ambush?*

Their position was five hundred yards from the projected kill zone. The concrete barriers, which acted as guardrails, prevented Junior's men from pulling off the highway. Retreat was their only option, or push forward.

Alex waited patiently, deferring to Charlie to take the first shot. Charlie was an expert and would know what to do. Alex took a deep breath and then waited. They approached closer. Closer. The procession stopped just short of the kill zone.

"What are they doing?" whispered Alex, exhaling out of frustration. She studied them through her scope. Colton moved his glasses up and down the highway.

"Four vehicles approaching from the west," said Colton. "Eastbound lane. Have they been out here all night? Have they been watching us?"

"Juliette One, Charlie One. Over," said Charlie into the radio.

"Go ahead, Charlie One," Colton replied.

"Four vehicles. Driver only. Came from beyond Crump. Mission revised. Fire on my lead. Roger."

Colton and Alex looked at each other. A change of plans meant exposing them sooner and creating a much more difficult shot for Alex because of the longer range.

"No problem," she said.

Colton keyed the mic. "Copy that, Charlie One. On your lead. Out."

Alex got her head back in the game, once again focusing on her potential targets. Through the scope she considered her options. At first, she looked for the easiest targets, those without cover behind vehicles or concrete barriers. Then she considered Charlie's line of sight and decided upon targets that would be more difficult for him to hit.

She narrowed it down to a couple of options as the cars sped past her on the left. Several men prepared to jump the barriers dividing the highway when the crack of Charlie's rifle echoed through the valley. The fifty-caliber round obliterated a man's skull, spewing brains and blood across the hood of an old Datsun pickup.

The remaining men stood in shock as Alex sought her target. She let out her breath and squeezed the trigger, sending a .308 round into the center of a heavyset man's chest, where the Remington Core-Lokt bullet expanded.

Two shots, two kills.

Now, chaos set in. The approaching vehicles heard the rifle rounds and immediately took up defensive positions near the kill zone. Junior's men scrambled for cover, but neither Alex nor Charlie rested on their laurels.

Charlie fired again, missing his intended target but finding the radiator of a Dodge Power Wagon. Alex fired twice, missing both times, but sending men scurrying for cover.

From this distance, the faint sound of shouting could be heard emanating from the bridge. Alex thought she could make out Junior's voice issuing commands. It didn't matter. *Just shoot.*

Time began to stand still for Alex as her mind raced, looking for a target. The men were well concealed, so she looked for any opening. The next shot destroyed a man's knee. *Not dead, but out of commission.*

Charlie scored another kill. Alex decided on another tactic. *Shut off their retreat.* She sent another round into the rear of the convoy, penetrating the windshield and instantly killing the driver.

The shouts were louder now. Charlie must have picked up on Alex's thinking because he shot out the windshield of another car in the rear of Junior's attack formation, such that it was. *Dead passenger. Check.*

The shouts became panicked. It was barely discernible, but one voice rose above the clamor—Junior's. The front vehicles lurched forward and began speeding across the bridge. Alex had to make a choice—hit the moving targets or shoot at the sitting ducks. She searched through her scope and found a familiar face. It was one of the men who had manhandled her at the jail, rubbing his nasty body against hers.

"Hello," she said calmly before shooting him in the chest. Romeo fell in a heap, draped over the white concrete guardrail, which was now splattered with his blood. She popped him again for good measure.

Charlie killed another man who was trying to squeeze into the backseat of a Jeep Wrangler. Alex immediately shot out the Jeep's tires, creating another handful of ducks to pick off. Charlie nailed the passenger with a head shot that passed through and through into the thigh of a man standing in the backseat. Alex shot and wounded the driver. It was going well until several rounds of automatic fire could be heard to their left.

"Daddy!" yelled Alex. "I forgot about them!"

"We're exposed up here," said Colton. "We've gotta go."

"Hand me my AR," shouted Alex. "Tell Charlie we're done."

"Charlie One, Juliette One. Buggin' out. Over."

"Roger that."

Charlie turned his rifle on the two vehicles that had eluded the kill zone. They'd placed themselves squarely between Alex and Charlie. Four of the men hid behind the concrete barrier facing Alex, and four of the men crouched between the vehicles, searching for Charlie's position.

"Daddy, take the Remington and meet me at the horses," shouted Alex. "I'll be there in a minute."

Colton gathered up the sniper rifle and remaining ammo and slid backwards into the trees. Alex left their sniper hide and found a position behind a fallen tree, which provided her cover. She glanced to her right and saw that Junior's men were getting organized.

A shot rang out as Charlie began his assault on this front pack. Alex joined the fray with a four-round burst that shattered the concrete barrier, missing low.

Junior's men returned fire, but their shots flew wildly over Alex's position. Charlie continued pounding them with gunfire, killing one.

The rest of Junior's men passed through the kill zone, so Alex turned her attention to steering them to the north of the highway into the now deserted Bridge View Estates. Stubby had told her that a battle fought north of the highway was safer for them.

As Junior's vehicles approached the break in the guardrail that led to Bridge View, Alex opened fire on the caravan. She riddled the lead car with bullets, forcing them to slow and, ultimately, bail out to the path of least resistance.

Charlie continued to shoot down upon the men trapped between them while Alex inwardly celebrated as one car after another turned off Highway 64 toward the north. When the last one exited, she inserted another magazine and opened fire on the two vehicles below her.

Alex's position was well concealed, and thus far, her targets were more interested in staying behind cover than engaging in the fight. Charlie hit another man in the shoulder. Alex shot one in the backside. Junior's men were caught in a deadly crossfire and would all die if this continued.

In a bold move, Junior's men stood and began firing in both directions. The drivers took their positions behind the wheels of their vehicles and the remaining deputies slid into the cars as they sped in reverse back toward the highway's exit. Junior must have communications between the vehicles, thought Alex. She made a mental note to tell Stubby.

After a few more rounds, she retreated through the woods and joined her daddy. Phase one of the second Battle of Shiloh was complete.

CHAPTER 25

Mid-morning
Veterans Day, November 11
Shiloh

The original Shiloh Meeting House, built by Methodists in the mid-nineteenth century, was an unassuming beam and mortar constructed building with few windows. General William Tecumseh Sherman located his division of Union soldiers along the ridge on both sides of Shiloh Church, awaiting the Confederate Army led by General Beauregard. He held the position for a few hours before being forced to retreat.

Today, a different type of army occupied the area around the reconstructed replica of Shiloh Church. Freedom-loving Americans opposed to tyranny in government on any level stood ready to do battle. The mood was excited as Alex and Colton gave Stubby a rundown of the events at the bridge. Alex estimated six to eight killed and another half dozen wounded depending upon Charlie's level of success after she left. Three of Junior's vehicles were disabled in the melee.

"He still has forty men," started Stubby. "Certainly not an army, but more manpower than we have. Some of these guys may have military experience as well."

"Do you still plan on engaging them here?" asked Colton.

"Yes," said Stubby. "We're hunkered down and ready. I've deployed the Mennonites toward the highway to act as scouts. They won't take up arms, but they're willing to do their part. They'll let us know as soon as Junior and his men head this way."

"Daddy, we've gotta go," said Alex. She quickly gave Stubby a hug and moved toward the door, when Stubby stopped her. He grasped her by the shoulders and looked her in the eye.

"Alex, you did great and I see that you're anxious. Just remember this. We're all fighting the same battle, just in different roles. You're part of a team now. Stay in communication with us because you can't get out ahead of us. If you do, Junior will be back in Savannah like white on rice. Understand?"

"Yes, sir, General Stubby!" She broke free from his grip, smiled and then provided him a snappy salute. He returned the salute, spun her around, and shoved her out the door to a room full of laughter. The tension was eased and the troops at Shiloh were ready.

Alex and Colton mounted up and their horses galloped through the trails until they reached the clearing at Wyatt Farm. Alex's hat flew off her head as Snowflake picked up speed, but it hit Colton squarely in the chest.

"Thanks, Daddy!" hollered Alex as Snowflake crossed through the open gates entering Shiloh Ranch. Shouts up ahead from Javy's men guarding the main house announced their return.

Madison came running out of the house to greet her family. She fought back tears and the two excitedly talked about their success on the bridge. Madison followed each from room to room inside the house as they changed into different clothing for the next part of the operation. Camo was traded for more nondescript khaki and black outfits. The sniper rifle was given to Bessie, who was a pretty good marksman, and Alex grabbed half a dozen fully loaded magazines for her backpack. She also strapped on a knife suggested by Stubby.

As the two bounded down the stairs with Madison in tow, they stopped to drink some water and inhale a bowl of hot oatmeal topped with apples. The meal warmed their bones and forced them to cool their jets.

Maria took their plates and in her best heavily accented English, she said, "You look like ninjas."

Alex and Colton evaluated each other and began laughing. "All black might have been better, but we certainly look like some kind of military some-somethin'," said Colton.

"Dress for success, right, Mom?" asked Alex as she stood, subtly announcing that it was time to go.

"Yes, honey," said Madison as she gave her daughter a hug. "Be safe."

"We will," said Alex, who quickly left. She didn't want long goodbyes. They were on a mission and she didn't want the emotional distraction. She recalled some of the mental toughness traits she'd picked up from Tiger Woods.

Alex had learned to believe in herself. Golf was a very personal game, not a team sport. It was one of the few sports where you were in complete control of your game. She'd learned at an early age that having a strong success drive and believing she was capable of achieving her goals kept her singularly focused on the task at hand.

By playing competitive golf in tournaments, Alex learned that you couldn't let anything distract you. The secret to performing at your best under pressure was to control what you were paying attention to in the moment: Don't concern yourself with negative things that might happen. Visualize success in every shot and be confident in your abilities.

Javy helped her into the saddle and Colton finally joined her. She could see concern and emotion on his face.

"Daddy, we have to leave this behind."

"Whadya mean?"

"We've got to play a role now, a dangerous one. But what we accomplish today will make our lives secure. It's like golf, Daddy. Play focused and emotionless."

"Yeah, I understand," said Colton as he subconsciously shook his body to rid it of baggage and inner distractions. "Let's ride!"

Nearly an hour later, they were tying off their boat at Croft Dairies and unloading their gear. Rhoda and Chase were already waiting for them.

"Stubby called ahead and filled us in," said Chase. "He said you killed it, Alex. Way to go!"

"Yeah, we took out quite a few of them," she replied. "Are they ready?"

"Let's just say that we're better off than forty-eight hours ago. Come on and get organized before we head into town."

Chase helped Alex off the ramp and onto the wet grass, where she lost her footing. He quickly assisted her and the two walked briskly up the hill, discussing the morning's events.

"I've whittled the group down to my feisty fifteen," said Chase. "After doing the live-fire drills, I found several of the girls to be squeamish although they courageously tried to hide it. We can't risk an emotional basket case once things get rollin'."

"Can you use them some other way?" asked Alex.

"Oh, for sure," replied Chase. "They'll be used as scouts along the highway into town and I'm holding a few to protect Miss Rhoda."

"Feisty fifteen, huh?" asked Alex as she laughed at the comparison to the soldiers in the *Dirty Dozen* movie.

"Yeah, they don't mind getting in the mud, messin' their hair, et cetera. They're built out of their leader's mold."

"You handpicked people like yourself, that's good," said Alex.

"Nah, not me. You, Alex. You're their dang hero. All these girls wanted to talk about was you and what you've been through."

"Really?"

"You'll see," replied Chase. "You're their icon, a fearless hero ready to fight the good fight. They really look up to you, seriously."

Alex and Chase rounded the corner of the house to a contingent of young warriors. The girls wore grungy clothes, including hiding their hair under ball caps and knitted beanies. Some had smudged their face with dirt while others made a point to dress like boys.

"Look, Alex is here!"

"Alex, how did it go this morning?"

"Are we ready to fight?"

Alex hopped up the stairs and stood over her Feisty Fifteen, plus Chase. Before she spoke, she looked at Chase and realized there was something different about him. He seemed *humble*. He had purpose now. Placing him in this position might end up being a great call.

"Okay, listen up, y'all," started Alex as she noticed Colton and Rhoda file in behind the group. Alex looked down at the Feisty

Fifteen, who soaked in every word. "Things will happen very quickly now. Junior brought most of his men across the bridge and they swept towards the north. Stubby will try to contain them, giving us time to take care of our business."

"That's good news!"

"Yes, yes, it is. But I counted fifty to start and they still have forty guys. I'm thinking there may be at least forty to fifty left behind."

"What's the plan?"

Alex removed her AR-15 and set it against the porch column. "We've got a job ahead of us. If we fail, they'll come after us with a vengeance. We've been playing cat and mouse with the Durhams for two months, but now that we've kicked the hornet's nest, it's time to exterminate them before they bite us."

Alex took a deep breath and continued. "We're gonna join up with Coach Carey and the guys. Listen to me, this is important. We have to follow Coach Carey's instructions. He knows the lay of the land and what needs to be done. Like they say in football, *there's no I in team.* At the end of the day, we'll confound the heck out of Junior's men. We'll make our way to Cherry Mansion or wherever the queen bee is hiding, and we'll end this once and for all!"

CHAPTER 26

Morning
Veterans Day, November 11
Shiloh

Stubby and the men quickly readied their defenses. The Wyatts' old tractor was used to block Caney Branch Road, which provided another route directly into the heart of the Shiloh and Pittsburg Landing. Three days before, they'd sent the old Bobcat that Javy and Stubby fixed up out to CR117 to pile debris to block access from their rear. Stubby didn't have the manpower for surprises. This left Junior one accessible route, CR22, which led them directly into his gunsights.

The biggest challenge Stubby faced was disabling Junior's vehicles. Naturally, he hoped the ranchers on the north side of the highway helped take a few of them out, but he couldn't count on it. Stubby deployed several methods, depending on the route Junior would take.

He created Molotov cocktails full of broken nails and screws. On gravel roads, the men dug ditches a couple of inches deep. Stubby and the neighbors gathered two-by-four studs and drove long nails through them. They secured the boards across the roads with the nails sticking up. After being covered with leaves, the nails were obscured and a tire-flattening hazard was created.

Meanwhile, he positioned his men in strategic locations where they could move from point to point depending on how Junior approached. He was unpredictable, and with the benefit of transportation, Stubby was disadvantaged. The element of surprise was their best asset, together with fighting in familiar surroundings.

He'd learned this the hard way in Vietnam.

"Alpha One, Juliette One. Over." The radio interrupted Stubby, who was deep in thought.

"Go ahead, Juliette One."

"En route, Alpha One. Will be switching comms to local in thirty minutes."

"Roger that, Juliette One. I'll inform Bravo One."

"Copy. Thanks," replied Alex.

Stubby laughed to himself. Alex Ryman, fifteen-year-old Rambo. *Never underestimate the determination of an extremely pissed-off woman.*

Stubby had instructed Alex to join the two-way communications system established by Coach Carey and the Tiger Resistance. These were two distinct and separate operations. If Junior's men did get wind of their ham radio chatter, he might not think to listen on the two-way frequency bands. Stubby was amazed that Junior hadn't picked up on the Tiger Resistance already. Unlike his brother, Junior had no military sense whatsoever. Rollie Durham would have posed a much different adversary on this day.

John Wyatt approached on horseback and Stubby greeted him outside Shiloh Church. "We're as ready as we'll ever be," said Wyatt as he slid off his chestnut stallion.

"Do you think he'll take the bait and turn down Hamburg-Purdy Road?" asked Wyatt.

"Yeah, Junior will bull ahead until he cracks his head on a block wall. That's what I'm countin' on. He'll come right down below us, not thinking of the consequences, hell-bent on whatever drives the boy."

"Alpha One, Charlie One. Over."

"Go ahead, Charlie One."

"Three more KIA. Remainder has pushed into Hooker's Bend. Scorched earth strategy. Repeat. Scorched earth strategy."

"Roger, Charlie One. Out."

Stubby clipped his radio to his jacket and rubbed his fingers through his hair. Junior was out of control. It would be a bloodbath up there, and when Junior didn't find what he was lookin' for, he'd head back this way.

Stubby suddenly wished he had more men, a lot more.

CHAPTER 27

Morning
Veterans Day, November 11
The Arnold Home
Hooker's Bend

SMACK! THUD!

The jaw of Ben Arnold probably broke on the last swing of the chair leg as it slammed into his face. His wife cried uncontrollably as she lay half-naked on the floor. Any attempts to go to her husband's aid earned her a swift kick to the ribs. Her son's body blocked the entrance to the small farmhouse, gutted with a large hunting knife. He'd attempted to run into the house when Junior and his men rushed down the Arnolds' driveway. Junior's man shot him in the thigh, which slowed him, and another ripped the knife through unarmed Bennie Arnold's chest, killing him instantly.

"Where are they?" screamed Junior as he grabbed Arnold by his salt-and-pepper hair and wrenched his face upward. Junior leaned into the man's face, which had been torn open by the blows.

"Arrrgh, waah, who," the words came out of the incoherent man's mouth.

"You do know! Somebody has to know!" screamed Junior as he shook Arnold's head violently, slinging blood on his sobbing wife. "You're gonna tell me or I'm gonna gut you like your kid. Now, once again. WHERE ARE THEY?"

"Please, mister," pleaded his wife. "My husband can't take any more. Leave him be!"

Junior let go of Arnold's hair and pushed him violently to the side, causing him to topple out of the remaining dining room chair.

"Good idea, Mizzzz Arnold," said Junior. "Maybe me and the boys should have a go at you while the man of the house watches through the only eye he's got left. Whadya think, boys?"

Nobody answered because they knew Junior wasn't really seeking an answer. He stood over the woman, who was making every effort to cover up where Junior's men had ripped her dress off. Nobody said a word as Junior crouched down next to the woman. He fiddled with her hair and then started to pull at her dress. Mrs. Arnold cried uncontrollably, holding onto her dress, with her husband barely clinging to his life.

"It won't be so bad, ma'am," snarled Junior. "After we're done with ya, we'll do the humane thing and kill ya so you won't have to live with the pain."

"Nooo," moaned her husband as he lay on the floor, staring at his wife. He lifted his arm and pointed towards the front door. "Thhhlowww."

Junior patted Mrs. Arnold on the thigh and returned his attention to her husband. He knelt on one knee and turned his head sideways to look into the man's face.

"What's that? Did something jostle your memory? Spit it out. Come on now."

The man coughed some blood, barely missing Junior's face, but he gathered the strength to speak.

"Thy-low. Thy-low!"

Junior reached back and yanked the woman's dress out of her clutches, leaving her body exposed. He gently wiped the blood off Arnold's face.

He whispered in Arnold's ear, "Where? Whereabouts in Shiloh?"

"Ubby. Ack Ubby."

Junior stood up and paced the floor. The woman began to crawl towards her husband and Junior flung her dress at her. "I knew it! I knew they were lying to me that night we went to that country singer's place. It all makes sense now. They said they were from Nashville."

Junior continued to pace.

"Can we please get my husband some help now?" begged Mrs. Arnold.

Junior ignored her. "Cherry said they only seemed to care about crossing the bridge. When he pressed them, they said they were going to Memphis. These people ain't stupid. They were never going to Memphis. They were going to that ranch where Stubby lives. I'll betcha they're friends with that other country fella in Saltillo too!"

"Please, mister, can we help him now? He told you what you wanted to know." Mrs. Arnold had resumed sobbing now and made no effort to hide herself. Junior turned and looked at them and tilted his head as if confused. Then, calmly, he pulled his .357 and shot them both in the head.

"Let's roll," he said to the four men in the foyer.

"Are we headed to Saltillo?" one of the deputies asked.

"No siree, Bob," Junior replied. "We're headin' down to Shiloh to even a few scores. That's where the real party is."

CHAPTER 28

Afternoon
Veterans Day, November 11
Hardin County High School
Savannah

The short trip up CR69 into Savannah was uneventful. A 1970 Ford F-150 farm truck led the way, with most of the girls huddled amidst hay bales to stay warm. Temperatures were dropping and a fog was settling in over the river and into low-lying areas inland.

"Isn't meeting here risky?" asked Chase. The shuffling feet of the group echoed down the dimly lit hallways. Alex briefly had visions of a typical school day at Davidson Academy, where she'd be walking with friends or catching the eye of a good-looking guy. Locker doors would be slamming and jokes would be exchanged as teenagers learned the art of social interaction.

It was the first time she'd thought of her normal life in a long time and she quickly gained the strength to shut the memories out of the present. She turned her attention back to Beau, who had provided her a long hug when he'd greeted her at the truck. She'd felt something. His embrace was more than a hey-old-pal-it's-nice-to-see-ya hug. It had feeling and warmth. She didn't want to let go. *Maybe this will all be over soon and we can see what happens between us.*

"We've been monitoring the deputies' activities since the night of the rescue," said Beau. He glanced at Alex and smiled. "Junior's men did a sweep of the high school just a few days ago and, of course, found nothing. We don't use the building often and nothing important is stored here. It made sense today because of the large group."

Voices could be heard from around the corner of the next hallway and the girls began running toward the sounds. Shrieks and cries of excitement marked the reunion of the guys from the Tiger Resistance and their female classmates, who'd been in hiding for two and a half months.

All of the teens were friends and some were family. Alex and Beau allowed the reunion to last ten minutes because they felt it would relieve the tension and create comradery amongst the newly created team.

Jimbo and Clay Bennett made their way through the crowd to say hello to Alex. She really liked these guys and would've been buddies with them at home. Beau introduced them to Chase and then he led Chase to meet the other guys. As they made the rounds, Coach Carey emerged from stage right and signaled for Alex to join him. She gave each of the Bennetts a quick hug and jumped on stage.

"Okay, everyone, let's get started," said Coach Carey, nodding in Colton's direction.

Only a few of the voices subsided. He tried again. "Tigers, all of you, let's focus. There'll be plenty of time to reunite after we kick some butt tonight!"

Coach Carey couldn't help going into *rah-rah* mode, which had the opposite effect of his request for quiet. The impromptu pep rally lasted another five minutes until it finally died down on its own.

"Good job, Coach," Alex whispered in his ear with a grin.

"Yeah, sometimes I can't help myself," he replied and then Coach Carey turned his attention back to the task at hand.

"Ladies, welcome back!" he exclaimed. He removed his hat and adjusted his hair. Alex thought Coach Carey looked tired, but in the low light, everyone looked gaunt. "I wish this was a homecoming in the traditional sense with a bonfire rally, a barbecue cookout, and some good old-fashioned football, but it's not. All of you have been thrust into the real world at a young age. We're all in a real bad situation where people don't follow any rules, including those given to us by God. As a result, we have to adapt our way of thinking to protect ourselves."

"We're ready, Coach," shouted Jimbo Bennett.

"Yeah," added several of the girls.

Coach Carey held his hands up, acknowledging their willingness to take on a difficult task. Colton gave him a pat on the back, encouraging Coach Carey to continue.

"At this moment, Junior and over forty men are terrorizing people across the river. Alex's and Chase's families, together with their neighbors, are waiting for our illustrious sheriff. I have no doubt that Junior will get what he deserves. Our job is just as important. We have to take out the head of the snake—Ma Durham!"

"Dang straight," yelled one of the guys.

"Save her for Alex!" shouted one of the girls.

"Yeah, that was the deal!" shouted another.

Coach Carey instructed Beau to wheel a whiteboard onto the stage and asked Alex to pull the lanterns together to provide better light. As the light and board united, a clearly marked layout of the town with certain landmarks could be seen by the group.

"As you can see," said Coach Carey, "there are four major checkpoints controlled by Junior's men, the most important of which, for our purposes, is the west bridge. He has men stationed at the jail, the hospital, and at the two major stores acting as warehouses—Lowe's and Walmart. There are still eighteen armed men guarding these locations and at least two more located at Cherry Mansion with Ma."

"We've got 'em outnumbered," said Clay.

"And I'll betcha Junior took his best men with him across the river," surmised Jimbo.

"That's true, boys, but make no mistake, although this may be the practice squad, they're armed and most likely scared after what Beau did to their buddies at the hospital that night. A scared man can be more unpredictable and dangerous."

"How're we gonna play it, Dad?" asked Beau.

Coach Carey returned his attention to the whiteboard. "Our primary goals are to take over control of the west bridge and capture

Ma. That means the bulk of our activity will take place on the east side of town."

"Wait, Coach, don't you mean the west side of town at Cherry Mansion and the river?" asked one of the girls.

"No, ma'am," he replied. "The Tiger Resistance is all about subterfuge. Trust me, we'll have teams in place to take the prize, but the rest of you will play an important role. If we can divert just two men away from the bridge, that cuts their manpower down by a third—a huge strategic advantage for us. If one or two more abandon their post at Cherry Mansion, then we'll have the numbers."

"Coach," started one of the guys, "when we take the bridge, won't Junior's men come back towards us?"

"They will, but we'll establish a wall of blockers along CR128 and fight them back."

The group began to mumble and whisper to each other. One of the most dangerous parts of the mission was preventing Junior's men from returning, en masse, to the west bridge and Cherry Mansion. Coach Carey wasn't thrilled at the thought of engaging experienced thugs in a gunfight.

"At that point, we'll have won the battle and we'll throw it in their face. Perhaps they'll disperse, or we'll have to take them out."

A hush came over the room as reality set in. *Take them out.* There would be shots fired in both directions. People died in gun battles. Alex decided to add a few words.

"Hey, y'all. I've been in gun battles. I've been shot at and I've killed before too. I prayed about it and made peace with it. These are horrible criminals that we're dealing with. They have killed or tortured your friends, family, and the community. We all agree it's time to stand up against evil. Blood will flow on both sides, but we'll not surrender until you have your town back."

"We're ready, Alex," said one of the girls.

"We are too," chimed in one of the Tiger Resistance.

"We're all Tigers now!" exclaimed Jimbo Bennett, causing the pep rally to begin again.

Coach Carey made no effort to tamp it down, but he instructed

Beau and Alex to move into the group and pair them off into guy-girl teams.

When the fifteen pairs were established and field assignments made, Coach Carey led the newly expanded Tiger Resistance in prayer.

"Dear Lord, thank you for the privilege of leading this brave group of young people as we embark on an unthinkable task against the evil enveloping our town. I thank you for each of the talents you've bestowed upon them and I pray that you give them the strength to use those gifts in the face of killers.

"Watch over them and protect them from injury. God, fill them with your spirit and courage as they fight for their families, neighbors, and the rest of your children. Amen."

CHAPTER 29

Afternoon
Veterans Day, November 11
The Woods
Shiloh

One of the Mennonite men on horseback flew down the gravel road toward Shiloh Church. By the speed of his horse and the look of fear on his face, Stubby knew it was time for battle. He received the report and immediately warned his men to get ready. He cued the mic on the Baofeng to contact his outpost at the intersection of the CR22 and Hamburg-Purdy Road, which meandered through the leafless oaks at the base of the steep ravine where Stubby stood alone.

"Delta One, Alpha One. Copy."

"Go, Alpha One."

"Sitrep."

"Vehicles approaching from the north. Five. No, check that. Six trucks and cars. Over."

Stubby held his breath. If Junior sensed a trap, he might make an effort to continue southbound through the blockade somehow. This plan depended upon Stubby's knowledge of Junior and the predictability of his actions.

"Roger, Delta One."

Seconds seemed like hours. Silence filled the air until a smattering of raindrops began to fall on top of the dead leaves scattered through the woods.

"Alpha One, this is Delta One. The convoy has stopped. Confirmed. Junior is in second vehicle. Repeat, Junior is in vehicle two, a blue Pontiac LeMans. Over."

"Roger that, Delta One. Continue to advise."

More seconds ticked away. Stubby wiped moisture from his brow, a combination of nervous sweat and a steadier drizzle. Any soldier who claimed to enter battle without trepidation was being disingenuous. Besides, fear of dying tended to keep you on your toes.

"Moving. High rate of speed. Headed your way. Out!"

Stubby had a minute to ready his troops. He switched to the Midland two-way radio.

"Game time, boys! They're comin'!"

Over the rustle of leaves and the falling rain, Stubby could hear the distinctive metallic clicks of rounds being chambered and charging handles being pulled. His men had superior positions for the battle—well-concealed high ground. Now, he needed their booby traps to work by flattening the tires of the lead vehicles and distracting the occupants inside.

The roar of the engines of the sixties and seventies vintage automobiles could be heard as they rounded the bend. The men were instructed to wait for Stubby's command after the lead vehicles were incapacitated. If the tire-puncturing devices failed, the last two men in Stubby's skirmish line, Jake and Javy, who were instructed to take out the tires. It was a well-thought-out plan with backup contingencies considered. The rest was *mano a mano.*

The dual exhausts rumbled toward him and then music came to his ears in the form of exploding tires.

POW! POW! POW-POW! HISS!

Stubby didn't hesitate as he keyed the mic.

"FIRE AT WILL!"

CRACK! CRACK-CRACK! CRACK!

Suddenly, Stubby's mind left the woods of Shiloh and transferred into the jungles of Cambodia. A war was a war when bullets whizzed by your head as the enemy returned fire.

He knelt behind a fallen tree and riddled the side of a vehicle with bullet holes. The sounds of broken glass, screams of pain, and shouts of instructions pounded his psyche. In his mind, he was forty years younger now and ready to take on the V.C., or Junior.

Bullets shredded the bark of the oak trees as Junior's men gained their footing at the back side of their vehicles. As instructed, Stubby's guys shot out the tires of the vehicles, rendering them useless for travel, but excellent to Junior's guys as a protective barrier.

He frantically searched through the heavier rain and the smoke-filled air. He sought out Junior, the man who was responsible for all of the deaths and torment in Savannah. Stubby wanted to kill Junior himself.

The gunfire continued with few casualties on either side. While it was impossible to be exact, Stubby felt like the bulk of the rounds exchanged were coming from his side of the battle. He began to be concerned with ammo discipline as his unseasoned fighters could quickly run out of bullets if they weren't careful.

From his vantage point, Stubby could see that little damage was being inflicted on Junior's men, so he took an unusual step. He queued the microphone button.

"Cease fire. Repeat, cease fire."

He turned and signaled for Tristan Wyatt to join him. Tristan slid down the last twenty feet of the slope as he lost his footing.

"Young man, I want you to give your father these instructions. Tell John to circle around the back of the cars and block the road. We need to close off their retreat. Tell him to prepare to advance toward the rear of Junior's men. Got it?"

"Yes, sir," said Tristan. The boy glanced towards the shot-up vehicles below their position. "Wow."

"Yeah, wow. Now go to your dad!"

Junior's men stopped shooting as well and they were reloading their weapons. Stubby cursed himself for not considering this contingency. At this rate of fire, his men could run out of ammo!

Running at a low crouch, Junior's men were scrambling back and forth. What were they planning? As the smoke began to dissipate, Stubby noticed something that he'd missed in the melee. Junior's car was hidden behind the lead vehicle along the grassy shoulder of the road. He quickly studied the other cars' tires. They were shot out, thankfully, but what about the blue LeMans.

Stubby closed his eyes and recalled the early moments before the gun battle began. How many tires had blown? Did Junior's driver swerve to avoid a rear-end collision and, as a result, miss the nails?

Think, Stubby!

He wasn't sure, but it didn't matter. He had to assume that the LeMans could still move, and a decision had to be made. *Should I position myself to take it out if it does move or take my horse and intercept Junior around the bend?*

Static from his two-way radio broke his train of thought.

"In position." It was John Wyatt's voice, reporting as Delta One.

Stubby could instruct the men to commence firing again, giving him the needed cover to scamper up the hill and take his horse to catch Junior trying to escape. However, this might provide Junior the distraction he needed to get out of there before Stubby could react.

The *Jeopardy* song played in his head. "Time's a wastin'," Stubby mumbled.

He carefully lifted himself out of the crouch and worked his way up the ravine to the top of the ridge. Using the large oak trunks as cover, he slipped away undetected. From the high ground, he could still survey the field of battle although details escaped him. He had a new mission—a face-to-face with Leroy Durham Junior.

He quickly mounted up and walked his horse along the trails used by Confederate and Union Generals alike. A walk turned into a gallop as the cars slipped out of sight. Time was of the essence now. He had to find a concealed position to take aim at his prey.

Stubby reached the bottom of the trail and secured his horse to a tree. He walked out into the middle of Hamburg-Purdy Road and surveyed his options. Stubby jogged down the incline toward a granite marker designating the wooded thicket labeled the *Hornet's Nest.*

Two vintage civil war cannons flanked the carved granite monument, which stood fourteen feet tall. A single soldier, musket by his side, stood hovering over the cannons, rain dripping off the bill of his cap.

Stubby liked the position. It provided several hundred feet of unobstructed line of sight down the road, and the granite would stop or divert any bullet. Stubby took a moment to read aloud the words of Captain Andrew Hickenlooper found on the placard.

"*Then the supporting infantry, rising from their recumbent positions, sent forth a sheet of leaden hail that elicited curses, shrieks, groans, and shouts, all blended into an appalling cry.*"

In a hushed voice, he whispered to himself, "I'm with you, brothers."

Stubby steeled his nerves and got into position. Soon, Junior would come roaring around that bend with as many as four men with him. Five on one.

Then he shouted, "Rangers lead the way!"

CHAPTER 30

Late afternoon
Veterans Day, November 11
The Woods
Shiloh

The rain was steady now as Stubby reached for his radio. "Gentlemen, maintain ammo discipline but open fire. Let's finish this!"

The sounds of weapons discharging echoed through the woods. It was impossible to determine whether Junior's men were firing back, and Stubby began to regret leaving the field of battle. He would regret Junior escaping toward a relatively unsecured Shiloh Ranch even more.

He rested his body on top of the monument and waited. He had a spot in the road where Junior would have traveled too close to Stubby's position to change course. Now, Stubby would rely upon his military experience and his weapon of choice, the powerful AR-10, to overcome what might be five-on-one odds.

Through the hail of gunfire being exchanged between the two sides, Stubby heard the powerful engine of the vintage LeMans roar, and the dual exhausts rumbled as the car approached. The distinctive chrome bumper entered his field of view and he forced himself to remain disciplined.

"Come to papa," Stubby snarled. The Pontiac was approaching sixty when it came into full view, and Stubby gently pulled the trigger twice, smashing the windshield and instantly killing the driver.

Junior, riding in the passenger's seat, grabbed for the steering wheel but was unable to gain control of the car as it careened out of control and up an embankment. The right front fender crashed into a rock outcropping, causing the vehicle to roll over onto its hood before landing upright in a ditch.

Stubby didn't hesitate. He poured more rounds into the vehicle, killing one of the occupants who attempted to crawl through the back window.

Several shots rang out and sailed wildly past him. He searched for a target, but the remaining men stayed hidden within the steel of the car.

CREAK!

The passenger doors were opening and groans indicated movement. Stubby fired twice more into the windows, sending pieces of glass flying through the interior. There was no response.

The frequency of gunfire in the background had slowed, making Stubby wonder if one side or the other had gained an advantage.

Without warning, a figure rose from behind the trunk and opened fire on Stubby with an automatic weapon. He ducked as the bullets ricocheted off the granite, chipping out holes in the sturdy structure. As Stubby rose to return fire, he caught the silhouette of a man entering the thick woods to his right—the Hornet's Nest.

Without fear, he remained slightly exposed with his weapon focused on the spot where the shooter had popped his head up before. Stubby waited, confident in his abilities, but keenly aware that another man might be circling around him.

Movement to his right. But he stayed focused. Eliminate one threat at a time.

Stubby got his chance as the head of a man rose to get a look at his target. A fatal mistake, as the heavy .308 bullet blasted through his skull. He turned his attention to the man who had eluded death thus far. Stubby's gut told him it was Junior. The Hornet's Nest would once again see bloodshed.

Stubby scanned the woods for movement before he keyed the radio.

"Delta One, Sitrep."

"They've retreated into the woods, running in your direction. Giving chase."

"Roger that, Echo One. Alpha One, do you copy?"

"Go Alpha One."

"Send two men up the road to the monument. One hostile on the loose."

"Roger."

Once again, Stubby had to remain patient. He wanted to give chase after the elusive sheriff, but he also didn't want to leave an opening to his rear for Junior to get through. So he waited.

The rain continued to fall and it was getting darker. Two figures approached him through the woods on his left, which caused him to lower himself behind the monument. They quickly scurried across the road in a low crouch.

"Stubby," said Jake in a voice just above a whisper, "it's me and Javy. You've got four dead plus the Pontiac. Are you okay?"

"Yeah, come here and get down."

Jake and Javy quickly joined his side and provided Stubby an update of the battle down the road. Their side had some losses, but so did Junior's men. Everyone on both sides began to run out of ammo, causing Junior's men to retreat for the woods. John Wyatt and Tristan chased down one of the stragglers and beat him into submission.

"Where are our guys now?" asked Stubby.

"They checked for survivors in the vehicles and took weapons containing ammo. Our ammo levels are low, but so are theirs. Several guys heard the click of empty chambers. Empty rifles and spent magazines are strewn all over. At this point, it's sidearms or hand-to-hand combat. In any event, they're awaiting orders."

"How many escaped into the woods?" asked Stubby.

"I'm estimating a dozen or so. We have the numbers and the guys are ready to go in after them. Just give the word."

Stubby thought for a moment. He didn't want to let go of this opportunity to take down Junior. Also, he needed to buy time for Coach Carey and the Tiger Resistance. If he didn't stop Junior, they could be overwhelmed over there.

Stubby turned to Javy and pointed up the hill towards Shiloh Ranch. "Javy, find a place where the road opens up into the field. Watch for the sheriff."

Javy nodded and took off.

"Echo One, Alpha One. Over."

"Go, Alpha One."

"Echo One, maintain your position and guard the rear. Send the rest of our unit after Junior's men. Be careful, no friendly fire. Let 'em fly!" Stubby resurrected the infamous Rebel Yell, which was echoed from mouth to mouth during the Battle of Shiloh.

"Roger that. They fly!" replied Wyatt, who was also an avid student of Civil War history.

"Jake," said Stubby, "hold your position here and watch for anyone trying to cross the road. You've got a clear line of sight in both directions. Just shoot them. Don't bother notifying me on the radio. I'm gonna turn it off anyway."

"You are?" asked Jake.

The rain began to pour down, but Stubby was undeterred. He pulled his boonie cap out of his ruck and wrapped a shemagh around his neck for warmth. He also switched his optics from daytime to night vision. This gave him a huge advantage over his prey. As night set in, his rifle would illuminate all threats.

He took one more check of his ammo levels and confirmed to himself that he was ready. He patted his AR-10 and whispered to Jake, "It's time to go hunting."

CHAPTER 31

Late afternoon
Veterans Day, November 11
Savannah

Two by two, the Tiger Resistance teams took their positions around Savannah. Each team was assigned to the secondary targets identified by Coach Carey for the purposes of neutralizing Junior's guards stationed there. At locations like the hospital, Lowe's and Walmart, Junior's men could be monitored for their reactions, or engaged as a method of diversion. After Coach Carey initiated the attack on the west bridge leading across the river, his primary objective, the teams were instructed to immobilize their targets' transportation first and then shoot to kill if necessary.

Most of the secondary targets were located on the east and north sides of town. Once they took the fight to the west gate, and ultimately Cherry Mansion, it would take too long for Junior's men to jog across town to have an effect. Disabling their vehicles was a first priority and it was something the Tiger Resistance could do quietly through slashed tires and sabotage.

The first order of business was to take control of the Detention Center. They kept a constant watch of the facility anyway, but had maintained a two-man team across the street, hidden in the old hotel, since Alex's rescue.

This afternoon, there were two of Junior's men, actual deputies prior to the collapse of the grid, that stood guard. Coach Carey knew them both. One was a prolific smoker and the other a consumer of copious amounts of alcohol. Based upon their observations, the smoker stepped out front every hour on the hour. Sometimes the drinker would join him, but not always.

Coach Carey wanted to eliminate the guards and commandeer the jail first, but quietly. Their attack on the west bridge would raise alarms across the town, but it would be over quickly. They needed control of the jail and its contents, which included the armory, access to operating vehicles, and the jail cells for their prisoners. Coach Carey only considered one possible outcome of the day's events—winning.

At the last smoke break, the drinker was already in full swing. He was boisterous and thirsty. Twice during the seven-minute outing, the drinker offered his companion a swig of bourbon, but the smoker declined. Every man had his vice, Coach Carey surmised.

After the men went inside following this break, Colton and Alex moved into position on the left side of the building, securely hidden around the corner of the brick structure. Beau flattened himself against the wall outside of the building to the right and waited. Their goal was to tackle and subdue them, lock 'em up and throw away the key, as they say.

Within thirty minutes, the smoker brusquely swung open the double glass doors and strolled into the damp air, blissfully unaware of what awaited him. He was alone.

His feet shuffled along as he moved his shoulders side to side to crack his back. He pulled out his pack and found it empty. With a couple of curse words for effect, he slung the empty pack like a Frisbee into the parking lot. He pulled another pack out of his shirt pocket and began to wander down the sidewalk in front of Beau.

The smoker began to pack his smokes by smacking the top of the pack into the palm of his left hand.

SMACK—SMACK—SMACK.

THUD!

The smoker never knew what hit him. Beau charged the man, lowered his head, and rammed it into the man's rib cage. With the breath knocked out of him, the man was neutralized, but still a threat.

Beau and the Bennetts had watched mixed martial arts, MMA, on FoxTV from time to time. The fighters were consistently warned against punching their opponent behind their ear and near the spine. Even a light strike could result in a knockout, but a more powerful punch could cause death.

Beau whaled on the man, throwing punch after punch in the so-called forbidden zone. Pent-up frustration combined with anger, mixed with a little fear, resulted in the first casualty of the evening. Tiger Resistance—1. Scumbags—0.

It was Colton who stopped Beau from killing the man. He ran across the entry to the jail to intervene just in time. They dragged the deputy between two late-model cars and cuffed him to a door handle. Then they ripped his sleeve off his bloodied shirt and gagged him.

As a trophy, Beau was rewarded with the man's service weapon and his duty belt, which included a holster, another set of cuffs, a baton, a mini-mag flashlight, mace and extra ammo. Colton grabbed the man's jail keys and the sheriff's department radio, which now gave the Tiger Resistance a great tactical advantage. They could monitor chatter between Junior's guys.

Alex remained in a crouched position, awaiting the drinker. Beau and Colton moved to a spot closer to the door, tucked on each side of the looted soda machines. Colton held the baton while Beau readied the flashlight. When the drinker came out looking for the smoker, they'd be ready.

At least ten minutes passed before there was any sign of their target. Alex stuck her head around the corner of the entry.

She whispered loud enough for the guys to hear her, "Should we go in and get him?"

"Just a little longer," replied Colton. "I don't want to hunt him in unfamiliar surroundings."

"It's familiar to me," Alex shot back.

Another minute passed and then Beau whispered, "Movement! He's coming."

Deputy Drinker wasn't nonchalant like his partner. He approached the doors with caution and his weapon drawn. The glass door slowly opened.

"Johnson, ya out thar?" the man said, slurring his words.

The door opened a little more and his arm stuck through with a pistol leading the way. Colton raised the baton over his head and waited. The deputy emerged a little more and the arm was ripe for the crushin'.

THWACK! CRUNCH!

Colton swung down with all his might, knocking the service weapon to the ground and causing the two long bones of the man's forearm to break cleanly. Deputy Drinker fell forward through the door and Colton swung again, striking the man squarely in the back and driving him to the concrete. It was the final blow to the base of the skull that likely killed Deputy Drinker.

Tiger Resistance—2. Scumbags—0.

Alex rushed into the opened door and raised her weapon, waiting for anyone else to join the fray. If their intel was correct, these two losers were the extent of the jail's guard crew that day.

"Daddy, we have to clear the building. You and I will do it while Beau disposes of this guy."

Colton collapsed the baton and slipped it into his belt. He pulled the Kel-Tec Sub 2000 off his shoulder and nodded to Alex. They moved into the dark hallway of the jail.

Colton followed Alex's lead. It hadn't been long since she'd been bullied up and down the hallways of the small facility. Room by room, they entered each doorway aggressively with the intent of startling anyone present and prepared to shoot anything that moved. By the time they reached the end of the hallway at Junior's office, they were satisfied their intel was accurate.

Coach Carey summoned a couple of two-man teams to guard the jail while Beau and Alex searched for the keys to the vehicles. Their next target was critical. If they took command of the bridge, Stubby's goal of isolating Junior could be achieved and Coach Carey's goal of storming Cherry Mansion would be easier. Ma would be cut off from her minions.

Coach Carey gathered his troops in the parking lot of the jail and laid out the plan. There was no cover to approach the west bridge without being seen. He planned to surprise the guards on the bridge with an approach from the rear. They loaded into three cars and sped toward the river. He hoped the men would assume the vehicles were reinforcements for Junior, as no one else in town had operating vehicles.

Colton drove one pickup truck while Alex acted as the shooter from the passenger's side and Chase was in the back. Coach Carey drove another vehicle with Beau hanging out the passenger's side with a shotgun. The Bennetts drove the third car. They were the replacement guards for the west bridge.

Once the shooting began, there would be no turning back. With the leaves fallen from the trees surrounding Cherry Mansion and the remaining charred remains of vegetation providing no sound cover, the head of the snake could be alerted.

Now, the Tiger Resistance had become the aggressor. Coach Carey called in the play.

"Tiger Tails, Tiger Tails, Savannah full. Blitz. Ready. On snap. Repeat. Savannah full. Blitz, on snap!"

The play would be set in motion on the first movement, in this case, the bevy of bullets shot in the direction of the west bridge.

Coach Carey led the way until he was within a hundred yards and then he waved Colton to pull up alongside him. In the darkness, he couldn't make out how the men guarding the bridge were reacting. Chase held onto a roof rack on top of the pickup and studied the bridge through his scope.

"Two men," he shouted to Coach Carey. "They're turning toward us. Just say when." Chase remained disciplined.

They approached the bridge and the men came into view. They were both hunkered down behind the concrete barriers with their weapons pointed toward the oncoming vehicles. Coach Carey flashed his bright lights in their direction. This caused one of the men to let his guard down and he rose to get a better look.

"Open fire!" shouted Coach Carey.

Everyone fired. The man's body twisted and spun as he was ripped to shreds with a variety of bullets. Who fired the kill shot was anybody's guess.

Tiger Resistance—3. Scumbags—0.

"Hold fire!" instructed Coach Carey. He led the two-car procession slowly toward the blockade. There was no movement. As they got closer, a man darted from between the concrete barriers, zigzagging through the maze toward the embankment leading to Cherry Mansion.

Alex took a couple of shots, but the man ducked, avoiding the rounds flying over his head. Alex flung the door open and ran toward the man, firing her weapon, but missing badly.

"Alex, wait!" shouted Beau as he scampered to join her. The man slid down the wet, grassy embankment and began to run toward Cherry Mansion. Alex didn't hesitate and followed. She turned and looked toward her dad.

"No, Alex, you can't!" he shouted to her.

"I've got this, Daddy," she shouted as she leaped over the edge, her blonde ponytail being the last thing seen of her.

Coach Carey shouted to Colton, "Come on, we'll draw attention on the other side to give them cover. Let's go."

The Bennetts jumped out of the car and took up their duties as the new guards of the west gate. Coach Carey recalled a team to help them. The bridge was secure. Now, for the *coup de grâce.*

CHAPTER 32

Late afternoon
Veterans Day, November 11
The Hornet's Nest
Shiloh

The sporadic gunfire eventually stopped, but the fighting did not. In the mud and darkness of the Hornet's Nest, men slashed at each other with knives and pounded each other with fists. Screams filled the air as death came slowly for some. The fighting lasted for hours and well into the dark of night.

Stubby's men had the benefit of knowing the lay of the land. They'd lived, worked and hunted around these woods for years. They also had motivation on their side. This was their fight, unlike the hired guns employed by Junior, who did his bidding in exchange for a better meal or a little power.

Hand-to-hand combat, by its nature, became very personal. Your opponent was trying to kill you, so as you defended yourself, you got angry. What motivated one man to fight was most times different from another man. But when defending yourself against any attacker, once you got angry, your will to destroy the enemy became more than self-preservation, it converted to an obsession to win.

Stubby could hear the fighting in his subconscious, but his focus remained on finding Junior. He conjured up his skills of combat tracking, which was not unlike hunting an animal except in one respect—humans were cunning and skillful, fully capable of concealing their path.

Despite the distractions of rain, darkness setting in, and the brutal battle to his left, Stubby moved methodically, looking for the telltale signs of a man muddling his way through the unfamiliar thicket of the Hornet's Nest.

The first thing Stubby observed was the fact Junior made no effort to cover his departure from the woods. Junior was heading north toward the highway without regard for a path or the signs he left in his wake. Stubby got into Junior's mind and determined that he was scared without his entourage to protect him. In the end, Junior was a coward who was now running home to his mommy.

The tracks left in the mud were obvious. When Junior turned off a trail, he bulled his way through the underbrush, leaving broken twigs and mud wiped on fallen branches.

Every once in a while, Stubby raised his scope and scanned the woods in front of him through night vision. With no sign of Junior, he pressed forward, certain that his skills wouldn't let him down.

Gunfire rang out in the distance. A flurry of activity that stopped as quickly as it started. The noise came from the northeast—Savannah! Their operation was underway. The timing couldn't have been better. It was too late for Junior's men to retreat and assist. There was only one way out of the Hornet's Nest for them—in surrender.

Another low-lying area full of muck appeared before Stubby. The footprints were closer together now, indicating that Junior was tiring. Stubby used these indentations left by Junior to pick up speed on his prey. He was getting closer, he could feel it.

Then, suddenly Stubby stopped. He crouched down and searched the woods through his scope once again. Nothing. He remained still and listened. The sounds of battle behind him had faded. Only raindrops pelting the earth around him could be heard. Carefully, he reached down and retrieved a boot stuck in the gooey mud. The inside was still warm. Junior had lost his right boot while making his way through.

This gave Stubby new resolve. This had just happened. In addition to the boot being warm, it wasn't rain soaked yet. Junior was close by.

Stubby moved quickly up an embankment and toward the peak of a hill. He slowed near the top and prepared for an ambush. As he reached the crest, he heard Junior's heavy breathing. The snap of a twig down the other side confirmed his hopes.

"There you are, coward!" Stubby mumbled aloud.

Descending a trail toward the base of the hill, Junior was hobbling, using trees for stability. *He must be injured. Take your time and play it smart.*

Stubby used his scope to study Junior's movements. He was favoring his shoeless foot. He was also armed with a pistol. This was not going to be easy. Stubby began trailing him but made an unforced error by stepping on a fallen branch.

SNAP!

He knew the moment that sound reached Junior's ears, the game would change. Like a cornered animal, Junior would turn instinctively to confront his pursuing predator.

BOOM—BOOM—BOOM!

Junior fired three rounds out of his antiquated .357 Magnum revolver in Stubby's direction but missed badly. Stubby inched closer, hoping for a clear shot, but the overhanging saplings were soaked with rain and prevented a clear path for the bullets.

Junior began to hop down the trail, groaning in pain, but putting distance between them nonetheless. Stubby picked up the pace, not out of concern that Junior might escape. He didn't want Junior to find a rock outcropping to use as cover. There was too much potential for surprises in the Hornet's Nest and Stubby didn't want history to repeat itself on this night.

He began to trot down the trail and Junior must've sensed the gap closing. He turned and fired two more rounds, which were nowhere close to Stubby's position.

"Give it up, Junior! It's over for you now. Stop!"

"Screw you, Crump!"

Stubby was becoming winded and his lower back was screaming, but he pushed through the pain. He slowed his pace and walked through a tree canopy at a low crouch. Junior fired again.

BOOM—CLICK—CLICK—CLICK.

Stubby smelled blood as he ran toward Junior. He found him

leaning next to a tall pine, fumbling with his cold, wet fingers to reload his weapon.

"Drop it, Junior!" snarled Stubby as he slowly walked to Junior. "You'll never get the weapon raised before I drop ya. It's over, so let go of your weapon."

Junior's shoulders drooped as he complied. The .357 hit the ground and several bullets clinked against the metal. Junior leaned back against the pine and looked to the sky.

He began to laugh. Stubby gave him a puzzled look and allowed the moment to subside.

"So, Crump," Junior began, "whadya gonna do, make some kinda citizen's arrest and take me to my own jail? They'll gun you down before you can open your mouth."

"I don't think so, Junior," replied Stubby. "You're done. Your posse's done. And so is your vile mother!"

"Shut up about my mother," Junior screamed and lunged toward Stubby, who easily stepped to one side and drove the buttstock of his rifle into the back of Junior's head. Junior landed facedown in the pine needles, moaning in pain.

Stubby weighed his options. He could put this fool down and walk away with no one the wiser. Or he could let him stand to account in front of all the people he terrorized and harmed in Savannah.

"Get up, Junior. You'll have to stand before God at some point, but first you'll stand before the people of Savannah."

CHAPTER 33

After dusk
Veterans Day, November 11
Cherry Mansion
Savannah

Beau ran after the guard and was gaining ground when the man suddenly turned and fired at him. The shots struck the trees to his left and Beau reacted by sliding to the ground behind a row of shrubs. The guard continued his escape and Alex raced past Beau in pursuit.

She dashed through the bushes and used the trees as cover to avoid any efforts by the guard to shoot her. Beau jumped to his feet and raced to catch up. Voices could be heard from up ahead and the sounds of vehicles headed from their right grew louder as they got closer to Cherry Mansion.

The man turned and fired again and Beau instinctively ducked. Alex stopped behind a tree, took aim and fired twice. The second round hit the man in the thigh, spinning him to the ground. Alex immediately fired three more rounds, which tore up the sod around the man as he crawled toward the cover of an oak tree.

Alex took a deep breath and squeezed off two more rounds, this time exploding the man's left knee and severing an artery in his thigh. Blood came gushing out of the wound as Alex left the cover of the tree and ran directly towards his prone body, never taking her gun sights off the man.

Beau ran alongside with his pistol waving in all directions. His adrenaline raced like no other time in his life. The feeling of exhilaration had consumed his body and he was ready for a fight.

As the two caught up with the wounded deputy, the man raised his gun and fired a round toward Beau, who hit the ground to avoid being shot. Alex, undeterred, fired two rounds into the back of the deputy's head. After quickly confirming the kill, she fell back against a tree and let out a deep breath. Beau hid behind another tree twelve feet away.

"Thanks," said Beau, breathing heavily after the chase.

"No prob, I owed you one," said Alex. She dropped the magazine out of her AR-15 and replaced it with another full thirty rounds.

Gunshots rang out from the direction of Junior's charred bungalow.

"Here comes the cavalry," shouted Beau.

"Beau, are you ready for this?" asked Alex.

"Yeah, seriously," replied Beau. "But how do you stay so calm?"

Alex tried to look through the heavily landscaped yard to see the entrance to Cherry Mansion, but her view was obstructed.

"I don't know," she replied. "Let's go after Ma. Our dads and Chase will keep the guards busy. You and I can slip into the house from the side without being seen."

"Do you remember your way around in there?" asked Beau.

"Oh yeah, I know exactly where Ma sleeps and where she likes to watch. We're gonna walk right in the front door."

Alex stopped and knelt at the body of the dead man. She took his weapon and handed it to Beau, who tucked it away. Finding nothing else useful, she condescendingly patted him on the chest and began moving toward the house with her weapon raised. Beau took one glance at the bloodied body and then ran to catch up with Alex.

They reached the corner of the house and observed their surroundings. A gun battle was taking place near the front gate, but all else remained still. The two moved around the corner of the house and climbed onto the front porch from the side, being careful to avoid detection from anyone looking out the windows. They stopped to get their bearings. It began to rain harder and the steady patter on the roof provided them some cover for any noises they'd make.

"They're probably directing their attention toward the backyard," said Alex. "Hopefully, they don't have any additional guards inside."

"Our guys said there were only two guards here tonight," whispered Beau.

"Did they mention Bill Cherry?"

"No, I don't think so. Do you think he's here?" asked Beau.

"Probably, c'mon," said Alex.

They took turns slipping past the large plate-glass windows until they reached the front door. Alex slowly turned the handle and found it unlocked. She looked at Beau and smiled.

"Are you ready, QB One?"

"Heck yeah," he said with a smile.

Alex pushed the door open and waited for a reaction from inside. It was quiet and still. She quickly pushed her way in and hid behind the door jamb of the parlor, where a meeting of Union Generals had decided the fate of the Battle of Shiloh many, many years before.

Beau moved inside as well and gently closed the door behind him. He took up a position in the dining room at the foot of the stairs and then Beau nodded that he was ready.

Alex put two fingers to her eyes and circled her hand around. Then she pointed toward the hallway that led to the back of the house. Beau understood her meaning. They were going to go in opposite directions to clear the first level and then meet up in the middle.

Within minutes, they found themselves together again. Alex whispered instructions to Beau.

"At the top of the stairs, there's a sitting area. Cherry's bedroom is to the right and Ma's is on the left, overlooking the driveway and the main part of the back lawn. I'll betcha they're in that room."

"Got it. I'll follow you," said Beau.

"There's one more thing," continued Alex. "I'll know if they're in the sitting area. I'm gonna kill them both. But if they're in Ma's bedroom, I remember that there's a squeaky board at the top of the stairs. I'm gonna try to step over it, but if I can't, they'll know someone is approaching. If the board creaks, we gotta move fast, okay?"

Beau nodded and pointed up the stairs. "Let's go."

"Watch my back in case Cherry comes out of his bedroom."

Alex gingerly took step by step until her eyes were even with the second floor. She scanned back and forth for signs of life, but the area was empty. She took another couple of steps and then saw the faint light of a lantern coming from Ma's bedroom. The door to Cherry's bedroom was open and dark.

Alex turned to Beau and mouthed the words *Ma's room.*

As she hit the landing, she took an exaggerated step over the creaky board. Beau followed her foot placement and the two were both safely into the sitting room. They heard muffled voices behind the partially closed bedroom door. The flickering light reminded Alex that Ma probably had built a fire to stay warm.

"Ready?"

"Hit it!" he whispered back.

Alex kicked the door open and ran into the room. Ma and Cherry were watching the gun battle below from a partially boarded-up window. Cherry swung around and started to pull a pistol when Ma grabbed him by the shirt to pull him in front of her.

BANG—BANG—BANG!

Three shots rang out from behind Alex. Beau had shot Cherry three times in the chest, sending him crashing against the wall. Cherry's mouth fell open momentarily before he dropped his weapon and fell face forward onto Ma's bed.

Alex remained focused on the old woman's eyes. She was unarmed. Slowly, she raised her arms over her head and grinned, revealing a missing tooth. Then she let out a cackle. It was a frightening laugh of a woman possessed with an inner evil that Alex couldn't comprehend.

"Shoot me," Ma hissed. "Then you'll be just like me. Come on, hussy, my boy chose you for a reason. He saw something in you that I didn't before."

Alex remained unflappable as she slowly walked across the room. Only the crackle of the fire could be heard, as the gunshots outside had ceased.

Alex ignored her as she closed the gap between them.

"I know the feeling you have, girlie," Ma said in a guttural voice. "I've killed many times and I liked it. You like it too, don't ya?"

"Shut up!" screamed Alex. "I'm gonna kill you because you deserve it!" She thrust the barrel closer towards Ma.

"Get angry, hussy. Do it. Your boyfriend ain't got the guts to do it. Look at him, he's green around the gills, ain't you, boy? Killin' ain't your thing, but girlie here likes it. Do it!"

Alex walked towards Ma and smacked her in the mouth with the buttstock of her rifle. Ma fell to her knees and looked up at Alex with a bloody grin.

"You'll regret not killin' me, hussy," snarled Ma before Alex struck her again in the nose, causing bone to crunch. Ma toppled over and Alex pounced on her. She yanked both of Ma's arms behind her back and cuffed her hands together using a set of Safariland Restraints found in the Detention Center.

Alex stood over Ma and stared at the feeble woman who used her evil to destroy the souls of innocent human beings. She immediately regretted not shooting her and later tried to come up with a reason why, but couldn't.

Alex turned her attention to Bill Cherry, the last living descendant of the residents of Cherry Mansion. She rolled him over on the bed to confirm he was dead. The gaping wounds in his chest allowed blood to spurt across the pants of the onlooking Beau, who promptly vomited all over the corpse.

"Are ya all right, QB One?"

"Sure," he replied as he retched again.

Alex took Beau's two-way radio and announced their victory.

"Tiger Tails, Tiger Tails, victory!"

CHAPTER 34

Dawn, November 12
Court Square
Savannah

As small-town America sprouted up in the modern era during the nineteenth century, these towns grew around trading markets and natural points of interest like rivers. States began to subdivide themselves politically by counties, which were controlled by local forms of government closest to the constituents they served. A county seat in Tennessee, like Savannah, was typically located in the center of a geographic area. Most Tennessee county boundaries were determined by how far a rider on horseback could venture in a day from the center of town.

The town square of the county seat took on a special importance. Usually located near the building housing the counties administrative offices, the town square became a location suited for political rallies, open markets, and social gatherings of the local residents.

A boom in technology, including television, online social media, and virtual shopping, left most town squares useless except for the occasional concert in the park or political protest, which surprising to few, rarely took place in the heartland of America.

On this morning in Savannah, a phenomenon occurred that would be recalled for years. As word spread of the evening's events, the townspeople of Savannah emerged from their homes. The sun rose in the east, as always, but it somehow seemed brighter and warmer on this day, even for mid-November.

Folks waved to each other. They spoke to one another discreetly and then they ventured farther from home. Gone were the buses hauling slave labor to the Vulcan Quarry. The streets were devoid of Junior's tyrannical deputies pointing their guns in all directions. Peace and tranquility had arrived in Savannah in a manner not seen since the end of the Civil War.

Coach Carey, Stubby, Colton, and Jake, exhausted from a busy evening with no sleep, were standing inside the courthouse, speaking with the Bryants, when they noticed people beginning to congregate around the gazebo in Court Square. Dozens became hundreds as Main Street began to fill up.

"How did they know?" asked Jake.

Coach Carey knew his neighbors well. He was best suited to answer. "These people have been living in fear of the Durhams since the solar storm. Collectively, I believe they've created a conscious of their own. If one Savannah resident died or was tortured, they all felt it too. When evil was contained last night, they must've known."

Colton eased closer to the upper windows and watched the masses of people approaching Court Square. Their faces showed cautious optimism. The fear was gone, but celebration wasn't in order yet either. Curiosity was prevalent in all. They'd be seeking answers.

During the night, the Tiger Resistance was successful in arresting some of Junior's men, wounding others, or convincing even more to drop their weapons and run off. It would take a newly appointed sheriff and his deputies to ferret out all of the scum, but with the help of the residents in identifying the bad guys, that could be accomplished.

"Coach," started Colton, "these folks are gonna have a lot of questions, and more importantly, they'll be seeking assurances. I suspect they'll be wary of circumstances for a while until some sense of normalcy can be instituted."

"I knew this time would come, but not this quickly," said Coach Carey.

"Speak to them from the heart," said Pastor Bryant. "They all know you. They're looking for leadership and you're the guy."

Coach Carey tucked his hands in his jacket and shook off the chill held inside the brick and granite structure. He nodded and turned to descend the sweeping marble stairs. The group followed him down and through the double glass doors onto the front steps of the Hardin County Courthouse.

As soon as the group emerged into the morning sun, the crowd started moving to the grassy lawn in front of them. At least two to three hundred people stood at the base of the steps, on the grass, and in the middle of Main Street.

"Good morning, everyone!" shouted Coach Carey, the warm, moist air from his lungs immediately condensing into a misty vapor. "If I haven't met you before, my name is Joe Carey, and I'm the, um, was the coach of the Hardin County High football team. I'm glad that all of you have wandered out of your homes this morning. As you can tell, something very important in this town's history happened last night."

"Hey, Joe!" shouted an elderly woman from the middle of the crowd. "It's me, Donna English, the school librarian. Are we safe now?"

The crowd mumbled and spoke among themselves. Clearly, this was on everybody's mind.

Coach Carey continued. "Last night, with the help of these gentlemen and many others who are unsung heroes, we took into custody and made citizen's arrests of Ma Durham and Sheriff Leroy Durham. They are currently locked in separate jail cells at the Detention Center."

He felt like he'd won the state championship and returned to a hero's welcome. The citizens of Savannah were jumping up and down, cheering. Hugs were exchanged and tears of joy were flowing. The relief that overcame this town created such an uproar that other residents who were slowly walking toward the congregation began running at full speed to join in the festivities. This was truly cause for celebration.

The spontaneous reaction urged Colton, Jake, and Stubby to exchange bro-hugs and slaps on the back. After Stubby arrived with Junior, the entire group became involved in setting up security around the same locations covered by Junior's men. Disgruntled deputies were the primary concern, but now the responsibility of protecting and marshalling the town's assets rested upon their group until a new government could be installed.

"Does this mean no more quarry operation?"

"That's correct," replied Coach Carey. "Slavery was wrong back then, and it's wrong in any form today!"

"What about the brothels? Are my daughters safe to come home?"

"Absolutely. In fact, you'll be proud to know that many of Savannah's own young ladies helped in the operation last night. It was their will to fight to return home that led to our victory."

The crowd applauded and roared with approval. Coach Carey allowed the cheering to continue and then he moved to calm the crowd.

"Do you have food to give us?" someone shouted.

"Yeah, when can we go into Walmart?" asked another.

Before he could speak, a man shouted from the crowd, and then several others followed his lead.

"What about the Durhams? Bring the scum out here so we can see 'em in chains!"

"Yeah, time to face justice, I say!"

"Let me at 'em! They took everything I owned!"

Colton leaned into Coach Carey. "This mob will rip them apart. We haven't discussed this, but folks are gonna demand justice. Whadya think?"

The angry shouts persisted and fists were pumped into the air. Within seconds, the giddily exuberant crowd changed to a vengeful, bloodthirsty throng ready to rip the Durhams limb from limb.

CHAPTER 35

Afternoon, November 12
Court Square
Savannah

Establishing governmental authority was not easy, which made the works of our Founding Fathers that much more remarkable. The United States Constitution was the greatest document ever written. Its structure was second to none, as checks and balances were designed to manage this great republic.

State and local governments followed the lead of the Founding Fathers and the system had served its purpose well for two and a half centuries. With the end of the world as they knew it upon the people of Savannah, they were about to experience the growing pains of any new government.

Although a foundation of principles was in place, the personnel designed to carry out the functions of government was not. This was an issue already addressed by many small towns in America since the collapse, and for Savannah, it had become the second order of business.

The first thing on the town's agenda was the disposition of Mayor Betty Jean Durham and her son Sheriff Leroy Durham Junior. The rain had moved out of the area and a beautiful sunny day of nearly seventy degrees warmed the spirits of the town, but not their hearts. Revenge and punishment was on everybody's mind.

Debates raged throughout the community of less than five hundred people. Folks from rural parts of Hardin County who hadn't experienced the Durhams' wrath firsthand were also present. The ranchers from West Hardin County arrived on horseback as word spread from neighbor to neighbor.

Coach Carey had promised everyone an opportunity to be heard, but he made it clear, until elections were held or a consensus was reached, the Durhams would remain in custody. But he promised them the right to be heard—a debate in Court Square—regarding the fate of Ma and Junior.

Many of the landowners from across the river arrived at the same time. The contingent from Shiloh Ranch included Stubby and Bessie, the Allens, and the Rymans. John Wyatt and Lucinda made the trip. Russ Hilton brought a group of men from Saltillo.

As the families rode across the bridge together on horseback, they debated the fate of the Durhams as well. Alex, Stubby, Jake, and Chase were firmly in the death penalty camp.

"They should meet their maker and be held to account," bellowed Jake.

"If this were the real world, that's what would happen," said Alex.

Bessie and Emily didn't understand why there needed to be a rush to judgment. "They're safely locked away," said Emily. "Get a mayor, sheriff, and judge put into place, and then exact the proper punishment. Follow the rules we had before, in other words."

Colton argued that there were inherent risks in holding these two. First, he argued, the psychological effect of leaving them in town would be a dark cloud over their rebuilding effort. Second, he didn't want to feed them. He proposed delivering them to the only true governmental authority that was close to Savannah—the FEMA and National Guard encampment at Jackson. Colton suggested delivering evidence of their crimes, including written statements from the victims, to the military police or commander of the facility. Let the Durhams stand trial and receive due process.

The group dismounted and tied their horses off alongside dozens of others. Some kids were asked to provide the horses buckets of drinking water while the meeting in Court Square took place.

Madison, who had remained quiet during the conversations about the Durhams, held hands with Colton as they strolled down the street. Colton made small talk with her, but she barely uttered a response. She hadn't formed an opinion on the demise of the Durhams, and although she was the lone voice of an outsider, making her thoughts known was important to her.

The crowd building in front of the gazebo at Court Square was twice as large as this morning's. Madison allowed the sun to soak into her face and she unfurled the scarf used to keep her neck warm while riding.

A sticker on the bumper of a Volvo caught her eye. Four simple letters—W.W.J.D. *What would Jesus do?* Madison had never been a fan of those bracelets and bumper stickers. To her, the phrase *what would Jesus do* implied that she should answer that question at every turn and she should do the same. She wasn't capable of turning water into wine, performing miracles, or feeding thousands with a loaf of bread and a fish.

Madison said a quick prayer, of sorts, to herself. *I give thanks that there is a God and that he's not me. I couldn't handle the pressure. Amen.*

Then Madison thought of a miracle that she could help perform in Jesus' name—healing. This was a community in dire need of healing. Healing through forgiveness.

As the group arrived at the courthouse steps, Coach Carey got their attention and waved them up the stairs. Once inside, a substantial group of the town's leaders were present. Introductions were made and small groups split apart to chat.

Madison sought out Pastor Bryant and pulled him aside for a private conversation. They whispered back and forth and eventually their heads nodded in unison. They'd reached an accord.

"Everyone, I'd like to say a few words before we get started," said Coach Carey. "This could easily turn into a three-ring circus and a riot. The people have clamored all day to force the Durhams to face their accusers. I have to abide by their wishes or we'll lose our legitimacy and stature within the town. Toward that end, I snuck Ma and Junior over here earlier and they're locked in a holding cell behind the criminal courtroom."

"Are we going to suggest a punishment for the Durhams?" asked Emily.

"I think we've narrowed it down to three options," replied Coach Carey. "One is to summarily execute them and be done with it, but how does that make us any different from them?"

"Here's how," interrupted Alex. "They destroyed the lives of innocent people. Those two are guilty beyond any doubt whatsoever. I vote execute." Beau slid over to Alex to hold her hand, a move not unnoticed by her mother. *He's calming her down.*

"I can see how you feel that way, Alex," said Coach Carey. "You showed remarkable maturity in not taking on that task on your own. Beau told me how you showed restraint."

"Yeah, well," she began to speak and then stopped herself.

Coach Carey continued. "The second option is to hold a trial, but several of you made an excellent point. This town needs to move on and the continued presence of the Durhams will prevent that from happening. But it is preferable to execution without a trial.

"The third option is to follow the law as we know it. Until we have our own government put into place, we could turn these criminals over to the federal government in Jackson. They are better equipped to house them and exact the appropriate punishment. We'll be done with them once and for all."

Everyone spoke amongst themselves and a decision was still not reached. Pastor Bryant quietly stepped to the staircase leading to the second floor and began to speak.

"May I suggest that we get the ugliness out of the way first? Allow the Durhams to face their accusers and atone for their sins. Then let me address our friends and neighbors. After that, it'll be in God's hands."

Coach Carey and two other men retrieved the Durhams from the jail cell. He walked them into the grand foyer of the courthouse, where they had to face the town's leaders first. Not a word was spoken as hate-filled eyes looked down upon the former mayor and sheriff. Madison began to wonder if the two were safer inside the building or out there.

Both of them were uncooperative as they were dragged into the sunlight toward the gazebo. Coach Carey had stationed armed men around the structure to prevent the mob from exacting punishment on their own.

Jeers and barbs greeted the former town leaders, who had used the collapse of the power grid to begin a reign of terror. Shouts filled the air and threats were directed at the Durhams. Once placed inside the gazebo, the two shielded their faces from the angry mob.

Then, the mud began to fly, but not in the form of political rhetoric. Gobs of mud from the rain-soaked turf were pulled up and slung at the Durhams. Soon, they were covered with dirt, sod and weeds. The scene was reminiscent of the rotten eggs that had pelted a newly widowed Betty Jean and her young sons, Rollie and Leroy, the night their house burned down in Adamsville. They were chased out of town and into Savannah that night. Now, Savannah would determine their fate.

Coach Carey allowed the demonstration to continue for fifteen minutes before he determined that it was counterproductive. The townspeople had made their point and the Durhams probably realized they were better off in custody than released to the mob. He escorted them back inside and then said to Pastor Bryant, "They're all yours."

Pastor Bryant entered the mud-filled gazebo and the crowd immediately quietened down. He spoke from the heart.

"My friends, nothing erases the past. There is repentance and atonement for our sins. Atonement helps us overcome our transgressions and mistakes. It heals our hearts of pain and cleanses our minds from doubt and grief.

"Retribution and revenge is not the answer. Ultimately, the punishment must be determined by God. However, forgiveness is within our ability and it is the next step toward healing. Our community needs to heal and come together as one. Forgiveness doesn't erase the past, but it heals the memories. Forgiving what we cannot forget provides us the opportunity to move forward into a new future.

"I pray that you will forgive the Durhams for what they've done so that we can start the healing process. Let us banish them from our community and put them into the hands of the government. We will rid ourselves of this bitter memory and begin to create new ones together, with God's approval and guidance."

Pastor Bryant bowed his head and walked towards the crowd. He took an inordinate amount of time with each person who needed prayer or consolation. After an hour, an agreement was reached.

CHAPTER 36

Morning, November 14
FEMA Camp Commander's Office
Fairgrounds Park
Jackson, Tennessee

Coach Carey slowly approached the checkpoint manned by two tan MRAPs and a half-dozen members of the Tennessee National Guard. An MRAP, which stands for mine-resistant ambush protected vehicle, was designed to withstand the blasts of improvised explosive devices. But as the war in Afghanistan was brought to an end, excess military surplus in all forms, from weapons to vehicles, were deployed to National Guard units and law enforcement departments across the country. In light of the violence and unrest that had swept the nation prior to the solar storm, many argued that the militarization of local law enforcement was necessary. Others claimed the presence of MRAPs on America's streets had a chilling effect on our way of life. In any event, they were now used to protect larger cities, like Jackson, and the FEMA camps contained within.

"Stop! Driver, exit the vehicle and keep your hands in plain view," ordered a deep female voice over the speaker of a HUMVEE parked behind the RG-33 MRAPs.

Colton rode in the passenger seat of the 1971 Chevy Suburban. Alex and Beau sat in the middle row of the vehicle and turned to keep an eye on the Durhams, who were bound and gagged in the rear row of the truck.

The group debated whether they should have made a reconnaissance trip north into Jackson before venturing out of Savannah with their prisoners. The roads were still considered dangerous and there was the matter of crossing through Decatur County, which had maintained roadblocks of their own at one point. In Colton's mind, if something went south, they'd execute Ma and Junior on the side of the road and get home safely.

Fortunately, there were no issues as they traveled the sixty miles to Jackson. Now, they were anxious to relieve themselves of the Durhams and start a new life at Shiloh Ranch.

Coach Carey exited the vehicle with his hands high in the air. Two sets of Guardsmen exited the MRAPs and circled their Suburban. The bound and gagged prisoners caught the attention of one of the soldiers, who spoke softly into the microphone clipped to his chest rig.

The female officer who'd addressed them upon arrival emerged from the HUMVEE. She approached Coach Carey.

"State your name and your business," she said brusquely.

"Acting Mayor Joe Carey of Savannah, Tennessee, ma'am. We're here to turn over two criminals who should be charged with murder, corruption, and other heinous crimes. We've brought affidavits and evidence to turn over to the authorities."

Without saying a word, she assessed Coach Carey and then walked to the Suburban, where she peered inside. Ma and Junior wiggled and pulled against their restraints in the back of the vehicle.

She took another look at Beau and Alex and then glanced into the front seat, where Colton held two throwaway rifles, as he called them. He'd warned Coach Carey about the martial law order placed into effect days after the grid collapsed. The National Guard had been actively confiscating weapons door-to-door in his neighborhood and Colton didn't want to lose their best weapons under circumstances like these.

In a wooded stretch of road several miles back, the group stashed their battle weapons and pistols. They each kept an old .22-caliber rifle used for target practice or squirrel huntin'. If the FEMA patrols demanded their weapons, they'd gladly give these up to avoid further scrutiny.

"We'll need you to turn over your weapons," the officer began.

"They're in violation of the President's declaration. Technically speaking, we could confiscate this operating vehicle, but this is one of several models declared by the Department of Homeland Security as persona non grata because it doesn't meet our minimum fuel consumption requirements."

"Really? Um, okay," said Coach Carey. "Thank you for that. I'll get our guns."

Coach Carey removed the four rifles and handed them to one of the Guardsmen. He stood by the driver's door, waiting for further instructions.

"Mayor Carey, follow me closely to our facility at Fairgrounds Park," he was ordered. "Do not fall back or attempt to travel in any other direction. It will not end well for you, understood?"

"Yes, ma'am," he replied as he quickly slid behind the wheel.

"So far, so good," whispered Colton.

"I guess," said Coach Carey. "I get the impression that these folks don't like to play games. All business. I'm ready to be done with this and get home."

The HUMVEE rumbled to life and the two vehicles headed toward town. Coach Carey had been to Jackson many times and was familiar with the Fairgrounds. It was a beautiful facility spread out over hundreds of acres adjacent to lakes and ponds. All of the buildings were painted bright white with red metal roofs.

They pulled through another security checkpoint as they turned onto the Fairgrounds. A large banner that read *FEMA Region IV Welcomes You* hung from two posts. Old Glory flew proudly from one and the Tennessee State Flag from the other.

"This is all new," stated Coach Carey. "They've added the ten-foot-tall chain-link fencing and the razor wire. This appears to be a prison camp more than a refugee facility."

"I guess that's good, considering we're about to drop off two murderers," added Colton.

The vehicles pulled into a parking area near the entrance to the main building and two Guardsmen quickly approached their vehicles and motioned for them to exit. Everyone in the group was given a pat-down search and Alex's knife was removed from her leg sheath. They placed it on the dashboard for her to retrieve as they left.

The back doors to the Suburban were opened and the Durhams were wrestled out of their seats. Alex and Beau carried the two file boxes full of affidavits and documents providing the incriminatory evidence on the Durhams.

"Follow us," gruffed one of the Guardsmen.

Inside the building, there was very little activity. The reception area resembled the visitors' welcome center of any small town. There were images of men and women wearing matching blue jean uniforms working on equipment or maintaining gardens. There were more images of soldiers having friendly interaction with women and children. Everything was designed to portray peace and harmony within the confines of the FEMA camp.

"Hello, folks," started an officer in a tidy military uniform. "I'm Major Don Scott, acting Commander of FEMA Camp Jackson. Welcome."

The major extended his hand to the group and then his eyes furrowed as he studied the bound prisoners.

"It's a pleasure to meet you, sir," said Colton. "We don't want to take up too much of your time. We're turning these prisoners over to be prosecuted for the crimes of murder, extortion, abuse of public office, kidnapping, false imprisonment, and anything else you can determine is appropriate. These boxes are filled with supporting documentation and affidavits for your use in prosecuting them."

"Well, okay," said the major. "Corporal, lock them up in holding cells eight and nine. Take the documentation to my office so I can review it."

Both Durhams protested and attempted to pull away from the Guardsmen. Their voices were muffled by the gags placed in their mouths on the trip up. The group had barely cleared the Savannah city limits when they agreed the Durhams would drive them crazy with their sharp tongues on the hour-plus trip to Jackson, so Beau volunteered the sleeves off his tee shirt to gag them.

Junior got a little rough with one of the Guardsmen and earned himself a shove in the back and a crash face-first into the floor. He was dragged out of the room by the two remaining guards.

"Thank you, Major," said Coach Carey. "As acting mayor until we can hold elections next week, I wasn't sure if bringing them here was the right thing to do. A decision had to be made and it appears we made the right one."

"I get it, Mayor, especially the *acting* part," said the major. "We've received reports of the activities in Savannah, but frankly, we don't have the manpower to police areas outside of our mission. Jackson, as you know, is located halfway between Nashville and Memphis, so we get a lot of traffic off the interstate. This is only one facility that we maintain here. The other two are at Union University and the Jackson-Madison County Hospital in town."

"It sounds like you're spread out all over town," said Colton.

"We are and we've been shorthanded from the git-go. As Memphis and Nashville descended into anarchy, more of our men were shifted there. In fact, I've been designated for reassignment to Nashville myself. I'm simply waiting for my replacement to arrive with a fresh set of troops."

"How are things in Nashville?" asked Colton. Alex, who had been studying the room and watching activities outside the windows, moved closer to her dad.

"Stabilizing," the major replied. "All the mid-to-large cities in America fell apart quickly. Gangs formed and looters ran roughshod through the neighborhoods. Fortunately, the National Guard was prepared in Nashville and we clamped down hard. We've added several more facilities to house the residents and soon the cleanup will begin."

"Cleanup?" asked Alex.

"Yes," the major replied. "Much of South Nashville went up in flames. Belle Meade mansion was lost to fire. Very sad."

Colton and Alex looked at each other. Alex began to tear up and Colton quickly held her.

"They lived in that area," said Coach Carey.

"I'm sorry, folks," said the major. "I didn't mean to bring you bad news. I mean, your home might've been spared. I wish I could tell you for sure one way or the other."

"That's okay, Major," said Colton, who extended his hand to shake. "Thanks for your help today. I think we'll be on our way now, if that's all right."

"Sure, folks, and thank you. I'll turn all of this over to the new commander as soon as he arrives."

CHAPTER 37

Evening, November 15
Main House
Shiloh Ranch

"They want me to be a county commissioner," announced Jake as everyone took their seats around the dining room table. "Well, actually, they wanted Colton, but since he's not a landowner, he wasn't eligible.

"That's fine by me," added Colton. "I have no interest in politics. Besides, it's a dangerous sport."

"In any event, as a county commissioner, I can keep an eye on what they're doing in Savannah and maybe even sway some opinions, if necessary," said Jake. "I don't really want to be heavily involved in Savannah's business, but I feel being on the inside will at least give us a heads-up if they're moving in the wrong direction."

Madison set plates in front of everyone as Bessie and Emily carried out bowls of mashed potatoes, carrots, and collard greens. She added her thoughts. "Maybe things will be different now. I mean, won't Americans eventually get settled in and realize that we have a chance for a do-over. A new start for our country based upon the teachings of the Bible and following the Constitution."

"I hope so," said Emily. "Do you think it's possible that the solar flare was God's way of cleaning house? I mean, it's crossed my mind, anyway."

"It's hard to say, Emily," replied Colton. "I do believe that America will be rebuilt from the bottom up. Small-town America and the rural communities will lead the way in providing a better life for everyone. The cities had become too large and too dependent on government to run things. I'd be willing to bet that the vast majority of casualties of this disaster have been in the large metropolitan areas, not places like Hardin County."

"Getting rid of the Durhams was a huge step in restoring order and moving forward," said Jake. "There will be some growing pains, but I'm optimistic."

Everyone got settled in their seats as the warm food produced steam rising through the candlelight.

"Jake, would you say grace?" asked Emily with a smile.

Jake gave thanks for their meal, their health, the health of all their neighbors, and the love this extended family shared.

Alex began eating, taking in everyone's opinions. She noticed that Stubby looked in her direction several times and finally she returned his glances. *Something is on Stubby's mind.*

"So, Stubby, what do you think of our future?" asked Alex, deliberately putting him on the spot. The two had learned to read one another and Alex wanted to beat him to the punch. Like Stubby, she was not so optimistic about their future.

"Well," he began, "we're definitely better off since we've removed that cancer from Savannah. They have elections coming up, as Jake said, and some kind of normal lifestyle can be achieved. The key is organizing the non-producers and providing them a way to contribute to this new society. There are many who are used to receiving from the government. Now, they all have to help make Savannah a better place to live and contribute to necessities like food production, hygiene, and security."

"Who's gonna be the new sheriff?" asked Alex.

"That's still up in the air until the election," replied Jake. "Coach Carey is a shoe-in for mayor, and the pastor's wife, Leslie, will be the vice-mayor. The leaders for sheriff include a former deputy who returned after the Durhams were run out of town. He never liked Junior, and when the solar storm hit, he retreated to his ranch in the far eastern end of the county. I think his name is Stanford."

"We need to distribute the guns to everyone that won't be needed by his department," said Alex. "You know, just in case."

"I don't think we'll have a repeat of the Durhams, honey," said Madison reassuringly. "Mr. Carey and Mrs. Bryant would never let that happen."

"It's not them that I'm worried about," said Alex. "We learned in Jackson that the cities are no longer safe. We've already seen refugees in the past month. There may be more on the way. If everyone is armed, then they have a better chance of protecting themselves, and the town, if necessary."

Stubby nodded imperceptibly.

Jake pushed his plate away from his belly so that he could rest his elbows on the table. "We're all going to Savannah on Sunday for the election and the barter market afterwards. I'll bring this up to Coach Carey. It might not be a bad idea to create a small army of citizen deputies."

Stubby continued to probe her mind, so Alex decided to let her opinion be known about the FEMA camp in Jackson. Something had been bothering her since they left and she wanted to digest the news about Nashville without clouding her judgment about what she'd observed in Jackson.

"Also," Alex continued, "something was *off* up there. The commander, his offices, the whole thing seemed *suspicious*."

"Whadya mean, Allie-Cat?" asked Colton. "The major couldn't have been nicer and more helpful. I didn't see any signs of trouble."

"Everything was too perfect, Daddy. For one thing, I didn't see any refugees. Looking through the windows toward some of the pavilions, there were tons of military equipment and supplies stacked neatly. I saw soldiers taking inventory or organizing pallets. I believe this was their headquarters and the reception area was designed to create an illusion for anyone who entered."

"What kind of illusion, Alex?" asked Madison.

"The kind that sucks people into a false sense of security. I would like to see where they house the happy campers shown in those pictures. The images were staged, phony. It reminded me of the pictures they took of us when we helped at Big Brothers, Big Sisters in Nashville. They posed us. Just like the FEMA camp pictures."

Stubby cleared his throat. "Propaganda."

"Exactly," said Alex.

"Maybe they're trying to repair their image?" asked Madison. "Remember, we didn't hear many good things about the Nashville FEMA camps."

Alex contemplated this for a moment, but her gut screamed to her that something was wrong. "Or their attempting to hide what's behind the curtain."

CHAPTER 38

Afternoon, November 18
Election Day
Court Square
Savannah

It was a beautiful Sunday in Savannah as folks attended church services around town and then made their way to Court Square. It was election day and the good folks of Hardin County would be choosing their leadership team to replace the tyrannical bunch led by the Durhams.

The decision to remove them from the jail turned into a plus for the psyche of the town. They no longer had to worry about voter intimidation and the ballot-box stuffing of the past. They were no longer afraid to leave their homes and interact with their neighbors.

Today, they'd be making their voices heard on who should operate their government. They would be voting on seven county commissioners, a sheriff, a vice-mayor, and a mayor. There weren't many candidates on the ballot and the vote was pretty much a formality to legally bestow power upon the individuals running for a formal title. It was the symbolism of free and open elections, and the freedom to assemble in the heart of town uninhibited by threats from others, that helped lift this town off its knees.

The vote took place from noon to four o'clock, during which time the first barter market was opened for business. The spectacle of bartering drew a crowd as much as the process itself. Most people didn't think they had anything of value anymore. Junior and his men had stripped them of their dignity and any wealth.

At first, the trading was awkward because both buyers and sellers were new to the concept. Without money as a medium of exchange, goods and services were traded based upon perceived value. One man, a former roofer offering his services, proposed to repair a hole in a man's shed in exchange for a gold watch. That deal went nowhere.

Another trade took place between a farmer and a local resident. He offered half a dozen apples in exchange for a can opener. Another farmer overheard this proposal and chimed in that he'd provide eight apples for the can opener.

Because apples were readily available this time of year, they quickly became a standard of exchange to go by. Then one of the farmers offered up a jar of canned apples. This was seen as more valuable than the picked-off-the-tree apple and more offers were exchanged.

Services were exchanged for services and goods were traded for goods. One thing was agreed upon by all of the attendees—the barter market was a hit and should be a regular Sunday event after church.

There was now so much interest in the barter market that Coach Carey had to resort to his megaphone to remind everyone to vote before the polls closed. After the polls closed, a handpicked group of six canvassers were chosen to count the votes and announce the winners before dark so folks could get home. When they emerged onto the front steps of the courthouse, the candidates all stood before them and awaited the results.

Once again, Coach Carey had to resort to the megaphone to get everyone's attention. Over the moans and groans of the citizens, he declared the barter market to be closed so they could conduct the business of the county.

As expected, he was elected mayor with Leslie Bryant his vice-mayor. Jake was elected a county commissioner, and former Deputy Stanford was now Sheriff Stanford. The winners accepted applause on their victory and immediately entered the large courtroom inside to cover a few major issues left hanging.

Everyone approved an ongoing barter market each Sunday. Mayor Carey quipped that it would happen whether they approved it or not.

They decided not to revise and reinstate the radio broadcasts over the local AM Emergency Band. With winter coming and food in short supply, the town didn't need any more mouths to feed.

After a short debate, it was decided to house displaced refugees lured by the Durhams into Savannah in abandoned homes around town. The refugees would be told that the housing was temporary, pending the return of the owners or their kin, and they would be monitored to insure proper maintenance of the home. They were also required to work for the county in some capacity. There were no free rides unless disabled or elderly.

Many topics were tabled for a future meeting, including the suggestion that arms be distributed to the residents, method of payment to the deputies, and the level of security deemed necessary in light of the changes brought about by the Durhams' arrest.

Sheriff Stanford was instructed to come up with a manpower plan for the county and submit it at the next meeting. The temporary deputies consisted of volunteers and they were far from a disciplined security force. Finding the right people and placing them into service would take many weeks.

Coach Carey and Mrs. Bryant took a tour of the grocery stores, which had been commandeered by Junior. They found an abundance of food that, based upon simple calculations, could feed the town until late spring. Jake volunteered to create a committee of ranchers and farmers on the west side of the county to develop a sustainability plan involving the Savannah residents as labor to help grow crops throughout next year as well as assist with the cattle.

Rhoda, who was elected the commissioner from the southeast part of Hardin County, volunteered excess milk from Croft Dairies to help feed the citizens in exchange for items at Tractor Supply that would help her expand the dairy's operations.

The group could find no meaningful use for the Vulcan Quarry and voted that it never be reopened. Cherry Mansion was ordered to be bordered up and condemned. Despite its historic significance, the group would decide later whether to tear it down or create a museum depicting its recent grim uses.

They agreed to meet again the Wednesday afternoon prior to Thanksgiving. Finally, they discussed the need to continue the goodwill among the residents. The people had been through a lot and the new community leaders wanted to put an exclamation point on their newfound freedom. A Thanksgiving Day celebration was proposed and approved.

The new leadership team would put the word out that a potluck *Welcome Home* celebration would take place Thanksgiving Day on Main Street for all to attend. Mayor Carey said he'd put together a scrimmage in the vacant lot to substitute for the usual Thanksgiving Day games on television. Vice-Mayor Bryant volunteered her husband to prepare a Thanksgiving Day sermon, which he could give from the gazebo in Court Square. All of the commissioners would reach out to their neighbors and ask for food donations.

This would be an event to give thanks for being alive and free from tyranny. It would also be the start of a new chapter in Savannah's version of post-apocalyptic America.

CHAPTER 39

Afternoon
Thanksgiving Day, November 22
Court Square
Savannah

The Bennett brothers proudly put the final touches on a Welcome Home sign and affixed it to the gazebo. The United States flag once again flew proudly above the Hardin County Courthouse. Folding tables had been gathered up from every meeting place, the store shelves of Lowe's and the aisles of Walmart. Hundreds of people had gathered for the Thanksgiving festivities on a sunny day in the mid-fifties.

Rather than hit the citizens with another healthy dose of preachin' right after church, Pastor Bryant blessed the food and suggested that everyone enjoy God's bounty. The scene was one to behold, and due to Alex's quick thinking, it was memorialized with pictures.

She charged her iPhone, a device she hadn't used since their arrival at Shiloh Ranch, and took dozens of pictures of the attendees. She also managed quite a few selfies with Beau. They were inseparable now and had even shared a kiss in private that morning after Alex arrived. In her mind, sufficient time had passed between their introduction to Savannah, her abduction, and the takedown of the Durhams, to pursue a possible relationship with Beau.

The world was different now. Movie dates ceased to exist. The Friday night lights of high school football were turned off. Lunch at The Bluebird Café was no longer an option. A young teenage couple who'd experienced more than most adults had to find other ways to allow their courtship to take place.

Alex invited Beau out to Shiloh Ranch, where they rode horses and she taught him how to shoot. Beau invited Alex to Savannah when he and the guys played a pickup football game. At night, everyone was expected to be at home. After all, a grid-down world was still a potentially dangerous place.

They shared their time together as much as possible and were excited about today because Beau was going to show off his football skills during the first annual Turkey Bowl in Savannah. Also, Alex wanted to spend some time with the girls of Croft Dairies. They'd returned home and she wanted to make sure her Feisty Fifteen were getting back to normal.

The breaking of bread and socializing continued. Alex promised to figure out a way to print the photos and she would pin them to the newly created bulletin board on the front of the courthouse.

People who had certain services to offer or products to sell could post a written notice on the bulletin board. This enabled people to transact business during the week, in between the barter markets.

A special bulletin board was established for those seeking information about missing loved ones. This included those who might have been sent to the quarry and never returned. The Vulcan Quarry operation had been well guarded by Junior's people and information leaks were few. The activities there were known to be dangerous and it was not unusual for a bus to return to town at night with several seats empty.

A suggestion box was also placed by the entry to the building. When information was readily available via the Internet or media, this archaic form of communication became a thing of the past. Now, the primary means of reaching out to the county commissioners was via the suggestion box.

Not everything was perfect, and obvious aspects of everyday life were overlooked, but the community was working together without friction or acrimony. The citizens of Savannah were bound and determined to make it work despite the horrors of the past eleven weeks.

With full tummies and happy hearts, everyone turned their

attention toward Pastor Bryant as he took his position behind a lectern set up for him in the gazebo. He started out by drawing attention to the sign above his head.

"Welcome home!" he shouted.

"Welcome home!" the crowd yelled back in unison.

"This is a homecoming in every sense of the word," started Pastor Bryant. "Although many of us never left Savannah, it hasn't really been home since the solar flare devastated our world. We have seen evil, looked it in the eye, and with God's help, drove it from our town!"

"Amen!" yelled the crowd. Pastor Bryant was a traditional Methodist minister and didn't have the dramatic touch that his evangelical counterparts had. Today, the wave of euphoria had swept over the entire town, and Pastor Bryant was feeling it as well.

He continued. "This morning, during church, I presented my usual sermon about the Pilgrims coming to the New World and their perseverance against all odds. If you missed it, join us next year at Graham Chapel and you can hear it then. Now, enough shameless advertising."

Pastor Bryant took a sip of water and began after the chuckles died down. "The real story of Thanksgiving is about freedom. Religious freedom if you are a student of history. It's also about political freedom. In the seventeenth century, King James persecuted anyone who did not recognize his absolute authority during his reign. If you dared to challenge the king, you'd be publicly executed or you'd disappear. Either way, all of your worldly belongings would be confiscated for distribution throughout the kingdom, all for the greater good of the realm.

"The original Pilgrims fled Holland and came to the New World via sponsorships by wealthy merchants and landowners. Once they arrived here, they found desolate wilderness and were forced to live off the land, something none of them had ever done. This is where the traditional story of Thanksgiving fits in.

"After only half the Pilgrims survived the winter, the Indians stepped in and taught them how to build shelters, plant crops, and lead a self-sustainable lifestyle. The Pilgrims eagerly built homes and created farms full of crops. Then it was announced that everything they produced went into a common store—community ownership—for the purposes of paying off their benefactors overseas.

"Each family was given one common share of the harvested bounty regardless of how much they produced. Those who produced little or nothing got one share. A family who produced enough for ten families got one share.

"This created a problem because soon, the number of takers rose and the makers' levels of production fell, which reduced the amount contributed to the common store. Governor William Bradford concluded that the most creative and industrious families had no incentive to work any harder than anyone else because no matter what they produced, they'd just get one common share.

"Bradford decided to shake things up by changing the system one spring. This time, everything you produced you kept for yourself and you were allowed to market your products for sale in a free-market manner. Bradford was pleased with the results and it resulted in a thriving community that produced lots of crops with which to trade with the Indians. Trading posts were created and goods exchanged throughout the New England colonies.

"The word of this newfound economic freedom reached the shores of Europe, which turned into what's been known as the Great Puritan Migration. An adventure that originally started out as the pursuit of religious freedom morphed into the creation of the greatest free-market society in the history of man—America.

"My friends, God puts before us trials and tribulations that force us to seek solutions. The early settlers came to an unknown world, seeking religious freedom, and through death and harsh conditions, they discovered the power of the free market.

"We have all persevered through the horrors. Now it's time to accept the direction God has sent us. We should thank him for his guidance in restructuring our community and accepting the gifts of new friends who lead the way back to freedom. Let us not ever take for granted our freedoms again."

CHAPTER 40

Afternoon
Thanksgiving Day, November 22
Court Square
Savannah

Mayor Carey reassumed his title of Coach Carey for a while as his Hardin County Tigers prepared to square off for the first annual Turkey Day Bowl game in Savannah. It didn't matter that the game wasn't being played on the football field down at the school. None of the kids or fans seemed to care that the game was located on a vacant lot behind La Dee Da's boutique and Ma Ma Fia's Café. It was football, a Thanksgiving Day tradition, and it represented normalcy for them all.

The teams were equally divided between white-jersey visitors and the burgundy-clad home squad. Beau, wearing his burgundy jersey with the number 1, would act as quarterback for both teams.

This was a flag-football game intended to minimize contact between the boys. The makeshift field, which the boys had marked with chalk earlier, was full of stones and tree roots. Coach Carey didn't want anyone to get hurt.

"You never know," he said to the fans as they lined the field. "We might be conducting spring practice in a few months. I'm gonna want a healthy squad to coach."

Beau adjusted the flags on his belt and Alex gave him a very public kiss, which was out of character for her. She whispered, "Good luck, QB One."

The *Kiss That Reverberated Around Savannah* was seen by her parents, the Feisty Fifteen, and all of the Tiger Tails. Savannah had a new king and queen—Beau and Alex.

The game got underway to the delight of the loud and boisterous crowd. Alex took up a spot behind Coach Carey and was joined by her parents.

"Hey, Coach," shouted Colton, "do they get this loud at the regular games?"

"Sometimes, but not usually like this," Coach Carey replied. "I think the crowd has a lot to crow about. I like it!"

"It does feel good," said Colton as he hugged Alex and Madison.

Many of the residents wore the school colors and some even picked sides if they had a particular favorite on the field. Alex noticed several of her new friends from Croft Dairies were also cheerleaders for the team. She was proud of the courage they'd shown in standing up against the Durhams.

The Bennett brothers were on defense for this particular set of downs and Beau was under center. In the spirit of the Harlem Globetrotters, and to stir up a little playful banter, Beau issued a challenge.

"Yo, Jimbo and Clay, I've got an idea. Why don't I tell you the play and you guys see if you can stop it. How's that?"

"How about we tear across the line and dump you on your—"

Coach Carey blew the whistle. "Delay of game!"

"C'mon, Dad, I was just playin' with 'em."

"March back five yards, Mr. Mouth," Coach Carey yelled back amidst the laughter of the crowd. The exchange between the father, his son, and the two adopted young men tickled the crowd, who began to taunt each other.

"Burgundy!"

"White!"

"Burgundy!"

"White!"

Jimbo Bennett yelled mockingly across the line to Beau, "Bring it, QB One!"

Beau glanced in her direction and winked. Alex blushed as she realized that Beau must have relayed her pet name for him to the guys. She was also flattered that he was talking about her. This was the first boy she'd ever liked, and she was enjoying the attention.

Beau, anticipating a blitz from the Bennetts, called a swing pass to his running back. The play began and, as predicted, the Bennett boys roared through the line, looking for blood. With a big smile on his face, Beau easily flicked a pass to his right and caught his tailback in stride, who raced for a touchdown.

The play didn't end there, however. Jimbo and Clay scooped up Beau and ran with him to their end zone, unceremoniously dumping him in the grass. They danced, high-fived, and celebrated as the crowd roared its approval.

Alex also applauded the fun, but then she heard something. Something in the distance. A steady rumble.

As the crowd continued to enjoy the festivities, she slowly backed away from her parents toward Court Square. She glanced toward Stubby, who nodded his head. He'd also abandoned Jake and Chase and moved deliberately toward the center of town.

The roar grew louder. The sound began to reverberate off the buildings and was clearly approaching from the east along Main Street. Stubby and Alex reached the back of the crowd about the same time and then began to walk briskly toward Court Square.

The rumble turned to a roar and others began to hear it. The celebration died down and the euphoria slipped away as the fear of the unknown settled in. Within a minute, everyone was slowly walking toward the courthouse and barely breathed as the continuous deep, resonant sound grew louder.

The lead vehicle of the military convoy appeared, followed by another and then another. The crowd had migrated from the football field toward the convoy. Alex and Stubby stood dumbfounded in the middle of the road.

As the citizens of Savannah filed onto Main Street, a voice boomed through a loudspeaker.

"Attention, attention. You are conducting an unlawful assembly in violation of the President's Declaration of Martial Law. You are to cease and desist immediately. Place any weapons on the ground and stand still with your hands up! You are all under arrest by orders of Major Roland Durham, commander of the Federal Emergency Management Association headquartered in Jackson."

THANK YOU FOR READING HORNET'S NEST!

If you enjoyed it, I'd be grateful if you'd take a moment to write a short review (just a few words are needed) and post it on Amazon. Amazon uses complicated algorithms to determine what books are recommended to readers. Sales are, of course, a factor, but so are the quantities of reviews my books get. By taking a few seconds to leave a review, you help me out, and also help new readers learn about my work.

And before you go…

SIGN UP for Bobby Akart's mailing list to receive special offers, bonus content, and you'll be the first to receive news about new releases.

eepurl.com/bYqq3L

VISIT Amazon.com/BobbyAkart for more information on his next project, as well as his completed words: the Doomsday series, the Yellowstone series, the Lone Star series, the Pandemic series, the Blackout series, the Boston Brahmin series and the Prepping for Tomorrow series totaling nearly forty novels, including over thirty Amazon #1 Bestsellers in forty-plus fiction and nonfiction genres.

Visit Bobby Akart's website for informative blog entries on preparedness, writing, and a behind-the-scenes look into his novels.

BobbyAkart.com

READ ON FOR A BONUS EXCERPT from

DEVIL'S HOMECOMING

The final book in The Blackout Series

DEVIL'S
HOMECOMING
BEST SELLING AUTHOR
BOBBY AKART
BOOK SIX OF THE BLACKOUT SERIES

PROLOGUE

When a deer stares into the headlights of an oncoming vehicle, its eyes fully dilate to capture as much light as possible. There is a brief period of time when the deer stares into the beams, seemingly paralyzed—mesmerized by the threat hurtling towards it. In reality, the deer cannot see at all during this brief moment and freezes until its eyes can adjust. As the vehicle closes the gap between it and the helpless deer, what happens next is in the hands of the driver.

Like an animal frozen in fear, humans have a similar *deer in the headlights* reaction to certain stimuli. Our mental state can cause a form of temporary paralysis from anxiety, fear, panic, surprise or confusion. Like the deer that freezes instead of running safely out of the vehicle's path, humans become stuck in time. While they perceive the threat, the fear response of standing still is a natural defensive reaction. Our bodies become rigid, our heart rates decline, and muscles become stiff.

In theory, our bodies are freezing as a defensive mechanism to make us less noticed by a potential predator. That's the theory, anyway.

If the driver slows to avoid a collision, the deer's eyesight will adjust and it will quickly bound off the road into the relative safety of the woods. But how does a human react when sensory perception processes the threat, clearing the way for a reflexive reaction?

Much has been written about a human's fight-or-flight response to a perceived event, attack, or threat to its survival. In animals, the reaction varies from escape, to fight when cornered, and in some cases, like the Myotonic, Tennessee Fainting Goat, they faint to *play dead*. In humans, the consensus is that men tend to fight while women tend to flee. It's just human nature.

However, in large groups, humans tend to follow the leader—especially when faced with an imminent threat to their survival.

From Hornet's Nest …

As the citizens filled Main Street, a voice boomed through a loudspeaker.

"*Attention, attention. You are conducting an unlawful assembly in violation of the President's Declaration of Martial Law. You are to cease and desist immediately. Place any weapons on the ground and stand still with your hands up! You are all under arrest by orders of Major* Roland *Durham, commander of the Federal Emergency Management Association headquartered in Jackson.*"

CHAPTER 1

Afternoon
Thanksgiving Day, November 22
Court Square
Savannah, Tennessee

"RUN!"

The gaping open mouths of the residents of Savannah couldn't speak, but one managed to find the word that brought them out of their collective semiconscious state. That simple word triggered a complex series of reactions.

"RUN!" repeated another.

Like popcorn kernels boiling in hot oil on a stove, eventually the kernels succumb to the heat and explode. In the blink of an eye, the psyche of the citizens of Savannah detonated, sending them scurrying in all directions.

Women and children were knocked down and trampled. Men momentarily stood in defiant disbelief at the disruptors of their Thanksgiving Day celebration. A few, however, kept a clear mind throughout and quickly analyzed their options.

"Colton," said Stubby, grabbing the arm of his new, trusted friend, "quickly, go to the horses. Take Bessie and Madison and return to Shiloh Ranch. Prepare to leave immediately. Begin taking as many things to the Wolven place at Childer's Hill as you can."

"What about you?" asked Colton.

"And Alex?" added Madison.

Stubby searched through the chaotic crowd, seeking out Jake and his family. His short stature prevented him from seeing over most of the people running in all directions. Then his eyes were drawn to the vehicles that slowly rolled onto Main Street.

The scene was reminiscent of his days in Cambodia when U.S. troops would descend upon a small village, frightening the children, to the dismay of its residents. Over time, the villagers became used to the intrusion, but their fear subsided when they learned the battle would take place elsewhere.

Now, in Savannah, Tennessee, it appeared FEMA had brought the battle to Smalltown, U.S.A. A convoy comprised of black MRAPs bearing the logo of Homeland Security coupled with several tan-colored Humvees spread out on both sides of Main Street. Camo-laden soldiers filled in the gaps with their automatic weapons pointed in all directions. Thus far, no shots had been fired.

"I need her and we've got to go!" he replied, shaking the parallels to Cambodia. He turned to Alex. "Do you still have the keys?"

"In my pocket," she replied without hesitation. "Are you thinking what I'm thinking?"

"Yeah, but we gotta go while they're distracted."

Stubby kissed his wife and Alex hugged her parents.

"I'll be fine," she whispered to them and then immediately began to run around the gazebo toward the Detention Center. Then she added over her shoulder, "Take Snowflake home too."

Stubby checked for the Allens one more time and took off after Alex. The two had a brief window of opportunity and they had to hurry.

*****

Colton grabbed Madison firmly by the hand as she attempted to protest Alex's decision. Both parents maintained concern for their daughter, who was still recovering from a concussion, but they had grown to accept Alex's new role in the community. She was a freedom fighter in a way, respected by everyone for the challenges she'd faced and overcome. Mostly, she was revered as the hero who took down Ma Durham.

"Maddie, she'll be fine," said Colton as he tugged her toward the bridge. "Bessie, are you okay?"

"Oh yeah, let's get out of here," Stubby's wife replied as she led the way through the throng of panicked people.

"This is Major Roland Durham, commanding officer of FEMA in Jackson. Pursuant to the President's Declaration of Martial Law, I command you to halt, drop any weapons, and put your hands over your head!"

Colton glanced over his shoulder as the three began to run toward the horses. Either the masses didn't hear Rollie's commands or their intense desire to flee overrode any consideration of compliance. This was fine with Colton because every moment the standoff continued, he and the women would be closer to safety.

They approached the grassy area where over a dozen horses had been tied off during the Thanksgiving Day festivities. The horses were spooked by the high energy emanating from Court Square. Their lack of cooperation and anxiety almost got Colton kicked as he retrieved Snowflake first and then the others.

"Halt!" Rollie bellowed over the loudspeaker. "No one is authorized to leave this area. Drop your weapons and put your hands in the air, or we'll shoot!"

Colton urged his horse up the embankment and onto the bridge. He pulled Snowflake behind him and, likewise, Bessie brought along Stubby's horse. The three riders made their way through the maze of concrete barriers, hoping that FEMA wasn't waiting for them across the bridge.

CLIP-CLOP—CLIP-CLOP—CLIP-CLOP.

The horses picked up the pace along the concrete bridge, which crossed over to the west. Both sides of the highway were cluttered with the debris of battles fought. The dead bodies had been removed, but the hulls of destroyed vehicles remained.

When Colton cleared the bloody stains of Junior's men shot by Charlie and Alex, he turned the group off the road and onto the fields leading into the Shiloh Battlefield National Park. He led the entourage into a patch of woods and stopped, allowing everyone to catch their breath and release their emotions.

The shouts and the booming voice of Rollie over the loudspeaker was barely discernible from this distance. The comfort of safety allowed Madison to gather her thoughts and realize that once again, her teenage daughter was at risk. She slid off her horse and collapsed in a heap in the cool grass.

"Colton, I thought this was over," she said as she began to cry. "I thought we could get our lives back to normal. I thought …" Her words trailed off as she began to openly sob. She was losing control.

Colton dismounted and joined his wife. "Maddie, I know. Me too. None of us anticipated this."

Madison was breathing rapidly to the point of hyperventilation. "Alex. Colton, she's just a kid. She plays golf. She's on Facebook. She studies algebra. She's not a soldier!"

Bessie came to Madison's side as well and tried to comfort her new friend. "Honey, Stubby will take care of her. He won't let her get hurt."

Madison shot back, "Stubby keeps putting her in the line of fire! She's not an Army Ranger. She's a kid!"

The words stung and Bessie subconsciously wrapped her arms around herself, providing a comforting hug.

Colton tried to comfort her further. "Maddie, please calm down. Alex is an extraordinary young woman who has grown throughout this entire ordeal. You've said it yourself. We have to trust in her abilities and Stubby's wisdom. Also, you've got to trust that God will protect her and Stubby in doing …" Colton paused and then continued as he looked into Madison's eyes. "Well, in whatever they're doing, okay?"

Madison nodded, although she didn't appear to have her heart in it. "What are they doing?"

"God only knows," said Colton as he looked back to Savannah, searching for answers.

CHAPTER 2

Afternoon
Thanksgiving Day, November 22
Court Square
Savannah, Tennessee

"Round 'em up, boys! We've got runners!" shouted Rollie over the loudspeaker. "You people have one last chance to stop where you are, or I'll consider your actions as hostile against the United States government and the power vested in me by the President under martial law. Do not make me shoot you!"

Two dozen men poured into the crowd from behind the convoy of FEMA military vehicles. They slapped people to the ground and physically beat anyone deemed uncooperative.

During the melee, Jake, Emily, and Chase had slowly retreated in a wooded area near the football field. They hid behind the three-foot-wide trunks of hundred-year-old oaks to weigh their options.

"We wasted too much time looking for everyone else," said Chase. "We've got to get to the horses now. This way!"

Chase hooked his arms inside his parents' and led them down a well-worn trail through the patch of woods towards Cherry Mansion. It was a path he was familiar with, having used it the night he accidentally blew up the propane tank that nearly killed Alex.

He was sure of himself—confident in his abilities. But what he'd learned was that his overconfidence was the most dangerous form of carelessness. Chase simply didn't consider the possibility of a missed shot and where the projectile would land if it didn't hit its mark. His desire to right the wrong that had landed Alex in the hands of the Durhams in the first place blinded him to the likelihood that he might miss with his second shot or his third. Confidence was good but overconfidence always sank the ship.

"This way." Chase encouraged his parents toward the bridge and the horses. Jake's chest was heaving and he was clearly winded. They reached an opening as they approached the rear of a group of local businesses, which gave Chase an opportunity to glance back toward Main Street. The soldiers had driven a wedge within the center of the crowd, effectively dividing them down the middle. They were systematically handcuffing people, who lay prone on the ground.

"Son, I've gotta catch my breath. Just gimme a minute." Jake immediately stopped before receiving a response and bent over, clutching his knees.

"Dad, we don't have much time," said Chase. "I hate to tell ya, but we're gonna have to run the last hundred yards or so to get to the horses. We'll be exposed on Main Street the whole time."

Emily pointed to the western horizon and nodded toward the setting sun. "It'll be dark soon, can't we wait 'til then?"

"Maybe, but it's a matter of time before the soldiers make their way to the bridge to lock it down," replied Chase. "Plus, they'll confiscate the horses. I don't think we can chance it."

Jake stood up and put his hand on Chase's shoulder. "You're right, son. We've gotta go. We don't wanna get stuck on this side of the bridge."

Chase nodded to his dad and he led the way along the alley littered with empty boxes and trash cans. In between buildings, he'd look to see if the soldiers had made a move toward the bridge. Thus far, they were still preoccupied at Court Square and the immediate vicinity in front of the courthouse.

The Allens eased along the back side of the last commercial business in line and faced the charred, skeletal remains of the Hickory Pit BBQ Restaurant across Main Street.

"They're coming," whispered Chase, immediately causing Jake and Emily to snap their heads to the east. "I see three men, all armed. We've got to go."

"Son, they're too close," said Jake. "If they don't run us down, they may just open fire and cut us down."

Chase looked at the approaching soldiers and then to the horses, which were tied up by the bridge. They needed a distraction. He immediately cursed himself for coming to this Thanksgiving shindig unarmed. *I let my guard down. We all let our guards down.*

Still a teenager, Chase was as unprepared for this post-apocalyptic world as anyone. Heck, he was still unprepared for life. He was mature enough to know that he couldn't carry the guilt of the danger he'd placed Alex in. He also didn't want to disappoint his dad. He needed to relieve himself of this burden. Self-redemption was the first step to exonerating himself from this guilt.

"I'm going to distract them, which will give you guys a chance to get away," started Chase. "Once I start, don't hesitate and run to the horses. Get out of town."

"Chase, no," his mom pleaded. "We're not gonna leave you here. We'll stick together and figure out another way."

"There is no other way, Mom," said Chase. "I'll be fine. Now, we have to act quickly."

"Son, what are you gonna do?" asked Jake.

Chase leaned out from behind the corner of the building. The three soldiers were getting closer.

"We don't have time, Dad. I'll be fine. I'll make my way to Miss Rhoda's and then I'll cross the river by boat. Get ready."

Before either of his parents could question him further, Chase was off, backtracking his way toward the alley. He darted from building corner to building corner, watching for the armed men walking toward the west.

Then he saw them. He caught a glimpse of the trio passing the third building from the end, dangerously close to his parents' position. He had to act.

Chase ran through the alleyway toward Court Square and then found what he was looking for—the distraction that would do the job. He reached into a trash can and began hurling empty beer bottles toward Main Street.

With a rapid-fire motion, Chase broke the bottles on the sidewalk, the sides of the building and onto Main Street. The shouts from the soldiers gave him the response he'd hoped for. Now, he had to lure them in his direction.

The sounds of heavy footsteps crunching glass and kicking debris filled the alleyway. Chase counted three soldiers. *Perfect!* He tossed three more bottles in their direction, breaking them at their feet.

"Stop!" shouted one.

"Halt!" yelled another.

Chase decided to get in one more lick. He grabbed a wine bottle by the neck and jumped into the opening. He hurled the bottle toward the lead soldier. The heavy bottle crashed against his riot helmet, temporarily stunning him.

Time to go. He began running back toward the woods adjacent to the neighborhood, backtracking into familiar territory.

SPIT—SPIT—SPIT!

Suppressed automatic fire erupted behind him as the soldiers attempted to shoot him. Chase ran like the wind, zigzagging through the woods to avoid the bullets. However, darkness had set in and he was running without regard for the low-hanging branches of the oak trees. His instincts allowed him to avoid the first branch, but his attempt to turn and check on his pursuers prevented him from seeing the second one.

THWACK!

The oak clotheslined Chase, sending his legs out from under him and landing his back against the ground with a thud. He tried to regain his footing and stand, but only made it to one knee. His vision was blurred and then he tasted the salty blood flowing out of his forehead into his mouth.

He tried to get up again.

THUMP!

The buttstock of a rifle came crashing down at the base of his skull, sending him face-first into the pine needles. He made one last feeble attempt to rise on one hand until a boot crashed into his ribs, sending him to the ground. Another boot stomped into his side, followed by another to his stomach.

Chase couldn't breathe, nor could he see, as his vision was blurred by the pain and the blood gushing from his forehead.

CRUNCH!

He was kicked in the face. Chase tried to cover himself with his arms, using his innate defenses to shield his body from further harm. Another buttstock crushed his hand into his nose. Another kick. And then another.

Chase was holding onto consciousness, his mind wandering from his parents' faces and then ultimately to Alex. The blows were relentless as Chase paid a hefty price for his redemption. Then his mind slipped into darkness.

CHAPTER 3

Afternoon
Thanksgiving Day, November 22
Hardin County Detention Center
Savannah

Alex slowly opened the glass door and entered the lobby of the Detention Center. The only light within the building was coming from the end of the hallway to her right, where the setting sun illuminated the sheriff's office and the adjoining conference room. She drew her sidearm, having left her beloved AR-15 at Shiloh Ranch because everyone thought it was *over*. The building was eerily quiet. *Where is our new sheriff? What about the deputies?*

She eased down the hallway toward the sunlight, her shadow stretching twelve feet behind her along the tile floor. *Something doesn't seem right.* Sometimes, silence said a lot more than you think.

Creak.

Alex resisted the urge to call out like they do on television shows. The character would ask *who's there?* That was so stupid, thought Alex. Of course the bad guys aren't gonna tell ya *who's there.* They really needed to get some new scriptwriters in Hollywood, she thought as she laughed under her breath.

Creak.

The noise was emanating from the end of the hall near the sheriff's office. Alex's palms immediately became sweaty as she recalled being left alone in there with Junior. He was vile and he smelled. Alex knew what he'd had in store for her. She'd narrowly escaped the barbarity he'd wanted to inflict upon her.

Alex lowered herself into a crouch as she inched closer, her gun pointed toward the open doorway of the conference room. She took a quick, deep breath to steady her nerves and then she burst into the room, slamming the partially closed door against the wall with a thud.

She checked the corners of the room and crouched lower to observe the space under the conference table. The room was empty.

Creak.

Alex spun around, pointing her gun in all directions. *Where is the noise coming from?* She approached a bathroom door and looked inside. The steel-bar-covered window had been broken and the cool breeze was blowing a sheriff's deputy's uniform on a hanger suspended from a fire sprinkler.

Alex laughed out loud as she released the tension. She mumbled, "That's what we should have done to Junior. Hanged him."

Then she heard heavy footsteps coming down the hallway. She gathered her wits and stood against the wall next to the door. She pointed her pistol at the center of the opening and waited.

The sounds stopped. Slowly, through the opening, Stubby entered the room.

"Hey," said Alex.

Stubby jumped and flung himself against the door jamb. "Jeez, Alex!"

"Sorry, Stubby," Alex said, laughing. "Did I scare you?"

"Yeah, maybe a little," he replied. "You're lucky I didn't shoot you."

"You would've never had a chance. I think we're clear, but the sheriff is missing," said Alex as she slid past Stubby and headed for the sheriff's office. "I think he slipped out the back."

Stubby holstered his weapon. "We don't have time to play around, Alex."

"I'm not playin'. I'm just not panickin' either."

Alex entered the office. She surveyed the wall of keys and looked at each in the diminishing sunlight. "We're gonna need wheels. Whadya think, big for more hauling room, or fast to get away from those guys out there?"

Stubby glanced out the side door into the adjacent parking lot. "Look for one labeled Ford Bronco."

Alex ran her fingers along the wall until she stopped and pulled a set of keys off the hook. She tossed them to Stubby.

"Do you remember the layout from when we were here the other day?" asked Stubby.

"Yeah, admin is in this wing. Jail is on the opposite end to the east. The kitchen, intake, and the armory are in the south wing of the T."

"I'm glad you remembered the armory keys this morning," said Stubby.

"Yeah, I planned on giving them to the sheriff after the game. So what's the plan?"

"I'm gonna drive around to the loading docks for the kitchen. The truck will be shielded from the prisoner intake on the other side of the T. You go to the armory and start hauling weapons to the loading dock through the kitchen. Focus on long guns first—battle rifles, not hunting weapons. I'll help you with the ammo. Those ammo cans could weigh fifty pounds each."

"Got it. Should we lock the front door?" Alex surveyed the wall for the keys to the double glass doors. Once they were located, she tucked her pinky finger through the ring. "Good. If they have to break in, at least we'll hear them coming."

Alex took off down the hallway and locked the doors. She stared for a moment at the activity around Court Square. People were lying on the ground everywhere with armed soldiers pointing guns at them and kicking their spread-eagled limbs. "Unbelievable," Alex muttered.

She strained to see through the waning daylight for any signs of Beau. He and Coach Carey had still been on the playing field with most of the Tiger Tails when the armored vehicles had rolled onto Main Street. Through the hectic few moments before she'd raced to the Detention Center, she'd forgotten about Beau and had lost track of his location. Now, as she had an opportunity to take a breather, she realized how much she missed him.

Alex shook off the thoughts of Beau and the others and got back to the task at hand. After Ma and Junior had been taken into custody, Alex's first thought was to secure the armory. She didn't trust anyone and was concerned that the guns would fall into the wrong hands. Also, she was fully aware of how scarce and valuable ammo was.

She had rustled through the desk drawers of Junior's office that day and found the keys to the solid steel doors protecting the cache of weapons. Alex then slipped them in her pocket and didn't tell anyone except Stubby. He'd appreciated her way of thinking, whereas she knew her parents would encourage her to return the keys to the new sheriff.

Alex had a different perspective and outlook on the world following the collapse of the power grid. Some people might call her cynical or pessimistic, but Alex understood early on how mean people were. There was a reason for the old saying *desperate people will do desperate things*. Alex had grasped the concept immediately in those hours before the solar flare hit, and the events of the last three months only reinforced her convictions.

She made her way down the unlit hallway, using an LED-lit keyring she and Chase had found while scavenging. She missed those days. There was a certain thrill of going through abandoned homes to see what you could find. It sure beat lurking through a dark, abandoned jail where, if the walls could talk, the screams of untold horrors performed by Junior's men would fill the air.

Alex really liked Chase and felt everyone was overreacting in blaming him for her capture. Alex knew the risks every time they went outside of Shiloh Ranch. Chase was a good guy, and Alex saw the potential in him. She pulled her hair out of her face and tossed it behind her. *Back to business.*

For the next ten minutes, Alex and Stubby emptied the armory of the Hardin County Sheriff's Department. Several dozen weapons and thousands of rounds of ammo were removed and placed in the back of the old Bronco. They were impressed with the number of weapons still available considering Junior's propensity to hire deputies. The ammo cache was a huge help, as the ranchers on the west side of the river had spent so many rounds on Shiloh Ridge the day of the battle with Junior.

"Let's grab the radios," said Alex.

"We need to go, Alex," Stubby whispered back.

"C'mon, they're near the intake window," Alex said as she hustled into the dark kitchen.

Stubby followed and the two made their way down the hallway to retrieve the Motorola two-way units, which they crammed into a small gym bag found in a property locker.

As they returned to the kitchen entrance, they heard a crash of glass and muffled voices. The two froze and crouched against the wall. Stubby handed Alex the gym bag full of radios and drew his pistol.

They listened to feet crunching glass on the floor. Then there was a momentary silence. Nobody moved until Alex heard a chuckle, followed by a louder maniacal laugh.

"Well, I'm baaack! Did y'all miss me?"

It was Junior Durham.

CHAPTER 4

Late Afternoon
Thanksgiving Day, November 22
Savannah

"Tigers! Follow me!" shouted Coach Carey when he realized that the government had arrived in the form of FEMA. He was certain they were not there to help.

As the rest of the town was drawn to the spectacle on Main Street like bees to honey, Coach Carey sensed trouble and immediately gathered his young charges, who were wise beyond their years. The Tiger Tails and several of the girls from Croft Dairies gathered around him in the cover of the oak trees near the end zone of their makeshift football field.

Over twenty teenagers waited, many on one knee, waiting for their coach, and probably former mayor, to give them direction. Coach Carey removed his cap and wiped the sweat off his forehead. Despite the chill of evening coming on, the stress and anxiety caused him to break out in a sweat.

"Listen up," he started. "I don't know what's happening, but it ain't good. The way they've rolled into town, throwing Junior's brother's name around, I feel like we've taken two steps forward and three steps back. We have to put the Tiger Tails back into play."

"We're ready, Coach!"

"Yeah, just tell us what to do!"

Coach Carey clapped his hands softly and then moved closer to the group so that he wouldn't be overheard. "Everybody go back to your original assigned areas. Ladies, stick with the guy you were paired up with. Does everyone still have their radios?"

"Yes, sir," many of them replied.

"Beau, where do you wanna start the channel rotation?" asked Coach Carey.

"Let's start at the top and work backwards," replied Beau. "Today's channel designation will be number 99, Joel Case. Tomorrow will be number 95, Don Scott. Got it?"

"Yeah, QB1!"

Coach Carey surveyed their surroundings and then stuck his head back into the huddle with the Tiger Tails. "The first thing we have to do is assess the situation. It's just like those first few days when Junior and Ma took over our town. We're gonna do recon and surveillance. Report to me periodically, but keep radio chatter to a minimum."

"Coach, is there anything in particular you'd like us to monitor?"

"First, let's establish a pattern of activity. Determine the number of soldiers being used. How often do they rotate? What are they protecting? Are they conducting specific operations?"

Beau added, "In other words, count 'em and tag 'em."

"Exactly, son. Something like that. Avoid engagement, but get close enough to determine their intentions. Try to pick up their radio chatter. Gather intel."

"We'll do it, Coach!" said one of the boys.

Coach Carey stood and gave the scene one more good, hard look. He shook his head in disbelief. His friends and neighbors were being handcuffed and dragged to a central location in the middle of Main Street.

On the far end of the football field, he saw three dark figures dragging a fourth, lifeless body across a gravel parking lot before losing their grip and dropping it in a heap. After hurling several curse words, they yoked the body up by the limbs and started toward Court Square.

Savannah was on solid footing now, he thought to himself. This wasn't necessary. *Just leave us alone!*

Coach Carey's thoughts were so loud in his head that he immediately looked to the faces of the Tiger Tails to see if he'd expressed his inner rant aloud. All he saw in return were several sets of eyes looking to him for guidance and strength.

"Okay, before we break, let's do a quick head count and make sure everyone is accounted for."

The group looked around and several began to count heads. Beau walked around the outside of the group and then became frantic.

"Hey, wait a minute," said Beau. "Has anyone seen Jimbo and Clay?"

"No," said one.

"No, come to think of it, we never saw them again after they started dancing in the other end zone," replied another.

Coach Carey walked into the middle of the field, exposing himself to the FEMA soldiers if they were to look in his direction. He circled around, desperately looking for a sign of his two adopted sons, whom he loved as his own. In the commotion, he'd lost track of the Bennett boys.

He jogged back to the group, worried that the body being taken by the soldiers might be one of the Bennetts. "Okay, let's stick to the plan, except now we need to keep an eye out for Jimbo and Clay. If your post is in the northwest quadrant, search through the woods and also for any known hiding places Jimbo and Clay liked to use. The rest of you, keep your eyes open for them as well. Please report to me immediately if you see anything."

"Dad, do you want me to go looking for them?" asked Beau. "We hung out together all the time, so I know their favorite spots."

"You and I will do it together, son. We'll find your brothers."

THANK YOU FOR READING THIS EXCERPT OF DEVIL'S HOMECOMING, book six of The Blackout series.

The entire six book series is available on Amazon.com.

You may purchase signed copies, paperback and hardcover editions of Bobby Akart's books on www.BobbyAkart.com.

www.ingramcontent.com/pod-product-compliance
Lightning Source LLC
Chambersburg PA
CBHW020934310726
48980CB00007B/762/J

* 9 7 8 0 5 7 8 4 8 9 0 3 2 *